Nygh

& Daie

Part 1: The Girl and Hanna

PAUL W. GIBBS

SonWright Books

Glossary

Sun-cycle: One day

Moon-cycle: One month

Sun-mark/mark: One hour

Moon-mark: One week

Season: One year

Land-mark: One mile

Blessed Day: Birthday

Handbreadth: Three inches

ONE

The small village of Lorraine lies in a remote area in the wilderness, far from any well-traveled roads. Every now and then, merchants will arrive to sell their wares, or someone who has become lost in the woods might stumble upon it, and the citizens are more than happy to put them up for a day or so until the new arrivals are ready to be on their way. Even though the citizens give hospitality to anyone who finds themselves at the front gate, the village does not receive many outsiders, which is the way they prefer it.

The citizens chose to live in the isolated village because they favor it over the larger cities. Life may be more difficult, and everyone must pull together so the entire settlement will survive, but not a single man, woman, or child would trade what he or she has. That is until now.

Mountain Raiders were approaching the village. Their campfires were sighted two nights ago, and the adults of Lorraine all knew, they might not survive for much longer.

The Mountain Raiders live six sun-cycles from

1

Lorraine, at a walking pace, in the mountain ranges to the north. Now, with the coming of spring, they have left their lands to restock provisions and other items they need to survive. It takes six cycles of the sun to walk from the edge of the mountains to Lorraine, but the Raiders would make the journey in three.

That gave the villagers of Lorraine just one more sun-cycle to prepare themselves, but they all knew that when the Mountain Raiders came, they left nothing behind when they returned to the lands where they dwell. They did not farm, they did not raise cattle of their own, and they did not barter for what they needed. They came, they took, and they killed.

Anything of usefulness, to allow them to live, the Mountain Raiders would take with them. Food, blankets, cows, chickens; they would even take as much wood, as they could carry, which made up the wall surrounding Lorraine. They would strip the village clean and even that was not the worst they would be leaving with when they were through. There was one more item the Mountain Raiders came for; it was what they needed to help increase their numbers. They would take any child, ten seasons or younger.

They would take the young boys and raise them to become warriors in the Mountain Raider's culture. Forced, usually by brutal beatings, to forget about all they left behind. The boys had their previous lives beaten out of them, and if they would not break, beaten to death.

Young girls taken had one purpose, to mate with the strongest Mountain Raiders. As soon as the girls were of the age of breeding, where they could conceive a child, they would produce children for the Mountain Raiders, and if they were not able, then the Raiders had no use for them; and anything the Mountain Raiders had no use for, was a waste, and removed.

The Raiders were only interested in the children ten seasons or younger because they knew that a child who is older, is more defiant and is too much trouble to break. The Raiders take the children when they are young, then make them into exactly what the Raiders need. More of their kind, to spread terror and death throughout the region.

With spring's arrival, the villagers of Lorraine thought they would be able to spend time in their fields preparing for a good harvest at the end of the season. Now, they were spending time preparing what little defenses they had; in hopes, they will survive the attack, one which they knew was coming.

After seeing the campfires, six brave men of Lorraine volunteered to make their way as close as they could to the Mountain Raiders' camp. Six men went out, not to try to stop the approaching horde, for each of them knew that was an impossible task. The men went out to obtain a better understanding of just how many of the Raiders there were, and when they would attack. All six knew that if caught, they would not be returning to Lorraine. If that were to happen, the only good thing was that none of the six had families left in the village, so even though their deaths would weigh heavily on the shoulders of the other citizens, at least they would not be affecting any loved ones they would have left behind. The six men, as well as all the other people of Lorraine, knew, that if all six make it back, it would not be long before they will have to defend the village, and any defense against the Mountain Raiders was only a delay from the inevitable destruction they would bring with them.

The six men left Lorraine before the sun was in the sky on the second day, from the time the villagers spotted the fires. They would have to move swiftly if they were going to reach the encampment before the sun rose on the third. Not just because the Raiders had a better chance at seeing them with the sun's light, but because the Raiders would once again be on the march.

Each man carried two crucial items. One was a weapon. Of course, out of the six, only two had swords. Two others had axes; axes normally used for cutting down trees, not ones that have ever tasted the blood of a human.

The last two men had bows, which they used for hunting animals in the woods surrounding their home. The people of Lorraine would hunt deer, rabbits, and other types of animals allowing them to survive in the wilderness. The two men carrying bows knew that soon, they might be aiming for something that would also be aiming for them. The men hunted animals, and when they did, they could take their time, track their prey, and ease into the kill. They would not have that opportunity with the Raiders. They would not wait for the men of Lorraine to steady themselves to release their arrows. No, the Raiders would not let them have the needed time.

The other item each man carried was a horn, made from the horns of the mountain rams in the region. Even these were from animals that had come down out of the mountains and died. For no man would go to the mountains to hunt, it was the home of the Raiders.

The men traveled fast and far until they came to be one land-mark, away from the Mountain Raiders' camp and time for them to separate. Two remained at the location, while the other four continued on. When the four were a half of a land-mark away from the Raiders, two stayed and took up positions, while the last two went the rest of the way to the camp to see if they could find out just how much of a threat would be coming down on their village.

It was dark, but the moon was almost full which allowed more light to shine than what the two men would have liked, but they had no time to waste. The Raiders would be at their village by the end of the next sun-cycle. The men had to return home with as much information as they could. Anything that might help the people of Lorraine defend themselves.

Even though they did not have much time, they

could not move too fast; now that they were close to the Raiders' camp. If caught, they would not be able to find out how many warriors were on the march, nor would they be able to return to the village with the information they came for. They needed to move with haste, but stealth was just as important.

When they were near the encampment and could not risk moving any closer, one of the men climbed a tree to take a better look. He had lived in Lorraine his entire life, and since the village was in the middle of the woods, climbing trees was something he has done since he was a child, just like every child in the village. He climbed up enough to where he would have the best view of the camp. It was a view he was not happy to see.

Mountain Raiders live in the cold harshness of the mountains where temperatures are so low water does not run freely until the summer comes; and only then does it run but a brief time. The Raiders are humans, yet not affected by the conditions of their environment. Even though their land is cold, in the camp below, they do not need the abundance of clothing they would normally wear. This allows them to carry more supplies when they return to their own lands, along with the young children.

In the lands near Lorraine, an item the Raiders did not need were tents. The season's weather was comfortable, and since the cold did not affect the Raiders, the cool breeze was no bother to the warriors. Without tents, the man from Lorraine could see the size of the force he was observing. He knew his village did not stand a chance against the sight before his eyes.

It took him a while, but within a full mark of being in the tree, he counted how many of the Raiders were making their way to his home, the home, which had maybe another cycle of the sun to stand.

He slowly and quietly climbed down out of the tree, and even though he was careful, he thought he was making too much noise and someone from the camp would hear him. More than once, he stopped moving because he thought he had made a sound that would bring the Raiders upon him, and with them, his death.

When he reached the ground, the man who accompanied him to the camp, stood there and waited until they were looking at each other. When they did, the expression on the face of the man who had made the climb, told his companion that there would be no saving their village. The second man turned his head slightly so that he was looking in the direction of the camp. He then turned back to the man and nodded, asking the question without saying a word. The man who viewed the encampment knew what the question was. For his answer, he raised his hand so the second man could see the three fingers he was holding up. The second man's eyes grew wide. He knew what the three fingers meant. Each represented a hundred Raiders counted.

Three hundred Mountain Raiders were a sun-cycle run from the village. Three hundred, against ninety citizens of Lorraine; that included men, women, and children. The elderly and the sick, as well as the six men who were out in the woods, spying on the Raiders. Lorraine would not survive.

The men moved quietly away from where they were, which was still too close to the camp to break into a run, even though every part of them wanted to. They wanted to run; run back to Lorraine, to let the other villagers know what they had seen, and what they would be facing, but they knew they had to move slowly, just so they would have a chance to make it home.

They had no chance.

Before they were fifty paces from where the man climbed the tree, a lone sentry of the Raiders stopped them from going any further. He was standing in front of them, two against one. The men of Lorraine knew they were dead.

They were the ones carrying the swords. Since they were going to be the closest to the camp, they would need the best weapons in the event they had to confront the enemy. The two knew that their fighting skills were no match for the one warrior standing before them, but that did not stop them from drawing their swords.

The man who climbed the tree moved forward, towards the Raider. After two steps, he broke into a run to take on the man from the mountains. He raised his sword, while at the same time, the Raider raised his weapon, which the man from Lorraine could not even tell what it was. The Mountain Raiders live in a hostile environment. They did not work forges to make weapons of metal, so they made them out of rocks or from the bones of animals that live in the wilderness. The sword the man carried would fetch at least ten times what the weapon the Raider wielded would, but it did not matter about the value of the weapon, only the skill, each man possessed.

The two charged. As they approached one another, the man from Lorraine waited for the strike that would take his life, the Mountain Raider, anxious to deliver it.

Even though the man from Lorraine knew this was more than likely the last moments of his life, he would die knowing that he was doing what he came out to accomplish. This part of his mission was not to get back to the village; it was to give the man he came with, enough time to escape.

The man who stayed behind blocked the first few attacks from his opponent. He was even able to force the Raider to block a couple of his own. As they fought, the man from Lorraine saw that his companion had done as they had planned. As soon as he saw him take off running towards the Raider, the other villager took off running to the right and around the sentry. Since the man who remained was sure that his companion had fled, he was able to accept the possibility of his death. After he parried the attacks of the Raider three more times, that possibility became reality.

He fell face down on the ground, his life leaving him with every breath he released. The Raider he fought ran off, to capture and bring down the one who had escaped. Just before the man took his last breath, he heard the sounding of the horn three times. He had given his companion enough time to get away and sound the alarm. It was the last thing he would ever hear.

The two men waiting at the midway point heard the call of the horn as well and knew what it meant. The two that had made their way to the camp did not have to conceal their presence any longer, the Raiders knew that they were there. At least one got away to sound the warning. The three blows on the horn traveled through the woods. Each man knew what it meant. One blow on the horn, for every one hundred of the Mountain Raiders, making their way to Lorraine.

The men at the midway point knew what they had to do. One of them took off running, back towards the village. The sound of the horn would carry through the air all the way to Lorraine, but he did not run to relay the information. He ran because he knew that if he could make it back to his village, he would be one more man able to stand at the wall, defending his home. He also knew that with three hundred Raiders, it would not be standing for long.

The second man at the midway point remained. He was one of the men carrying a bow and stayed to give his companion a chance to make it home. If they had both left, they would be waiting for an attack from behind. No, he would stay and do what he could, to give his companion the opportunity to flee.

The man who remained heard the horn once more. The one sounding the horn, would blow three times, wait until the count of ten, and then sound the horn again. From the first time, the man at the midway point heard the horn, he would count, and when he reached ten, he heard the horn. This was part of the plan, so when he reached ten but did not hear the call from his fellow villager, he bowed his head slightly and offered a small prayer for his fallen comrade.

He still did not move from his self-assigned position. He would wait for one of two possibilities. Maybe the man sounding the horn had dropped it and was now making his way to the midway point. He would wait and see. What he saw next was the second reason he had remained.

He did not know how many Raiders had spotted the two men who went to the camp, but with the light of the moon, he saw a group of Raiders coming towards him.

This man has lived forty-two seasons. He had spent most of his life hunting the deer in the woods surrounding Lorraine and had never fired his bow at another human. That was about to change.

The moon was bright enough to allow him to see figures of black moving through the woods. It was enough for him to take aim and fire. He felt encouraged when the first arrow he let fly connected with one of the Raiders. The feeling stopped when the warrior he struck, did not fall.

He had enough time to reach behind him, pull out another arrow, and set it in his bow. He had enough skill, that when he fired the second arrow, it reached its destination, not three fingers width from the first arrow he had placed in the Raider. He might have had time to fire another, but the shock of what he had just seen stopped him from realizing what he needed to do.

He had been hunting in these woods for most of his life and had never had to use two arrows to take down any creature he was stalking. Tonight, not only did he have to use more than one, but the man he fired upon, and struck, was coming right for him, with the arrows still protruding from his chest. By the time he realized that he should fire again, it was too late.

The Raider came charging. When he was five paces away from the man from Lorraine, the Raider move to his left so that his weapon lined up with the throat of his victim. The weapon, the jawbone of a mountain goat, broke through the bow the man had up in front of him, and continued forward until it came out the back of the man's neck. The head landed on the ground before the body did and as the body fell, the Raider, who had made the kill, continued his run through the woods. He knew that there was more prey to slaughter.

The man who ran from the midway point took up the call as soon as he heard the silence. Like the man he was with but stayed behind to give him a chance to flee, he listened for the sound of the horn to end, counted to ten, and waited. When he did not hear the horn, it was his job to continue to sound the alarm.

As he ran, he blew the three calls, waited until the count of ten, then sounded the horn again. He would continue to perform the duty he was out there for.

He had been a half a land-mark from the camp of the Raiders. As soon as he heard the first sound of the horn, he started his run back to the village. He had a good lead on any Raider from the camp when his comrade had sounded the warning. That caused him to be even more surprised when he felt something hit him from behind.

He fell to the ground, and with the force that struck him; he did not have any control over how he landed. He did not stay down for more than three blinks of his eye, but when he positioned himself back up so that he was on his knees, he noticed three things. One was that he could not move his left arm. The second, was when he looked at the left side of his body, he saw he no longer had one. Whatever hit him had sliced clean through his shoulder, removing the arm from his body. The third and worse item he noticed was the Raider running toward him. He had enough time to see the Raider run past him, leaving a knife, made from stone, between the eyes of the man from Lorraine.

As the Raider passed his kill, he spotted the axe made from wood and stone, and without breaking his stride, he reached down and snatched it up. The left arm of his victim he left on the ground. He had no use for it. The axe he could use again.

Now, there was only one man at the one land-mark from the camp. His comrade began his run back to Lorraine as soon as the warning had sounded. The man who stayed also had a bow. He had lived and hunted in these woods for most of his life just like his father, who had gone ahead to the midway point of the Raiders' camp. His father had trained him since he was five seasons old. He taught him how to kill deer, rabbits, and even squirrels high up in the trees. His father would take him out near the small lakes in the area and they would hunt the waterfowl that use the land near the water to make their nests. The birds would be on the water, but a sitting bird was too easy of a target. Either he or his father would take a stone and throw it at the birds to make them take to the air. Then they would each fire as many arrows as they could into the flock and take down as many as possible. If six birds took to the air both father and son made sure that four would come down.

His father had taught him how to kill animals. He never taught him how to stand and fire at someone coming to kill him.

The man had the arrow in his bow and raised, ready to fire. When he saw the shadows move, he knew what he needed to do. Maybe if he had not tried to count the numbers of the advancing group, he would have been able to fire one or maybe even two shots. He was still counting when a club, made from something harder than his skull, came crashing down on his head. He could fire two arrows and bring down two of the waterfowl without missing a breath. Breath that he would never take again.

The last villager, who came out into the woods, had his horn, and as soon as he did not hear the warning coming from behind him, he took up the call. He kept the horn but dropped the axe after he took off running. Somehow, he knew that it would not do him any good against the ones coming for him, so he decided that it only added weight; weight that would slow him down, in his attempt to return to Lorraine.

He had left his brother back at the location, one land-mark away from the camp. His father had gone ahead to the midway point. He continued to run, all the while, forcing his tears not to flow. He knew he would not see his father or brother again. His only task now was to make it back to the village.

He had lived fifteen seasons and was chosen for this position because he was one of the fastest runners in his village. Whenever he and his friends would race around the wall of their village, he would win nine times out of ten. Usually, the tenth time was when one of his friends grew tired of losing and playfully tripped him up. It was ok with him; it was all in fun.

Now, he was not running for fun; he ran for his life. The Mountain Raiders were only a sun-cycle away from his home. Since he had been one landmark away from their encampment he was closer to his village, but still had a hard run ahead of him. He had to travel a sun-cycle in less than that time. He was not sure if he would make it or not.

He continued to run and only stopped when he could not take another breath. He had ceased sounding the horn. He knew that even this far away from the village, they would have been able to hear the warning and he needed to save his breath to make it home. He had covered a great distance and knew that he was over halfway to his village. He looked to the sky and saw the sun was just beginning to rise. It was morning. By his estimation, he would make it back to Lorraine before sunset. Just the thought of getting behind the walls of his village brought a measure of security to him.

He heard the noise off in the distance, coming from behind him. It was not a horn; no this was the yelling of the Mountain Raiders. With the rising of the sun, they were once again on the move. Now that they were only a sun-cycle away from Lorraine, their eagerness and anticipation for the battle was what they were expressing. They were working themselves into a rage. Something they could use to lay death on the small village they were heading for.

The young man from Lorraine knew that he could not rest any longer. He took off running in hopes of making it home before the Raiders came down on him. He could only hope.

He ran because his life depended on it. He did not even think about the fact that if he did make it back to Lorraine, he might die as soon as the Raiders breached what little defenses the village had. It did not matter; he was running because that was all he could do. The only other thought that came to him, was that he wished he had never won so many of the races he had with his friends. Then maybe he would not have been the one running for his life.

To his credit, if his friends had not tripped him up, when they raced, the young man would have won every time. He was fast, and when he broke the tree line and saw his village just across the open ground, his hope increased.

He and his friends had raced many times from the front gate of Lorraine to the edge of the woods and back. He saw himself doing just that clearly in his mind. Now he only had to run half that race and he would be home.

He was fast but not as fast as the Mountain Raider who had been following him. The Raider could have not only caught up to the young man but could have passed him at any moment of his choosing, yet he did not. No, he wanted the young man to make it home. At least most of the way.

When the young man from Lorraine was halfway between the tree line and the front gate, he believed that he would make it. He looked to his right and saw that the sun had not yet set. He had made it home in less time than what he thought he would. With that bit of inspiration, he pulled forth every last bit of strength he had to increase his speed to make it home. It was not enough.

The young man was fast, but the spear that entered his back was not only faster, but with the power behind the throw the Raider had made, the spear exited through the chest of its target. It was not because he felt the spear enter him that he stopped running, it had severed his spinal cord, so he probably did not feel anything. But the sight of the spearhead made from stone and the wooden shaft protruding an arm's length out of his chest shocked him enough to stop his run and fall to his knees. He looked ahead and saw the gate to Lorraine. He was so close, but he knew, he would not make it any further.

The man standing at the top of the wall of Lorraine watched the scene play out in front of him. He saw the young man run across the open ground. He saw the Raider exit the tree line but stop, lift his spear, and hurl it at the young man running towards the gate. The man, safe behind the wall of his village, did not even have time to yell to the young man to drop to the ground or warn him in any other way. The spear went through him, and he fell to the ground, landing on his knees. That was the position he stayed in.

He was the leader of Lorraine, and he had seen the last of the six, die just a stone's throw away from the front gate. Six men had gone out; none of them made it back to the village. The man looked up from the now-dead villager and saw the Raider still standing at the edge of the woods, where he had waited just for this moment. The moment when the man would look the Raider in the eye. The man behind the wall had heard the three calls of the horns. He knew that there were two hundred and ninety-nine more of the brutes making their way toward Lorraine. He could even hear their screams of frenzy off in the distance.

The two held their stare until the Raider was sure the other knew that death was coming for him and everyone behind the wall. Then the lone Raider turned and ran back into the woods, to join his fellow warriors.

The man on the wall looked to his left and saw the sun was almost setting. He heard the shouting; it was growing louder. He then turned back and looked at the tree line where the Raider departed into. He knew that the Raiders would be at his village soon and there was nothing he could do to stop them.

The Mountain Raiders did not exit the tree line. They made their camp far enough back in the woods, so the people in the small village would not be able to see them. They were not afraid of an attack from the villagers; no, they kept themselves out of sight to make the people in the village agonize over what would be coming for them.

The Raiders would wait until first light before attacking. Throughout the night, they would shout and scream, and make as much of an uproar as they could, to put fear into the villagers. They wanted every man, woman, and child in the village to know that when the sun rose in the sky, many of them would die and the young ones would be returning with the Raiders. For tonight, let their mothers and fathers tell the children that everything will be ok. Let them have a small measure of hope, which would disappear as soon as the Raiders came forth with their numbers.

This was their way. This was how they not only survived, but thrived. Whatever village the Mountain Raiders chose to attack, did not stand for long. It has always been their way. It would be again.

TWO

Hanna knew two things without a doubt. One was that she was five seasons old. The other, she was happy.

She lived with her mother and father and played with the other children in the village of Lorraine. She got along with almost all of them, except for Darius. He was a boy the same age as Hanna, and he always teased her whenever they were around each other. One of the things he did to annoy her was when Hanna had her hair tied back, to hang in one long braid, Darius would sneak up behind her and pull on it. Before Hanna could turn around and return the torment, he would have already run away.

It bothered Hanna when Darius would do this because everyone in the village would always tell her how pretty her hair was. Her parents had never cut it once, and at five seasons old, her golden hair came down past the middle of her back. So, when Darius would tug on it, Hanna wanted to turn around and punch him in the nose.

Every time Darius would pull his little prank, Hanna would tell her mother. She would say that he only did it because he liked her. Hanna told her mother that she did not like Darius and that he was nothing but a stupid boy. That was what she would tell her mother, but every time she asked her mother to tie her hair in a braid, her thoughts were on if Darius would notice when he saw her. It brought a smile to Hanna's face.

Hanna was always happy. She would help her mother in the small garden they had behind their home, and every now and then, her father would let her help him with something he was building. He was the carpenter in the village and with Lorraine being in the middle of the woods, he was never short of supplies. He would work on items that some of the other villagers would request from him, but when he was not undertaking a job of that nature, he would make items that he would be able to sell or trade to one of the few merchants who passed through Lorraine. Since the village was away from any major roads of travel, he had to have enough items made to bring him the coins or supplies he and his family needed, until the next time someone happened to come through their village.

For the last two sun-cycles, Hanna thought she was the only one happy in the village. Her parents would not allow her to go outside to play, and when she heard them talking, it seemed as if they were doing it in a way to make sure Hanna did not hear what they were saying. At first, she thought that maybe they were discussing something they wanted to surprise her with. Her Blessed Day, the day she was born, was only three moon-cycles away, so maybe they were planning a big gathering to celebrate. She started thinking about if Darius would be there. She hoped he would.

It was on the second day that Hanna could tell something else was bothering her parents. They still only talked in whispers, so Hanna did not know what was going on, but she knew it must be something important because her parents were always nervous. Her mother would jump at any little noise she heard. Once, Hanna, tired of staying inside, decided to step just out the front door of her house, but as soon as she had it opened, her mother yelled at her, grabbed her by the arm, and pulled her back inside, slamming the door behind them.

Her father stayed outside for most of the time the sun was in the sky. She would watch him through the window and see him talking to the other men of the village. By the looks on their faces, Hanna could tell that they were worrying about something; although, she did not know the reason. It was as if whatever the adults were talking about, was a secret.

Hanna had a secret of her own. One she has had for as long as she could remember. Even before she could speak a single word, someone else was speaking to her. It was not her mother nor her father; when they talked to her, she could see them. No, she had never seen who was behind the voice she heard in her thoughts; she did not even know where it came from.

Just when Hanna had begun to speak, the voice told her that she could not tell anyone about it. When Hanna asked why, the voice told her that she was special and that no one else would be able to hear the voice, and it was a secret the two of them shared. Hanna and the voice could communicate with one another just by thinking about what they wanted to say, so Hanna did not have to speak the words aloud. Hanna liked the idea of having something special. Something no one else had.

When her mother and father started acting differently, the voice told Hanna that she did not need to worry. Her parents and the other adults of Lorraine were only doing what they thought was best, but if Hanna would wait, and trust the voice, then she, along with everyone else in the village, including Darius, would see something amazing. When Hanna heard that, a smile grew on her face. She could not wait to see what the voice was referring to.

At the end of the third day when her parents had been acting differently, the voice explained to Hanna what was happening. At first, she was afraid. The older children in the village would tell stories about how the Mountain Raiders would come down and take the young children from their beds and make stew out of them. Hanna did not believe the stories, mostly, but she began to understand why her parents were worrying.

The voice told her that there was nothing to fear. That it would make sure the Raiders never reach the front gate and her family would be safe and so would everyone else in the village. Just to make sure, Hanna asked if Darius would be safe as well, and the voice promised her that even he would be.

On the fourth day, her parents pulled her out of her bed before the sun had risen. When her mother led her outside, Hanna thought that everything was back to normal, because this was the first time she had been out of the house, since her parents began to act differently, except for when she had to use the relief shack, and even then, either her mother or father went with her. But when Hanna saw that they were going to the center of the village, and then they both entered the building where the younger children of the village went to learn, Hanna saw that her parents and all the other adults were still acting very strange.

The voice spoke to Hanna and told her that everything would be fine. Hanna believed it because the voice had never spoken to her falsely before, so why would it now?

Once inside the building, Hanna looked around and noticed that the only people present were women and children. Of course, she looked to see if Darius was there, and she spotted him on the other side of the room. He was sitting beside his mother who was holding his younger sister in her lap. Hanna was hoping that her mother would take her over to them, but they went to the opposite side of the room.

Her mother found an area, sat on the floor, and pulled Hanna down next to her. She did it with force and Hanna had no problem in understanding that she was to stay seated by her mother and not move.

As Hanna glanced around the room, she saw that most of the women had troubling looks on their faces. Some of them appeared to be trying to hold back tears, but some were not having much success in making that happen.

The building was where Hanna would come, three times a moon-mark to learn to read, write and count. Only the young children would attend and since there were only fifteen of them in the entire village, neither the building nor the room was very big. There was enough space for the children, the elderly woman who taught them, and the chairs they all sat on. Chairs that Hanna knew her father had made, and she was always ready to remind Darius of that fact. Now every woman and child no matter how old they were, was in this room. A room built for sixteen, now held three times that number.

When Hanna's mother pulled her down to sit beside her, she told her to remain quiet. Hanna thought it was unfair that she was not allowed to speak, but her mother and the other women could. However, she did as her mother instructed her to do. She sat there and listened to what the other women and her mother were discussing.

She heard the words "Mountain Raiders" in almost every sentence from everyone that spoke.

From what Hanna could tell from the whispers, was that the Raiders would be attacking her village at first light. Even Hanna could not stop herself from worrying and she was beginning to put more belief in the stories the older children of the village would tell her and her friends. She did not want the Raiders to take her away and make her into a stew. With that thought, the voice spoke to her and said that she would be safe, as well as everyone in her village, including Darius. When the voice told her the last part, Hanna could not help but smile and looked across the room to see the boy who would pull her hair. They made eye contact, and even though she smiled at him, he could not return the gesture. She could tell that he was believing the stories more than she was.

She stopped looking at Darius when she heard one of the women close to her mention something about clover-root. That word caused Hanna to pay attention because she knew what it was. Every child in the village of Lorraine knew, because their parents taught them about it, as soon as they were old enough to walk outside and could understand words.

It was a plant that grew in the woods and when she was two seasons old, her father and mother would always point the plant out to her when they would see it. What was more important is what they would tell her. They would say, "Hanna whatever you do, you must never, ever, eat the clover-root. It is dangerous, and it will kill you, within moments of eating the plant." They must have been telling the truth because even the voice told her that she must never eat it. It was dangerous, and she would die, and not even the voice would be able to help her.

Remembering what she knew about the plant, Hanna started to wonder why the women were talking about giving some to the children if the Raiders enter the village. Hanna was going to ask her mother about what she heard, but the voice told her not to worry and that the Raiders would not enter the front gate. Hanna decided that since the voice always told her the truth, she would believe it this time as well, and not bother her mother with questions, who looked as if she was worrying enough already.

Hanna looked around the room and saw more of the women were having trouble holding back their tears. She wanted to tell them what the voice had said because she thought that if everyone knew that everything was going to be ok, the women, and the children, would stop worrying. The voice told her not to say anything. Soon, the entire village would see that everyone was going to be safe, and Hanna herself would be the one to make that happen and bring smiles to the faces of all the villagers. Hanna liked that thought because she enjoyed smiling and she wanted others to smile as well.

The elderly woman who taught the children of the village stood up in the middle of the room. She began talking, and when Hanna heard her mention Ourgós, the creator of all things, Hanna knew that she was praying. When the elderly woman began to speak, Hanna saw everyone in the room bow their heads and close their eyes as the prayer continue. She looked over and even saw that Darius had his eyes closed. She also saw tears running down his cheeks. She did not like to see Darius cry. Hanna then turned to her left and looked at her mother, who also had tears running down the side of her face.

It was at that moment when Hanna heard the voice speak to her in her mind. *"It is time. Do as I say, and your village and everyone in it will survive. And they will be happy that you saved them from the ones who have come."*

Hanna believed the voice. It had never lied to her before.

Everyone in the room had their heads lowered and eyes closed. This gave Hanna the opportunity to sneak away from her mother. At first, when the voice told her what to do, she was uncertain, because she knew her mother wanted her to stay next to her. The voice told her that this was the only way to make sure that her mother, father, Darius, and everyone in the village would be safe. Hanna wanted everyone to be safe, especially Darius.

She quietly slipped away from her mother and made it to the small room behind her. This was where they kept all the decorations the village used for their festivals. No one hardly ever went into the room. There was no other door, only the one Hanna entered through, but there was a window, covered with wooden shutters, which someone could open to let light in when needed. The window was too high for Hanna to reach so the voice instructed her to pull the small chair that was in the room up to the window so that she would be able to reach it. She did what the voice said, and as she moved the chair, she saw that her father had made this one as well. She could always recognize the items he built.

With the chair next to the window, Hanna climbed onto it and could now reach the window. She had to lift the small wooden bar that kept it closed, which had swollen some, due to moisture, causing her to struggle with it. Once she had it removed, the voice told her that she was very strong and brave and that she was doing an excellent job. That made Hanna smile.

With the window opened, Hanna climbed through and jumped down to the ground. It was a good distance for her, but with what the voice had told her, about how brave she was, Hanna did not even think about the drop. The voice said that she was the one who was going to make everyone safe, and she believed the voice.

Once outside, Hanna was at the back of the building and when she looked across the way, she saw the rear part of the wall which surrounded the village. She looked up to the sky and saw that the sun had still not come up, but she could tell, it would not be long before it did. She remembered hearing one of the women say that the Raiders would come at first light. Hanna knew that was not far off.

She did what the voice had instructed her to do next, and that was to run to the back wall. Hanna liked running. She would race the other children and sometimes, she would win. That is except when Darius was racing as well. The first time she had beaten him, she saw that it made him sad. Afterward, whenever she would race him, she would just happen to run a little bit slower than he did. It was worth it to see him smile. Even though he would then run up to her and pull her hair.

She made it to the back wall and asked the voice what to do next. The voice then told her to walk to her right until the voice told her to stop. Hanna had gone about twenty paces when the voice did just that. It was the next instructions that Hanna did not like.

Ever since Hanna could remember, her parents had told her that she was not to go beyond the village wall by herself. It was for her own safety, and she believed them. Now the voice was telling her to do what her parents had forbidden.

At this section of the wall, there was a hole. More than likely made by some animal that had forced its way through, to get into the village, either for shelter, food, or both. The hole has been there for over fifty seasons and since it was so small and so old, no one even remembered that it existed; at least none of the adults. The young children would go up to the hole and dare one of their friends to go through it. Of course, since their parents told all the children that they were not to go outside the wall on their own, none of the children ever took the challenge. It might have been because of the stories the older children told the younger ones about the Mountain Raiders, which may be why the parents never scolded them for telling the stories. It was one more way the adults could make sure the young children never left the safety of the village.

Hanna remembered what her parents had told her about leaving the village, and the stories of the Mountain Raiders, she was now ready to turn around and go back inside. She was even trying to figure out a way to get back in through the window, but the voice needed her to do what it wanted. It needed Hanna to listen. The voice promised that she would not get in trouble and that her parents would be happy that she not only saved them but everyone in the village. The voice knew Hanna was starting to doubt what she was doing and wanted to head back to her mother. The voice could not let her do that. To stop her, it told Hanna that if she did not do what it was telling her to do, her mother, father, and everyone in the village would be dead as soon as the sun rose in the sky and that the ones coming would take Hanna away.

She did not want her mother and father to

die, and she definitely did not want the Mountain Raiders to take her, so she knelt down and crawled through the small hole in the wall. The edges to the exit were sharp and when Hanna stood up on the outside of the wall, her dress caught and the side of it tore. The voice told her that her mother and father would buy her a new dress because of how brave she was. Hanna liked that idea; she did not get new clothes very often. Maybe she would get one with pockets on the front so she would be able to put things in them. The voice told her that she would.

The next instruction for Hanna was to run to her right and go to the edge of the wall. She did, happy at being able to run. When she reached the corner, the voice told her to turn right and continue to run until the voice told her to stop. Hanna had no problem with more running and when she was just past the midpoint of the wall, the voice told her to turn left and head towards the woods. Hanna knew that she was not to be outside the wall by herself. She also knew that if she were to go into the woods, her father would take a switch to her bottom, and she would not be able to sit down ever again. The voice told her that she would not be going into the woods. All she had to do was make her way over to the big rock, just off the corner of the front wall.

Hanna knew the rock. Whenever her father would let her go into the woods with him, he would take her by the big rock and allow her to climb up on top of it. It was about twice the height of what she was, and her father always had to help her. She was still hesitant about going any further, that was until the voice reminded her that if she did not follow the commands, her parents would die. Hanna started her run for the big rock.

Before she reached it, the voice told her to stop and pick up a branch lying on the ground. Hanna did and when she found one and looked at it, with it standing next to her, she saw that it came up to her shoulders. The voice told her to keep making her way to the big rock. She did, taking with her the stick she had in her hands, with the back end of it dragging the ground behind her.

When Hanna reached the rock, the voice told her to hide on the side, away from the village. Hanna liked that because she always enjoys playing hideaway with the other kids. Darius never could find her. The voice told her to wait there, and not to come out until told to.

Hanna knelt on the ground, holding the stick in her hands. In all the seasons, the voice had communicated to her, she never said anything aloud; she only heard the voice in her mind, and the voice knew her thoughts that she thought to it. But now, being outside the village, alone, Hanna wanted to hear at least her own voice. "Can I come out now?" Hanna asked.

In her mind, the voice replied, *"Not yet."*

Hanna was beginning to worry. Especially when she thought, she heard her mother calling her. No, she was not calling her, she was screaming for her. Hanna could tell that her mother was angry which caused her not to come out from behind the big rock. She heard her mother calling again, and this time there was something different about it. She could hear the change in the way she was saying her name as if she was pleading with Hanna to come to her.

It was not long before she heard her father calling to her also. His voice was deeper than her mother's voice, but she could still hear the fear in it every time he yelled her name. She did not want them to worry about her, so she decided she would go back to the hole in the wall and return to the building. Before she could make a move, the voice relayed one word to her, *"NO!"*

The voice had never addressed her in that manner before. The voice was always nice to her, it told her that it was her friend and that she was special. Now the voice sounded as if it was angry, which confused Hanna. Her mother and father were going to be angry with her for leaving but she also knew they would be worrying about her. Now the voice was angry as well.

The voice could not let the child go back. It needed her and this was the moment when the child would see what the two of them were capable of. The voice had to keep the child from returning to her parents for just a little while longer, so it communicated to Hanna, only this time in a more caring tone. *"Child, if you listen, and do as I say, I will come to you, and you, and your parents, will be able to see me. Won't that be wonderful?"*

Hanna could not help but smile. After all these seasons, the voice would come to her and she would be able to see who had been talking to her, for as long as she could remember. "Yes, I want to see you," Hanna said aloud, and then smiled.

"Then you must do as I tell you. Can you be strong, and brave, as I know you are? Can you be brave for your mother and father?"

At the mention of her parents, Hanna gave her answer. "Yes, I can be brave."

"Good, I am proud of you. It is almost time."

Hanna was happy. The voice never lied to her before, so why would it now? She would save her mother and father, and the rest of her village, and they would all be happy that she did.

Hanna did not know what came first. The first light of the sun or the yells coming off to her right. She looked up and saw that the sun had cast its rays into the sky. She then turned her head in the direction the shouts were coming from. Since she was still hiding in the middle of the big rock, she was not able to see what was making the awful noise. The voice had told her not to move, but since she was going to stay behind the big rock, she thought the voice would not be angry with her.

While still crouching, she made her way to the edge of the rock and that was when she saw the big humans, running out of the woods. She knew these were the Mountain Raiders the women and her mother had been talking about. After seeing, and hearing them, Hanna wanted to return to her mother and apologize for running off. She wanted to, but with the sight before her, she could not move, and she knew that if they saw her, the big humans would come and take her away, and make her into a stew.

The Mountain Raiders started their run at the first light of the sun. It was not even above the tree line off to their left, but they knew that before it cleared the tops of the trees, the small village would be no more, and they would be gathering up the spoils of their conquest. To the three hundred men, exiting the woods, this was an easy and rewarding victory.

Normally, the sun would not have risen to its highest position in the sky until later. That was about to change. This was when Sun would show the girl of five seasons that Sun was greater than anything in creation, and Sun would bless the child with some of that greatness.

Sun had waited for five seasons, communicating with the child, making her come to trust Sun. Making the child the perfect tool for what Sun needed. Sun knew the name Hanna, but why would Sun even speak it to the child? Sun was one of the strongest, and one of the First made, and had no reason to acknowledge the child except for Sun's own purpose. But Sun did need the child, and because of that, Sun would save the child, its parents, and the entire village where it lived. Sun did not truly desire to show the pitiful humans any part of what Sun could do, but Sun needed the child and now the child would know how great the voice speaking to it truly is.

It was not time for the sun to be high in the sky, but not long after it showed its first light, it continued to climb, and it was not long before it was directly over the small village below. Shining bright red in the sky, every living creature on the same side of the world stopped to see the sun rise quicker than it had ever done so before. Including the Mountain Raiders who were midway across the open field in front of Lorraine. They did not trust magic. They did not trust anyone who used it. And with the sun rising so fast, all three hundred of the Raiders stopped in their tracks to look at the sun directly over their heads.

The men of Lorraine, positioned on the walkways at the top of their village walls, saw the Mountain Raiders take to the field when the first light of the sun appeared. As soon as the horde left the woods, every man looking across the way was seeing not just their own deaths, but that of their family as well. They saw death coming towards them.

Their focus was on the mass before them and at first, they did not notice the sun in the sky. It was only after the Raiders stopped their advance that the men of Lorraine looked up and saw the sun had continued to rise and was now directly over their heads. Like the Mountain Raiders, all they could do was stare at the sun, while they used their hands to shield their eyes from the blinding light.

"It is time," Sun thought to Hanna, while she continued to watch the Raiders, now standing motionless, halfway across the open field. Sun could not hold the position for very long, so Hanna had a limited amount of time. For Sun to advance faster than what Sun normally would, Sun had to use a great deal of power. For even though Sun was strong, Sun was going against everything Ourgós had made Sun for. Sun did not have time to wait for the frightened child to come to her senses on her own. For the first time, Sun called her name. *"Hanna, you must move now! Take the branch with you, and run across, in front of the village wall. Drag the branch behind you to place a line on the ground."* Hanna heard the voice but was too scared to move. Sun had to be more assertive to provoke the human child to do as Sun commanded.

For what Sun was going to do, Sun needed precision and control. While holding the position in the sky, Sun focused one sunbeam down into the area with Hanna. Sun had to maintain control, or else the child would burn to ash and Sun needed her.

Hanna had placed her right hand on the rock to give her body more support when she saw the advancing horde. It was on that hand the sunbeam touched her. The pain was so great that not only did

Hanna snap back to her senses; she stood up from where she had been crouching down. Now Sun had her attention, *"GO!"* Sun yelled in her mind.

Hanna had heard what the voice had said so she did not need to have Sun repeat the instructions. Hanna came from behind the big rock and did what the voice had told her to do. She ran with the branch behind her, letting the back end drag the ground. Her fear had not left her, in fact, she was more afraid now than she was when she was hiding. She was out in the open, with the Raiders halfway across the field, off to her left. She knew that she could not look at them. If she did, she would not be able to continue her run.

When she reached the area in front of the village gate, she heard someone call her name. She could not stop herself from turning her head to her right to see who it was, even though she recognized the voice. She saw her father at the top of the wall, and after he called her name, all he could do was watch, as she ran in front of the village. She turned her head to look in the direction she was running and she finally reached the end of the wall.

"Now, go back, and stand in front of the gate, next to the line on the ground," the voice said to her. Since it did not tell her not to, Hanna dropped the branch before she turned around and started running in the direction she had just come from.

Once again, as she was making her way back, she heard her father yell her name, and right after he stopped, she heard her mother call to her as well. As she was running, she looked ahead and up to the top of the wall where she saw her parents. She thought about running to the gate so they could let her in.

"NO! Do not go to the gate," the voice yelled in her head. *"You must stand in front of the village, next to the line you made in the ground."*

"But…" That was the only word Hanna could say before the voice reprimanded her.

"If you do not do as I say, your mother will die! Your father will die! You will die, and I will not allow that. Now, do as I command you!"

Hanna did not like the way the voice was talking to her, but she liked what the voice said even less. She did not want to die, nor did she want her mother and father to die either. Because of what Sun told her when she reached the area across from the gate, she turned to her right and saw the horde of Raiders still standing halfway on the field.

"Hanna!"

She heard her mother call to her. And in hearing her name she heard the pleading she was doing to get her to come to her. Hanna wanted to, but she did not want her mother to die, so she stayed where she was.

The Mountain Raiders were over the shock of all that occurred since they exited the woods. First, the sun rising fast into the sky, then the sight of the small child running in front of the village wall. More than a few of the men in the raiding party wanted to make sure they claimed the small girl first. If she was brave enough to be outside the village on her own, then they all knew that when she was old enough to breed, she would birth strong men for the Mountain Raiders. It was seeing this child, standing out in the open alone, that encouraged the Raiders to continue their run across the open space, and now all three hundred were out of the woods; heading for the village to bring it down.

"Hanna! Run to the gate!"

She heard the words behind her and knew that they did not come from either of her parents, but from the leader of the village. She turned her head to look over her right shoulder and saw him standing next to her father. She then looked at the faces of all the people standing on the walkway. The women of the village had joined the men as well. Maybe it was because of what happened with the sun, or maybe it was because of what Hanna had done, she was not sure. What she did notice was that the looks on the faces of everyone changed suddenly, and they were no longer looking at her. All except her parents, who were still watching; holding each other in their arms, crying.

Her mother and father wanted to run to their daughter to bring her back into the walls of the village, but the leader of the village would not allow them to open the gates. That would put all the other villagers in danger as well. All Hanna's parents could do was watch as the approaching horde was moving closer to their daughter.

Hanna turned her head and realized what caused the people at the top of the wall to take their focus off her. She saw the Raiders once again running towards the village. Running towards her.

"LOOK AT ME!" the voice thought to her and for some reason, which she did not know, Hanna knew the voice was coming from the sun. *"Look at me,"* the voice thought softly to Hanna. With the comfort she felt from those words, Hanna looked up at the sun. For some reason, it did not blind her eyes. *"I will not hurt you. You are my warrior, and you will fight for me. For that reason alone, you, your parents, and your village will survive."*

A question came to Hanna, and she spoke it aloud, "What do I do?"

"Look back on the ones that are coming to destroy you and raise your arms up to the sky. Up to me." Hanna did as the voice instructed. She watched the Raiders make their way across the open field and raised her arms above her head. *"Wait,"* the voice said to her.

"Hanna!" her mother and father both yelled, knowing that they could do nothing to save their daughter.

"Wait," the voice said again. Hanna waited. The Raiders were almost upon her. When the Raiders were ten paces from her, the voice thought to her, *"Speak the word and let them know that my warrior has arrived."*

Hanna knew the word. She did not know how

she knew, but she knew. When the Raiders were four paces away, Hanna spoke the word, "Burn."

With that word spoken, a fire sprung up out of the line Hanna had made, using the branch she had drug behind her. The flames were as tall as the wall surrounding Lorraine. The temperature of those flames was as hot as the sun itself. They rose from the line on the ground and then they moved forward. A line of fire, which reached from one end of the village wall to the other, moved away from Hanna engulfing every Mountain Raider in its path.

It lasted no more than the time it would take a person to take ten breaths, but when it was over, and the flames had reached all the way to the tree line, it died down and disappeared. All that remained on the open field was piles and piles of ashes; the only thing left of the Mountain Raiders. The flames were so hot that they melted their bodies. Not even a single weapon remained. Rock, wood, and bone were all ravaged by the intense heat from the wall of fire.

Hanna lowered her arms and looked at the sight before her. She then turned to her right and saw that the sun was now just above the tree line; at the position, it should be. She then turned back to look across the open field and saw the dusty remains of the band of evil men who had come to destroy her village. But even those would not be around much longer, because they were being blown away by the gentle breeze.

The voice was correct. She had saved her village. She had saved her mother, her father, and even Darius. She had saved them all and the voice told her that they would be happy with what she did.

Hanna turned around to look at the people standing at the top of the wall. She saw her mother and father and they were both looking at her, but they were not the only ones. Everyone had their eyes on her. But unlike what Sun had said, they were not smiling, even though Hanna had just saved them all. No, they were looking at her, the same way they had watched the Mountain Raiders who had come to kill them. They were looking at Hanna, with fear.

THREE

I f anyone living in Bonehaven knew where Lorraine was located, they would be able to tell someone that it is on the opposite side of the world. The exact opposite. But since there was not a single person in Bonehaven, who even knew of Lorraine's existence, they knew not where it was.

Bonehaven is located in a valley within the Corrine Mountains. People came to the city for one of two reasons. The first being if they could not find work anywhere else in the general region, a person could always find work in the mines that ran through the vast mountain range.

Ore was in abundance, and always in demand. Not so much for the people who worked the mines. Yes, they made their living off it, but as soon as it was out of the mines, it went to the refinery and then sent off to other lands. Lands that prospered from the sweat, blood, and death of the citizens of Bonehaven.

The other reason a person might come to the city was if they were running from something. More than likely, a price was on their head and every other place they had tried to seek refuge became overwhelmed with more people who were willing and ready to collect.

If someone needed work or somewhere to hide, Bonehaven was a place a person could call home.

The citizens accepted outsiders to the city, but not because of their generous hospitality. It was because the life expectancy of a worker in the mines was fifteen seasons. The ore was abundant, but so were cave-ins, and other unfortunate events that can happen when digging deep into the ground. Not to mention the high death rate because of the killings committed by some of the citizens. They were the ones who supplemented their wages from working in the mines, by taking the coinage of others that ended up in the wrong place at the wrong time. Even if that place was the person's own home.

Even though there are murders, thefts, rapes, and every crime in existence in the city, Bonehaven does have a set of laws and even its own city guard. If one of its members were to come across a crime in progress, the member of the security force would step in and enforce any law which was on the books. That is if the person needing assistance had sufficient funds on them at the time or would be able to acquire those funds as soon as the citizen of the city guard stepped in and handled the situation.

There were laws, but like everything in Bonehaven, there was a cost to have those laws enforced.

Mining went on in the mountains continuously with two shifts, each shift working half a sun-cycle. The workers would mine ore for fifteen sun-marks then have fifteen sun-marks of rest before they were back to work. Day and night, it was the same routine. The excavation of the ore, the loading of it into carts, then hauling it to the surface, then to the refinery; which also worked continuously, day and night; night and day. It was a never-ending cycle.

The people who own the mines did not live in Bonehaven. They were too above the likes of the citizens of the city, but they had people in place to ensure their profits did not decrease. A mine could be owned by one person or a group of people. A person could own a single mine or multiple ones. There were even mines owned by a couple of holy temples. Of course, those owners did not allow any of their workers time off to go and worship in any of the temples. They would not have to because there were no temples in Bonehaven. There were plenty of drinking halls and brothels, but not a single place of worship.

The owners of the mines made sure the workers put their best efforts into making them coinage. The owners did not just own the mines, they owned the city. If someone wanted to invest in the city of Bonehaven, by opening a mine, a law stated that the owner of the mine was responsible for the housing of the workers and had to supply a mining store where the miners would be able to purchase any goods they would need to take care of themselves. The owners provided the workers with housing and even a store, although all of this came at a cost. The owners would make sure the miners had sufficient wages to survive. It just so happened that when a miner paid for their lodging or their supplies, they were paying back the very people who had given them their wages in the first place. And of course, the supplies the miners bought, had a great increase in price compared to what the owners paid for the items themselves.

It was a vicious cycle. One that would never end. The miners received wages for bringing up the ore, but by the time they paid for their lodgings and any supplies they needed, any coinage they collected, was almost, if not completely gone. It was a general consensus in Bonehaven, that a person did not come to the city so they could work their way up and out of the place, they went there and that was where they would stay. Death was the only way out of Bonehaven, and at least that did not cost anything.

Wherever there are men, there are two things that would also be available. That is hard drink and soft women. Both in Bonehaven can kill a man; and has.

The owners of the mines also owned the drinking halls and brothels. So once again, they would be receiving some, if not all the coinage they gave the men for their wages. But after paying for lodgings and supplies, the miners did not have much left over. If they wanted a drink or some time with a woman, they had to come up with the funds from somewhere. Either they would forgo some of the supplies they would normally purchase; soap was one of the items not in great demand in Bonehaven, or they might purchase only half of the food they would normally eat for a moon-cycle. They may go a little hungry, but at least the hardness of a drink, or the softness of a woman, would take their minds off the life they live.

Some men were fortunate and had a woman of their own. That helped when they needed to seek the comfort of her arms, but it also meant they had to purchase enough supplies to feed themselves and the woman they were taking care of. The man and woman did not have to be in a marriage to one another, in fact, they might not love each other, or even like one another. In Bonehaven, when a man and woman decide to live together, it is more out of a mutual agreement, one benefiting them both. The man would take care of her needs, and she would take care of his. With these types of arrangements, the man usually ended up spending more time working in the mines than he spent at home.

One of the laws the miners had to follow was that they could not work more than fifteen sun-marks per sun-cycle. If a worker wanted to make more coinage, he had to go to another mining company and seek employment. But since this was against the law, the man would only receive half of what he was making at another mine. It was not that his wages were half, it was the fact that the overseers of the mines took half of their wages for themselves. If caught allowing a man to work another fifteen sun-marks in another mine, the overseers would be in trouble as well. To compensate for the risk they were taking, they would take half the worker's wages. Of course, half the wages they took from the miners had to go to the people over them. It was a vicious endless cycle.

Another rule the owners of the mines enforced was that if a miner was not able to work because of an illness or for any other reason, then they would not only lose their wages for the shift but for the next shift when they came back to work. If a miner happened to be so sick that he could not work for an extended period, then when they returned to work, they would have to work the same number of days, that they were out sick, with no wages. Most of the time when this happens, the person sick hopes that whatever was causing them to be ill would be enough to kill them. Two sun-cycles without wages would cause any man to struggle to get back to where he was before. Missing a half of moon-mark or more, a person would be dead, because they would not be able to pay for the lodging or the food they needed. With this rule in place, many miners went into the mines, ill.

If there was one good thing to say about Bonehaven, just one, it would be that there were no orphanages. Yes, there were children, but they were not orphans. They might not know who their parents are, but if a child was living in Bonehaven it meant they were available for work. Work without wages. In the eyes of the people who ran the city, children were a very cheap labor force.

All the children in the city were born here. Even in the furthest parts of the regions, the lifestyle in Bonehaven was known, and no man or woman would ever bring a child to the place. Any parent that would even think of doing so, was an unfit parent, to begin with, and more than likely had already abandoned their child at an orphanage or a temple.

If a man had taken a woman into his home, and they had a child, they might keep the child until they were old enough to work in the mines and earn wages. That is at the age of eighteen seasons, which is the age the law of Bonehaven says that an individual is no longer a child, because the sooner they are an adult, the sooner they can perform the work which allows Bonehaven to thrive.

If the parents felt any love for the child, they may just let them stay with them until the child is able to get a place of their own. That did not happen too often, because even though a child of the age of eighteen to nineteen received wages, there was a tax set down by the owners of the mines that came out of the young adult's earnings. It did not matter if they worked just as hard as the older miners did. The owners decided that the child should pay a tax because they were lucky to even be born. This is where the tax got its name, The Lucky to be Born Tax.

Of course, this was only for the male children, only they could work in the mines. In Bonehaven, women had the opportunity to choose between three jobs. Cooking, being the first, and cleaning being the second. The third took place in the bedroom. Most of the time.

When a woman gave birth in Bonehaven, the first thing she wanted to know was if the baby was a boy or a girl. If it were a boy, the mother would have some hope that maybe the child would be able to survive in the city. But if the midwife said those words, "It's a girl," a little part of the mother died inside. She had carried the girl for the term of her pregnancy and even if the woman did not admit it to anyone else, or even to herself, part of her loved the child and did not want a girl to be born into the life the mother has. Those feelings usually only last until the midwife has done her job and leaves the woman to take care of the crying baby, but the feelings were there. Deep, deep, down inside.

Another law on the books of Bonehaven, and probably the only one truly enforced, without any question; was that no male could lie with a girl, seventeen seasons or younger, as he could with a woman. With this law in place, anyone caught taking advantage of a girl, not of legal adulthood, received the death penalty. It was the only law that came with an immediate death sentence if broken.

There were two myths as to why the young girls

of Bonehaven had this small amount of protection. One was because people thought that the men who had come up with this law had mothers, sisters, or daughters of their own, even if they did not know who they were, and because of that, it was a soft spot in the hearts of the men who built Bonehaven. The other myth is that when a girl turns eighteen, and if she is pure, she would fetch more coinage when sold into service. The second myth is more likely to be the truth.

Bonehaven law states that the mother was responsible for taking care of the child for five seasons. She had to make sure the child had food and shelter. However, the law did not say how much food the child had to have. Many children did not live past six moon-cycles, because they died from starvation. There was no punishment for the woman if a child died. With the conditions of Bonehaven, the city officials knew that life was hard, and if a child died, then it was just a part of life. A woman, who gave birth once, can give birth again. There would be another child soon. If not from the mother, then some other woman would become pregnant. That was a guarantee.

If the child happened to live beyond its first two seasons, then the moment it could start working it did. If the mother worked in one of the many brothels or drinking halls then the child would work in the same establishment, cleaning at first. A child of two seasons was closer to the floor and they would start with that task. Even though they were two, they received training on what to do. Although that lesson usually came with a beating, or at the very least, a hard slap across the face.

When a child turned five seasons, the mother had to decide what she was going to do with the child. It usually only took the woman one season from the time the child was born, to make up her mind. If the mother had a small amount of love for the child, she might take up to two seasons, but no longer than that.

Since the mother gave birth to the child, the law states that she is the only one who can make the decision on their future. She could decide to keep the child and raise it, which did not happen often, because that took away from any coinage she might be able to make, or coinage from the man she may be cohabitating with.

Or she could sell the child, which she could do in a variety of ways.

She could sell it to one of the brothels. The child would work there until they were eighteen. When that day came, if it is a boy, he will go to work in the mines. If it is a girl, she will continue to work in the brothel. Although she would not be cleaning anymore.

If the mother worked in a brothel already and had become pregnant from performing her duties, more than likely she had already arranged for the child to work in the same place where she and the child were living. The boys less than five would wash dishes and do other manual labor. Then when the boy turned eighteen, he would head to the mines. A girl whom the mother had already planned for, would continue to clean the brothel, but she would also start to learn how she would be earning her keep when she reached the appropriate age.

She would watch the way the other women, including her own mother, would flirt, and talk to the customers. When the girl turned sixteen, she would wait in the bedroom closet, belonging to one of the women while they performed their services in the upstairs rooms. There was a small opening in the closet door so the child could watch. When the customer left, the woman would ask the girl what she saw and if she had any questions. Most of the time they did not, because, by the time they were sixteen, they had already seen everything that went on in the establishment.

Another option the mother had for her child, was to sell it to one of the drinking halls. This was popular for the boys because the owners could use them to lift boxes and other items, as well as clean the floors, which consisted of spilled drinks, and other types of liquids that came from customers who were too drunk to make it outside before they relieved themselves. It was not too often that a girl went to one of the drinking halls. Drunk men and young girls were not a good combination, and the owner did not want to get in trouble with the local authority if one of the customers became too friendly with a young girl.

The mother could decide to sell the child in a private deal. This means she would sell the child to a man or woman who had a need for them. This happened when a person took an interest in the child and made the mother a proposition. A lot of mothers were willing to take an offer given to them because it was quick and simple. As soon as the mother and the buyer agreed upon the amount, no matter how old the child was, the mother would receive half the coinage at the time the mother and buyer made the agreement, and the rest when the child turned five, and handed over to the person who made the purchase.

If something were to happen to the child before the final transaction took place, the mother was under no obligation to return the coinage she received at the time she made the agreement. More than likely, she had already spent it and did not have enough to return the amount. It was also a rule, not a law, that if someone was to go about this method to acquire a child, then it was just their unfortunate luck that the transaction did not take place. It was not a matter of the way they went about it, purchasing a child by this method was standard practice. People just did not care that someone was out of some coinage. Someone in Bonehaven had to be.

Once a child traded hands in a private deal, the purchaser was responsible for taking care of the child. Once again, the law did not have any strong standings on what that care consisted of. The law still protected the girl if she were seventeen seasons or younger, so no man could bed her.

Individual buyers might purchase a child for different reasons. They may want the child to help take care of their lodgings. The buyer would take care of the child from the age of five until they were eighteen. Afterward, the purchaser might tell the child that they would have to obtain a job and give part of their wages to the one who bought them when they were five.

Though they might just tell the child to leave and never come back.

It was a common practice in Bonehaven, for men to take in young boys and raise them as their own sons and when they turn eighteen, they stay with the man who was almost like a father to them, or as close as one could have in Bonehaven. Some men knew that they were more than likely not to ever marry and would never have a son of their own blood, so this was a way they could have someone carry on their name. With this type of adoption, the boy taken in would take the man's last name. When the man passed away, the boy would inherit everything the man had. That usually only meant the boy did not have to leave the lodgings where he and the man lived. Coinage was not something passed on to the next of kin. There just was not any to leave.

Bonehaven. It is a place where people would go,

to work and to die. There was not much else to do in the place. The name itself had become a mockery to the citizens. They would say that their city was a Haven. A place where a person could come and live. They just had to work their fingers to the Bone to make that living. It was a vicious, endless cycle.

FOUR

T he child did not know happiness. She did not even know the word existed. It was not a word spoken often in Bonehaven, especially around children.

Not only did the child not know happiness, the child did not even know her own name. She was sure that at one time, she had one, but over the seasons, she had forgotten it. Most people would never forget their name. It was what they went by for as long as they could remember. But when someone calls a child, useless, pathetic, stupid, slow, a waste, pitiful, dumb, trash, and many other words adults would shout out to get the child's attention, then it was those words the child responded to. It had been that way for as long as she could remember. It was her life.

Even though adults used names that would suggest there was something wrong with the young girl's mind, the child was very smart. So smart, that she knew that no matter what word someone would call her, they were only words, and words could not hurt her. She was so smart that when an adult would yell at her, she kept her mouth closed and did not speak a word. That was probably why most adults thought she was not right in the head. But even a child who had limited mental capability, could clean, and do other types of work if trained, and if the child had trouble learning, after the third or fifth beating they would grasp the concept of what to do.

This young girl never received a beating for not doing as instructed. No, she received beatings because she did not talk, and adults became frustrated when they would ask her a question and she would not respond. After repeating the question, a second time, and the girl did not reply, she received a slap across her face. Sometimes she would be able to accept the strike with only a turn of her head. Other times the blows came so hard and so fast she could not stop herself from falling to the floor. Usually, the next phrase that came from the adult was, "If I hit you enough times you will answer me." The child never did. She would get back to her feet and look at the adult who had struck her. Sometimes the adult would strike the girl again, and once again, she would fall to the floor, but still did not speak.

The child learned something early in her life. Adults were trainable. She stumbled onto this by accident, but it was a very important lesson and even though it brought the child much pain, it brought her much more satisfaction.

She first discovered this bit of information from

the woman who had taken care of her for the first few seasons of her life. Even when she was very young, the girl did not say a word. At least not so any adult could hear her. She kept silent because the voice told her that if she were to do this, then she would see how the rest of the world was. The voice did not lie.

When asked a question and she did not respond, the woman taking care of her would strike her across the face. The woman would then tell her to speak, but the child kept quiet and received another hit, even stronger than the first. The child still did not speak. The woman would command her to speak and strike her a couple more times, but eventually, during the first encounter where the child was testing the woman, after about five hits, the woman just stopped and walked away. Having become frustrated with the child, she gave up trying to force her to speak.

After a few days, the woman once again wanted the child to answer her. The girl did not say a word and once again, the woman struck her, but this time it only went on for a count of three hits before the woman stopped. A couple of days later, the woman again asked the child a question. The child did not answer and once again, the woman struck her. But this time she only slapped the child once before the woman gave up and walked away. After that incident, the woman never asked the child a question again. She would tell the child what to do, and the child would follow the woman's instructions. But since the woman never asked any questions, the child never had to reply, nor was she ever struck by the woman again. The child had trained the woman to learn that no matter how many times struck, she would not talk. The woman learned that it was a waste of time to try to get a reply, so why even bother. To the woman, life in Bonehaven was too short to force a stupid girl to speak.

The voice told the girl, that this was the way of existence. It was one person's will against another. And in the battle of wills, it does not matter how many beatings you take, just as long as in the end, you are the one who wins. The child knew then that before someone would break her will, she would break theirs.

She was able to test this theory again when she began working in the brothel with the lady taking care of her. One of the young girls was responsible for teaching her how to clean the building. The child was two seasons old, but the one showing her what to do was older. In less than a season, she would be learning exactly what her job would pertain to in dealing with the men that came to her. Until then she had to train this child to take over her duties.

The child learned quickly but she still would not speak. When the older girl would ask her a question but did not receive a reply, she would strike the child across the face. It was the way she had learned, so it was the way she was going to teach this child. She did not know that the child was actually teaching her. After about the third confrontation between the two, the older girl grew tired of having to waste her energy on beating the girl. She decided that she would just teach the young child and leave it at that. Besides, in a couple of seasons, she would be upstairs in the rooms and would not have to deal with the stupid girl.

Once again, the young girl's will was stronger than the older girl. All she had to do was not surrender to the will of the other, and she knew eventually, the person would lose their will to force her to speak. The child may not know what happiness is, but she was surviving on her own terms.

For seasons, the voice would talk to the child. She would hear it in her mind and could even speak to the voice without verbally saying anything. But when she was alone, and there was no one else around, she would talk to the voice aloud. No, the child was not dumb, the child was very smart. Maybe even too smart to be living in Bonehaven. She still did not know her name, but she did not need to. Since the voice was always with her, it did not need to call to her to get her attention. She did not need a name. Even though she might have wanted one.

One night when the girl was four seasons old, she was cleaning downstairs in the brothel where she was living. As usual, the woman who took care of her was upstairs, and the girl who had spent the first few moon-cycles training her, did not come downstairs at night any longer, so the young girl kept busy by cleaning something. If she had a rag in her hand, and she appeared to be working, there was less likely a chance that someone would yell at her or give her another task to do. She learned early that if she chose a job to do, and went about doing it, the adults left her alone. They did not want the hassle of dealing with the dumb child.

While she was wiping down one of the tables in the waiting area, the place where men could have a drink before they went upstairs with one of the women, the young girl noticed a man watching her. The other girl had taught her that if any man tried to touch her, then she was to report it immediately to one of the matrons. The man was looking at her, but she knew that she did not have to worry about him trying something.

The next night the same man came back to the brothel. The young girl saw him again, sitting there watching her. Once again, all he did was watch, until one of the matrons told the child to take care of something else. The child obeyed, without question, even though she wanted to continue to keep an eye on the man.

On the third night, the young girl made sure that she was in the waiting room, at the same time as the previous two nights. As the child was hoping, the man was there and once again, as soon as the child stepped into the room, the man's eyes were on the young girl.

She did not know why the man was always staring at her, but she wanted to. She even thought about going over and speaking to him. That idea only lasted until her next breath, because even though she was curious, she did not want anyone to hear her talk, or else they would expect it from her all the time. And since they would know she could, they would not stop beating her until she spoke, or she was dead. The young girl knew that it would come to the second option first. She stayed in the waiting room until instructed to do something else. She would be back tomorrow night.

She had come into the waiting room in hopes to see the man, but he was not there. She waited as long as she could, wiping down the same table, five times before even moving on to the next one. Focused on waiting for the man, she did not notice one of the women who worked in the brothel was talking to her. Since she did not respond in any manner, the woman came up behind her and struck the child across the head, knocking her to the floor. While lying there, she looked up at the woman who had just hit her. They stared into each other's eyes, and each of them saw something. The child saw the woman that she was going to kill for striking her. The woman saw in the child's eyes the hatred she had. A hatred that showed if she could, the child would stand up, take the closest sharp object, and stab the woman until she bled to death. The woman saw it and walked away, not even telling the child what she had wanted, or why she had struck her.

The child stood and walked out of the room. She was heading for the kitchen to grab one of the cook's knives and find the woman who had just struck her. *"Not yet,"* the voice said to her. *"If you strike her down because she made you angry, then she is the one who has control of you. Even if you kill her, it is because of what she did, that caused you to act. Never let someone control your actions, they are yours to control."*

The child stopped walking. She understood what the voice had said. She was still angry, but she would not kill the woman. Maybe someday she would, but not now. She was in control of her actions. She was in control of her life. *"That is correct my child,"* the voice said to her in a soothing, comforting, tone, which calmed the child even more. She could trust the voice.

She turned around to find a task to do. Deciding that the man was not going to show up this night, so there was no need to go to the waiting room. Just as she was about to walk away, she looked up and saw the man who had been watching her for the past few nights coming down the stairs. As soon as he saw her, and as he continued to make his way to the lower level, they never took their eyes off each other. When he stepped off the stairs, he stopped and continued to look at the girl. They stared at each other for a few breaths then he walked away, heading for the exit. That was the last time the young girl saw the man for quite some time.

One night while the child was cleaning one of the downstairs rooms, the voice spoke to her. *"I need you to see something."*

The girl looked around and saw no one was near her so she spoke to answer the voice. "What?" the girl asked in a whisper.

"I cannot tell you; you have to see for yourself. But you must be quiet and do as I say. Can you do that?"

"Yes," the child answered. She trusted the voice. It was always nice to her.

"Leave where you are and go into the hallway off to the left." The girl did as the voice had instructed her and was now standing in the hallway in front of a door. *"Open it, take some of the linens out, and hold them in your arms."* The girl did as the voice instructed her. *"Now go to the level above."*

The girl did hesitate to respond, and since she was out in the hallway, she only thought of what she wanted to say to the voice. *"I am not allowed. The women will be starting their work in a little while and I am not old enough to go up there when they are with the men."*

The voice knew the girl was telling the truth, but it needed the child upstairs. *"You will not be long. And what I want you to see, is up there. You want to see it, don't you?"* The child thought for a moment and passed to the voice that she did. *"Then you have to go up the stairs."* The voice had one more thing to say to entice the young girl. *"But if you do not want to, you do not have to. It is ok if you are afraid."*

"I am not afraid," the child said aloud and looked around to make sure no one heard her.

"Then go up the stairs. Take the linen with you. If someone should see you, and ask what you are doing, just point in the direction down the hallway, and they will think that you are taking the linen to one of the rooms."

To the young girl, it sounded like an easy thing to do, and besides, the voice was her friend.

The child walked to the stairs and started to climb them. One woman did pass her, coming down, but did not even acknowledge that the child was there. After four seasons of keeping quiet, most of the women who work in the brothel believed the child was slow minded and was not worth the effort to speak to.

The child made it up the stairs without anyone else seeing her. *"Go down the hall and turn left,"* the young girl did what the voice said. *"Head to the third door on the right and go inside."*

The girl wanted to say something again. She knew that she was to stay out of the rooms while the women work, including the room belonging to the woman who took care of her. The older girls were the ones who clean the rooms on this level. The girl standing in the hallway, in front of the door, still was not old enough.

"It's ok," the voice said, *"There is no one in the room so you will not be seen."*

The girl trusted the voice, so she opened the door and stepped inside. The voice was correct; there was no one in the room. When she was in far enough, she closed the door behind her and then looked around. *"What did you want to show me?"* the girl thought to the voice.

"First you must go over to the door on your right, open it, and step inside. Once you are in, close the door behind you."

The girl saw the door the voice spoke of. It had not been wrong so far, so the girl did what the voice said. She opened the door to the small closet, stepped inside, and closed the door behind her. *"What now? I can't see anything in here."* The child was beginning to question what the voice wanted her to do.

"You must wait a moment; it will not be long now. But for you to see what I want to show you, you need to slide the handle that is on the back of the door. I know it is dark in there, but just use your hand to find the latch."

The girl did and when she had a hold of the small wooden knob, she slid it back to the right. Light from the room came into the small area, and the girl was now able to see into the room on the other side of the door. "What am I to see?" the girl said aloud since no one was around.

"You must be quiet, or someone will find you." The girl did not want that to happen, so she kept quiet.

It was not long before the girl heard the door to the outer room open. *"Look into the room, but remain silent,"* the voice said to the child, and when she looked through the small opening, she saw the young woman who had trained her to do the jobs assigned to her. The young woman had not spoken to her, since the day she had gone up to the second level of the building. Now the young woman was in the room by herself. She was not alone for long.

The girl hiding, heard the door open and shut, and then saw a man walk over to where the bed was, where the girl who had trained her was standing. She was not standing for long. The man put his hands on the girl's shoulders and pushed her to the floor to her knees. The girl then began to undo the strap the man had around his waist and then she pulled the man's trousers to the floor. The girl saw the young woman, rubbing her hands against the man. *"What is she doing?"* the girl thought to the voice.

"Watch," the voice replied to her.

The young woman continued to rub her hands on the man, and then the man reached down and pulled the young woman up to stand in front of him. "Get that dress off and get on your back," the man said in a demanding tone.

The young woman did as the man said. She slid the dress down to where it was in a pile at her feet. She then stepped out of it and climbed into the bed. The girl in the closet was watching the woman so she did not see the man remove his shirt and step out of his trousers, now on the floor. She only saw that the man had no clothes on when he climbed into the bed and positioned himself on top of the young woman.

It was only a moment later that the man was moving up and down on the young woman. He was making grunting noises, but it was the face of the young woman the girl was watching and focusing on. The young woman's face showed that she was in pain. But what the girl did not understand, was that if the man was hurting her, why was she not doing something to stop him. Why would she allow him to hurt her?

The girl did not understand that this was what took place in the rooms on the second floor where she had lived her entire life. She was too young, which was why the woman who ran this establishment, just like in all the other brothels in Bonehaven, waited until a girl had reached the age of sixteen before introducing them to what the women working in brothels did. What every girl who worked in the brothels would end up doing.

The young woman, the girl was watching, had just turned eighteen. To the eyes of the citizens of Bonehaven, she was now a woman. And as a woman, she had to earn her coinage. For two seasons, she watched from rooms just like where the young girl was hiding now, watching her. Tonight though, it was time for the young woman to stop watching and start working. Tonight, she was no longer a young girl. She was just a woman. One of many that work in the brothels. One of many that would never work in any other place. Until the day, they died.

The men of Bonehaven were not allowed to touch a girl under the age of eighteen. That did not mean they could not watch them and ask the matrons of the brothels when they would be of legal age. Many men paid in advance to be with a pure girl on the day she was of legal age. Some matrons of the brothels would even auction off those times to the highest bidder. Men who somehow had the coinage would pay seasons in advance to make sure they could be with the young woman they had been watching for so long. Touching was against the law, but it was not against the law to watch, wait, and want.

The girl in the closet did not take her eyes off the scene on the other side of the door she was behind. Not even when the man let out a loud, long grunt and then fell completely on top of the young woman under him. The young woman still had her face turned towards the closet so the girl could see her. Since there was a light next to the bed, she could see the tears running from the young woman's eyes. She could see the blood seeping from under the young woman's bottom lip that had come from the woman biting into it, to try to ignore the pain she was feeling. She could see the look in the young woman's eyes; the look was as if she were already dead. If the girl did not see the young woman take in quick breaths because she was trying to stop herself from crying, then the girl would have thought that what the man had done to her, had killed her.

The man finished with what he came to do, climbed out of the bed, and put his clothes on. He then left the room. Not giving the young woman another look or even another thought. To him, he got what he wanted out of her.

The girl was about ready to open the door to the small room and go to the woman. Yes, she might have been mean to her, but she looked as if she might need some help. *"No, you must not move until I tell you to,"* the voice said, and the girl thought that it might be best to listen to the voice.

She heard the door to the outer room open. She did not see who it was, but she heard what the unknown woman said, "Get yourself cleaned up. You have another buyer." The woman closed the door after she said what she needed to.

The girl in the closet looked at the young woman on the bed. She only stayed lying down for a few breaths after the woman closed the door, and then she sat up and swung her legs over the side of the bed. It looked as if even that bit of movement caused her pain. She then slid off the side of the bed so that she landed with her feet in the dress that was on the floor. She bent down and pulled the dress up, but the girl saw that even this caused her some discomfort.

The young woman took a step towards the door

but then stopped and turned so that her back was towards the bed. She then sat down on the bed and began to cry.

The girl in the closet decided that she was not going to go to the crying woman. She had allowed the man to do what he did to her, and if he hurt her, then she should have done something to stop him. It was her own fault. She should have been in control of her actions, not the man. The girl was still watching the young woman and saw that she had started wiping her face with the back of her hands. She then stood up and walked out of the room.

"Now you can leave," the voice said. *"Make sure you take the linens, and if anyone asks what you are doing with them, just point with them."*

The girl did what the voice said. She even slid the small covering on the inside of the door back in place, even though the voice had not told her. The girl thought that it would be best if she left everything the same way it was when she entered the room.

She exited the closet and closed the door behind her. Since she wanted to be out of the room before the young woman returned, she ran to the door, and when she opened it, she only paused long enough to make sure no one saw her exiting. She closed the door behind her and headed back the way she had come. She did not run, she walked at a normal pace. The girl thought that if she were running and someone spotted her, they would think she was up to something other than her assigned duties.

When she made it back to the top of the stairs, with no one seeing her, she saw a woman coming up. She had her head down, so she did not see the girl yet. The girl looked around and moved off to the left of the top of the stairs where there was a white statue on a pillar. It was not big, but neither was the girl. She hid behind it and waited for the woman to walk down the hallway. When it was clear, she took a quick look over the banister and saw that the stairs were empty. She ran down the stairs, to get back to the first floor.

She turned down the hall and made her way back to the closet where she had taken the linen and returned them. She wanted everything back in the same place before she had started her little adventure. She then closed the door and started back into the main area, but before she entered it, she stopped and put her back up against the wall. *"What was that man doing to her?"* the girl thought to the voice.

"That is what the women here do," the voice thought to her.

"Does it always hurt them?" the girl asked.

The voice did not respond right away. It knew it had to be careful in what it told the girl. *"Let's not talk about it right now. You should continue with your duties or someone is going to notice that you have not been around."*

The girl thought that was a good idea. She also thought that with what she had just seen, it might be best if she forgot about the entire event.

The voice did not tell the girl, but it thought the same thing. It did not want to discuss with the girl what she had witnessed. At least not at this time.

FIVE

The girl did not know why the woman was making a fuss about the way her hair looked. She did remember that the woman had said something about if it were not for the girl's raven black hair, she would have not even thought that she was hers. The child ignored it pretty much the same way she ignored everything the woman would say.

The woman woke the child up early in the morning and bathed the child herself, in a wooden tub she had brought to the room where they stayed. The same room the girl and woman had lived in together for five seasons. Five seasons to the day.

The woman slept in the bed, and the child slept on the floor by the closet. The closet that the child realized almost a season ago had the same viewport she had watched the young woman and man. Every time she thought about that night, she forced those images away. She wanted to forget it completely. So much that she never even asked the voice about it.

Now that the child was cleaner than she had ever been in her entire life, the woman brushed her hair and made sure that it was nice and glossy.

When the woman finished, she said something the girl did not understand. "It is for the best." The child was facing the woman when she spoke and noticed something in her eyes. The child thought that the woman was maybe jealous that the girl's hair was so beautiful and hers was not. What the child did not know was that even though the woman's hair was more grey than black, when she was the age the girl is now, her hair was just as beautiful. Beauty fades in Bonehaven.

The other thing the girl saw while looking into the woman's eyes, was that they were glistening with tears. The look the woman was showing made the girl think that these tears were something different from when she had seen other people cry. She just did not know what they meant and did not have time to think about it any longer because there was a knock at the door.

The woman stood up from kneeling in front of the girl and turned the child so both were facing the door to the room. "Enter," the woman said.

The door opened and in walked a man. The girl immediately recognized who it was, even though she did not know his name. It was the man who had been watching her. Only she had not seen him for quite some time. Now he was here in the room where she had been living for as long as she could remember.

The man walked into the room and closed the door behind him. He looked at the woman and then positioned his head so that he was looking at the girl. He nodded twice then looked back at the woman. He then walked over to them and handed the woman a bag. From the way it jingled, it sounded like a lot of coinage. The child knew what coinage was.

The man then turned, walked back to the door, and opened it, but did not step out into the hallway. He looked back at the girl and said one word, "Come."

The girl did not understand, but felt the woman behind her, give a slight push on her shoulders, and then said, "Go with him. He is responsible for you now."

The girl looked up and behind her so that she could see the woman's face. Once again, she saw her eyes glistening with tears. She did not know why, but she decided to do as the woman had said. She was always good at doing what people told her to do. Just as long as she did not have to talk to them.

She walked towards the door, stepped out into the hallway, and started making her way to the stairs. She did not even turn around when she heard the door to the room where she had stayed all this time, close. She did not turn around to look at the man who had come to the room and was now walking behind her.

When she reached the bottom of the stairs on the first level, she stopped. She did not know what to do next, but she did not have to decide. As the man behind her walked past, he reached down, grabbed her hand, and continued to walk through the building. When they reached the front door, they exited and walked down the street. The girl had no idea what was going on, and she was starting to believe that she was not in control, so she turned to the only one who has always been with her. The only one who had ever been nice to her.

"Where is he taken me?" she thought to the voice.

"I will speak with you later." The voice could tell that the girl was becoming very troubled. *"Do not fear. I will never leave you."* The girl had to believe what the voice said. The voice was all she had. She, herself, did not even have a name.

The man took her through the city. This was the first time she had been out of the building, except when she went outside to use the relief shack. It amazed her, to see all the sights and especially all the people. For all the seasons she has been alive, she never knew that there were so many people around.

They arrived at a building and the man brought her inside with him. While still holding onto her hand, they walked up to the fourth level and into a small room; even smaller than the one where she had spent the few seasons of her life.

When they were inside, the man closed the door behind them, and finally, let go of the girl's hand. He walked over to the bed, reached behind him, and pulled out a knife he had concealed in the top of his trousers. He then leaned down and placed the knife under the mattress. When he stood up and turned to face the girl, he noticed that she was looking at him. "You stay out of there, you understand?" The girl must have been worried because for the first time in her life, she replied to someone who had asked her a question. She did not say anything, just nodded to let the man know that she understood. The man then walked away from the bed, hoping that the girl's eyes would move away from it as well.

He went over to the small table in the room and pulled a black bag over to him. He stuck his hand inside, and then brought it back out, along with a small loaf of bread. He turned to face the girl, who was looking directly at him. "Come here," the man said.

The girl was used to obeying when instructed to do something, but when the man gave her a command, she did not just obey because that was what she would normally do; no, she did what the man said because when he talked, there was something in his voice that made the girl think that if she did not do as he instructed, then he might hit her. With the size of the man, she knew that if he did strike her, she would fall to the floor, and there was a good chance she would not get back up.

When she made her way over to the man, she stopped when she was a pace from him. For a moment, she thought he was going to strike her, but when his hand came up, he held out a piece of the loaf of bread he had taken out of the bag and broke it in half. She did not reach out to accept it. "Take it and eat it all. You have to have your strength for what we are going to do." Once again, the tone in the man's voice caused her to do exactly what he said. She took the bread and began eating, right where she was standing.

The man moved away from the table and took the other piece of bread with him. Before he was completely behind the girl, she quickly turned around so that he was in her line of sight. The girl thought it would not be a good idea to let this man get behind her. She wanted to see what he was doing at all times.

The man went over and sat down on the side of the bed. He sat there eating his half of the bread, while at the same time, he watched the girl. The same way she was watching him while she ate her meal. Neither one of them spoke. The girl because she never said a word to anyone; the man, because he was a man of few words.

He finished his meal before the girl and when the girl was through, he stood up and walked back over to the table. The girl turned her body to make sure the man was in her sight. When he reached the table, he pulled the black water bag off it and was about ready to hand it to the girl but realized that it was too big for her to properly lift. Since it was the only thing he drank out of, he did not have any cups for her to use. He placed the bag back on the table and looked at the girl who still had her eyes on him. "Put your hands out like this," he said while at the same time, he stuck his hands out and down to show the girl how he wanted her to cup her hands together. "Keep them like that," he said, and she did while he picked up the water bag, pulled out the stopper, and began to pour water into the girl's hands.

Even though she knew that he probably wanted her to drink the water she waited until he said she could. "Drink it all." The girl did, but when she brought her hands up to her mouth and started to drink, she made sure she did not take her eyes off the man.

She drank the water slowly and as she was watching the man watching her, she noticed just what he looked like. He was taller than the woman who had taken care of her. His hair was long and black. Not as black as hers, but still dark enough that it stood out from other people. The beard he had, hung down off his face. It looked as if he never shaved, but he kept it trimmed enough so that it did not look untidy. It was black as well but there was also some grey in it. He had wide shoulders, and from what the girl could tell, the thickness of his upper arms was the widest she had ever seen on any of the men who had come into the building where she lived; or better yet, where she used to live.

It was the eyes that she noticed most of all. There was something about the way they looked but she did not know how to describe them. The only word she could think of was "deep." Yes, his eyes were deep, and if she were to stare at them too long, she did not know what she would see in them. For the first time since she entered this room, she turned her eyes away from the man.

He must have taken that as they were both finished with the awkwardness because he stepped away from the table and walked to the other side of the room. As he moved, she put her eyes back on the man. Just as long as she did not look into his eyes again, she would be ok. "Come here," the man said to her, and she walked over to the other side of the room where the man was standing on the other side of the bed.

The man reached over, pulled one of the two pillows off the bed, and placed it on the floor. He then turned and looked at the girl. "You sleep there." The girl was not tired, in fact, she had only been awake for a few sun-marks. Even though she could not see out the windows in the room, because thick dark cloths covered them, she knew that it was not even midday. But the man had told her to sleep there, and she knew she should obey him.

When he had stepped back and away from the pillow, the girl moved over and positioned herself on the floor with her head on the pillow. She made sure she laid on her back so that she could see the man standing over her. It was at that moment that she remembered the night she had watched the young woman with the man, and she could not help but worry that he was going to do the same thing to her. She worried so much that she held her breath, then the man walked to the other side of the bed and climbed into it. She thought she was safe for the moment and began to breathe again.

She heard the man move on the bed, sounding as if he was trying to get as comfortable as possible. He finally settled into one position and the girl thought that was the last she would hear from him for the moment. Then he spoke to her, "Get as much sleep as you can. You will not be here long."

The girl did not sleep. Even if she were tired, she did not think she would be able to close her eyes with everything that had happened today. The man did though, the girl could tell by the snoring he was making. The girl had to turn to the only one who had been with her all her life. *"Are you there?"* she called out in her mind and waited for the voice to answer. Even though it replied right away, to the scared girl, it seemed like an eternity.

"I am here," the voice said in a soothing tone.

"What is he going to do with me?" the child asked.

"It is best if we do not talk about it," the voice said, and the girl could tell that the voice was keeping something from her.

"Tell me!" the girl thought to the voice.

The voice waited a moment, letting the girl wonder if it was going to tell her something. What the girl did not know was that the voice did know what the man was going to do. That did not mean it was going to tell her. *"Remember the night where you hid and saw the man and young woman."*

"Yes," the girl thought, and she knew what the voice was telling her, but waited until it confirmed her fears.

"The man might do that to you," the voice thought to her. It did not lie to the girl. The voice said, "might."

"He cannot touch me. I am not of age yet," the girl thought to the voice.

"That is true, but in this room, no one is around," the voice did not lie to her. It just made her think of what could happen. *"Or he might sell you to another one like him. Then they might do..."* The voice did not continue. It wanted the girl to visualize the same thing she saw that night with the young woman, only instead she would be the one the man was hurting.

"Help me!" the girl thought, but the voice did not reply. *"You have to help me get out of here."*

"Where would you go?" the voice said. *"You live in a world where people do as they please. If you were to leave this room, once you made it out of this place, they would bring you back to this man, or take you to someone else. No, it is best if you stay where you are and hope that he does not...,"* the voice did not continue.

The girl thought to herself for a moment. Then thought to the voice. *"Can you help me leave this place?"*

The voice waited a moment before answering. *"Yes, but anywhere you go in this city they will find you."*

"Then I will leave the city," the girl thought to the voice.

It waited a few more moments before speaking to the child again. *"No, it is too risky. Even if you were to get out of the city, they would hunt you down and bring you back. There are a lot of people, and they could send everyone after you."*

The girl was beginning to lose hope. Everything the voice told her she believed. It never lied to her before, why would it now.

"Maybe there is a way," the voice thought to her, and it could sense the hope returning to the little girl. *"I might be able to help you get out of the building and out of the city. I will even be able to stop anyone from ever coming after you."* The voice paused, *"No it is too dangerous. You are too young and are neither brave nor strong enough."*

"Yes, I am!" the girl said aloud and thought for a moment that the man had heard her. When she heard him snoring, she knew he was still asleep. She started thinking to the voice again, *"I am brave enough. I am strong enough. I will get out of here with or without your help. I am in control."*

The voice knew the young girl was ready. *"Very well, I will help you."*

"Then I can leave?" the girl asked.

"Yes, but not yet. You must wait until night. When I am at my strongest."

"What are you going to do?" the girl asked.

Even though the girl could not see it, and if the voice could, it would be smiling. *"Something spectacular and you will finally see me."* With that, the girl could not help but smile. Not only would she leave this place, but she would be able to see who she had been talking to for all these seasons. *"Get some sleep child. Tonight, you leave this place."*

Even though it was not even midday, the child slept.

She opened her eyes when she heard the man making a noise on the other side of the bed. She positioned herself so that she was on her knees to see over the top of the mattress. The man was on the other side of the room looking out the window. The sun had set, and the night was out. That was what he was waiting for. It was also, what the voice was waiting for. For the night to come. The man always went out at night. That was when he took care of his business. The voice was not sure if the man would go out tonight, especially since the voice knew what the man had planned for the next day.

The man sensed the girl was watching him and turned to see the top part of her face on the other side of the bed. He let the cloth fall back over the window and stepped away. As he walked over to the bed, the young girl stood up and took a couple of steps back. The man gave her a look but did not say anything. He just bent over, lifted the mattress a bit, and pulled something from underneath it. He placed it behind him immediately, but the girl was sure it was the knife, she had seen earlier.

The man pulled his shirt down to make sure that it was over the top part of his trousers, so no one would see the knife. He looked at the girl and they held each other's stares. The man was the first to turn away. "Do not leave this room," the man said, just before he opened the door and walked out.

A part of the girl wanted to do exactly what he had said, in fear of what he would do to her if she did leave, and he found out. She thought that maybe it would be best if she just stayed in the room. The voice could not allow that. *"Are you ready?"* it thought to her.

Hearing the voice again, brought back the desire and the willingness to leave the place, "What should I do?" she asked the voice aloud since she was alone in the room.

The voice was quick to reply. The child had to leave, and it did not have much time for what it planned to do. *"Go over to the table and take the bag the man had the bread in."* When the girl moved over to the table, she grabbed the bag the voice had spoken of. *"Take the water bag as well."* The first bag was heavy enough, but with the added weight of the second, the girl was not sure if she would be able to carry them both. *"You have to be strong remember,"* the voice said, knowing what the girl was thinking. With the encouragement of the voice, the girl was ready to move on. *"Now quickly, leave the room before the man returns."* The voice had been watching this man ever since he had taken an interest in the same girl the voice was interested in. It knew the man went out every night and did not return until just before sunrise. Although it did not tell the girl, she did not need to know.

Just before the girl opened the door to leave, she stopped and turned back around to look at the bed. *"What are you doing? You have to leave now."* The voice thought to her.

"I have to see something," the girl said aloud, and walked over to the bed; the same side the man had been standing on before he left. She had to sit the two bags down so that she would have her hands free. Once they were, she placed them under the mattress and lifted it as best she could. It was enough, and she saw something that brought a smile to her face. Under the mattress, the man had more than just one knife. In fact, there were more than just knives. There were swords, sticks, metal objects that looked like stars, and even some very thin wire. The girl did not know why they were there but one of those items was coming with her.

She knew the swords were too big to carry, and since she did not know what some of the other items were, she chose a small knife. The blade was no longer than a grown man's middle finger, and the handle was about the same length. It was small enough that the girl could slip it in the bag with the food, so she would not have to worry about dropping it. While holding the mattress with one hand she grabbed the small knife. Luckily, she was fast enough to take it, before the weight of the mattress became too much for her, and it fell back down on the bed. But not in the spot it was before she had lifted it. She went to the other side of the bed and pushed on the mattress so that it was back in its original position. It might have taken her time to get the knife and fix the mattress, but the knife she could use, and as for putting the mattress back, she knew that before she left she wanted to make it look as if she had never touched the knife hidden under the mattress.

"You must go now," the voice said.

The girl did not say anything. She was proud of herself for thinking about the knife. She did not know how, but she had a feeling that the man had more than one item hidden. She picked up the bags and left the room.

She did not run. Just like the night when she spied on the young woman, she knew that if she ran, she would draw more attention to herself. She walked out of the room, down to the ground floor of the building, and then she walked out into the night.

"Head to your right," the voice said, and she did. Now and then, the voice would tell her to go in a different direction, and she would obey, without question. She knew the voice was the only one that was going to be able to lead her to safety.

It took her three marks, but finally, she passed

through the front gates of Bonehaven. Even though there were guards posted; they did not see her. The same way that there was not a single person in the city, who had seen her leave. The moon can cast shadows, just like the sun, so the voice guided the child through the city and out of it, making sure that she was always in the shadows.

The girl was tired and since she was out of Bonehaven, she wanted to stop and rest. The voice told her that she was still too close to the city, and the people can still come after her. It convinced her to continue through the night, and when it was day, she could rest. The voice had helped her to escape so she trusted it.

When it was almost morning the voice led her to a group of trees off the road where she would be able to rest. Since she was only five seasons old and had been traveling all night, rest is what she wanted most of all.

The child slept until the evening. She would have continued to remain where she was, but the voice woke her and told her that she had to start walking again. When the child appeared that she was going to go back to sleep, the voice told her that the citizens of Bonehaven had plenty of time to search for her there. They would now start looking outside the confinements of the city. That made the girl grab her things and continue with her journey. To ensure she did not start to think about stopping again, the voice told her that she would not have to travel for long, and then it would make sure no one from Bonehaven would be able to come after her. The girl liked what the voice said.

When she traveled far enough, the voice told the child to turn around and face the city behind her. She did and saw that she was looking down at it. She was now away from Bonehaven, where she could see it in the valley, as well as the mountains on each side of it that went high into the sky.

"Are you ready?" the voice asked.

"For what?" the child asked aloud.

"To see how great, I am." That brought a smile to the child.

Moon knew that it did not have much time. The only reason it would be able to do this, was because Sun was doing the same thing on the other side of the world. Sun was moving higher into the sky, going against what Ourgós had set Sun to do. Because Sun was breaking Creator's plan, Moon could as well. As Sun was ascending in the sky over Lorraine, Moon was rising into the sky over Bonehaven. Moon would show the child what power Moon had.

When Moon was at the highest peak, it spoke to the child. *"Raise your hands in the air and look up to me."* The girl did just that. She saw the moon high in the sky and knew who had been talking to her all these seasons. To the girl, Moon was bright, Moon was full, Moon was beautiful.

"Now look back at the city but keep your arms raised high over your head," Moon said to her, and

then gave her one final instruction for what Moon had planned. *"Now say the word."*

The girl knew the word. She did not know how, but she knew. She looked down on the city and spoke, "Pull."

As she spoke, Moon used the control of gravity and forced the mountains standing on the sides of Bonehaven to shake. The force was so strong the mountains began to crumble and fall over the city. By the time it had stopped, there were no more mountains. There was no more Bonehaven. Piles and piles of rocks, which had once been the tall and mighty mountains, were the only thing now visible at the location. Bonehaven was still part of the world, but from that moment on, part of the world covered it completely.

"Did I do that?" the girl asked Moon.

"No, I did," Moon spoke to the girl in her thoughts but even she could tell that Moon was not as strong as Moon used to be. With what Moon had done, Moon used up a lot of strength. Strength which Moon would recover in no time at all.

SIX

Moon had a reason; Moon always had a reason for what Moon did. Moon did this to show the girl that she could trust Moon. That no matter what, Moon would always be there with her. Did Moon care for the girl? Maybe, to a certain extent. Moon had chosen the girl to be Moon's warrior. As Sun had done on the other side of the world, and what Sun did, Moon would do as well.

Moon had chosen the girl on the night she was born. She had been born in the middle of the night when Moon was highest in the sky. Moon heard the child cry out when she came from her mother. When Moon saw that the child had been born in Bonehaven, Moon knew that with the way the city was, the child would grow up in harsh conditions. Conditions that would make the child into what Moon needed her to be.

Moon looked over the child constantly. Guiding her, telling her what she should do around other people. But most of all Moon wanted the child to learn to trust Moon; and over the seasons, she did.

The night the man started watching the girl, Moon thought that the man might try to hurt her. Moon could not allow that, but Moon could not stop him if he did. Moon was powerful, even more powerful than Sun, at least in Moon's opinion; but Moon could not interact with the humans and other beings in the world below. Moon knew the man could be a problem if he took an interest in the same child Moon wanted.

Moon could talk to the child at any time. It was a gift Moon gave her on the night she was born. Moon could not talk to other humans directly, but Moon could listen in, and listen, Moon did.

On the fourth night that the man had gone to the place the girl was staying, the man went upstairs to talk to the woman who took care of the girl, her mother. Moon listened and discovered something that might cause a problem with what Moon was planning.

The man and woman talked. They talked about the girl. About how the man was sure, the child of this woman was his. At first, the woman told him that there was no way to know for certain. Many men had come to her over the seasons to buy her time so that she could take care of their needs. Since the child was four seasons old, there was no way that either of them could tell if the man was the child's father or not. Especially since she was born so many seasons ago.

The man knew.

The night before the man started watching the girl, he had come into the brothel wanting to spend some time with one of the women. As soon as he saw the girl, he knew the child was his. He saw it in her eyes. They were the same as his. There was only one word to describe them, deep. It was a trait passed down in his family's bloodline. There was no doubt in his mind; the girl was his.

The man was not sure if the woman believed him when he told her how he knew the child was his; but when he told the woman what he planned, the mother did not care if the man was the child's father or not. What he was going to do, was something she thought would never be possible.

The woman was hard on the child. Even hit the child a few times until she realized that it would not do any good. To her, there was something wrong with the girl. She only hit her to get her to talk and respond. She did not see a problem with it because the woman who raised her, did the same thing. Even though she was hard on the girl, did not mean there was not a part of her that did not love the child. That love might be deep down, under all the hardship she suffered through, but there was still a bit of love there. When the man explained to the woman what he was going to do, the mother could not help but think that he was going to be a blessing to her daughter.

The man was a hard man. Even before, he came to Bonehaven. The only reason he had come to the city, was because of the price placed on his head. A reward so big that no matter where he went, someone would always find him and try to collect. And every time they tried to take his life, he ended up taking the life of the person who had come for him.

Before he came to Bonehaven this man was an assassin. One of the best. One of his assignments was to kill a very important man; and when given an assignment, he completed it. Always.

The target's father, a powerful and wealthy duke, put his own contract out on the man who had killed his son. Since the man had been part of the Assassin's Guild, then the guild itself would not accept the contract. They were the ones who had sent the assassin to kill the duke's son in the first place, so they would not kill the one working for them. If they had, then there would not be very many assassins left.

The duke still wanted the man who killed his son to die, so he offered half of his lands, and half of his wealth to anyone that could find the assassin and bring him his head. Since the Assassin's Guild would not allow any of its members to go after the man, it was only desperate men wanting to become rich, and fools wanting fame, who tried to collect the reward. If they actually knew who they were going to be facing, they would not have even bothered trying.

The Assassin's Guild would not allow any of its

assassins to go after the man, and even if they did, there probably was not a single one of the guild's members that would have accepted the contract. They knew about the one who had made the kill and they did not want to even think about going up against him. The man was the best. Like his father before him, and his father before him. Being an assassin was in their bloodline. Of course, the ones who had trained each family member said that it was not what was in the blood that made the members of the family so efficient at what they did, it was in the eyes. Those deep eyes. So deep, that not even death would look in them. And if death would not, then who would?

After the man had killed the duke's son, he continued with what he had been doing. But by luck, or by fate, word got out that he was the one who had killed the son of the duke. Since then, no matter where he went, there would always be someone trying to collect the price on his head.

He dealt with being the one hunted for a number of seasons. Someone would come for him, and that person would die. But after so many attempts on his life, he was growing tired of all the death. He knew that no matter where he went in the civilized world, someone would always find him, and force him to kill. He decided to go to the one place no one would go if they did not have to, Bonehaven, a place that was uncivilized.

For many seasons, he lived in the city and worked

in the mines. He might have been an assassin for most of his life, but he was not afraid of manual labor. Every day he worked in the mines, and then went back to his lodgings, slept, and then the next day he would perform the same routine. He was content with the way he would spend the remaining seasons of his life.

Every now and then, he would get the desire to be with a woman. It was the responsibility of the women working in the brothels to make sure she could not conceive a child during the time she was working. The women had a leaf from a plant, which they were to take once a day to ensure that they did not become pregnant. Since there were a lot of children born to these women, it was obvious that it did not always work. Some say the leaf did not work at all but was used anyways so the women would be able to tell the men who bought her time that they were taking the leaf and not fertile, which took all the responsibility off the man. Which is the way they wanted it.

The man knew the girl was his, the minute he saw her and it was at that moment that he felt, for the first time in his life, that he needed to think about someone other than himself. When he met with the child's mother, he told her what he was going to do.

He had not killed since he had come to Bonehaven. After he saw the child, he knew he would again, for her. He told the child's mother that he would raise enough funds so that he could take the child out of Bonehaven. When the mother heard that, she did not care if the man was the child's father or not. If he would take the child out of this place, then she would let him. Deep down she did love the child, and if one of her daughters could have a life outside of the desolation, then she would give the child the chance.

It was risky. The man might be lying to her, and instead of doing what he said, he might sell her to someone else or do something worse. The mother had to risk it. If the man was lying to her, then she would never know, and she could just believe that her daughter was somewhere living the life she never had. Even if it were a lie, she would believe the lie.

The man did not lie to the woman. After he left the brothel that night, he began with his plan. He still needed coinage to feed himself, and to pay for his lodgings. With what he made from working in the mines, even if he did work another shift, he would never be able to save enough to make a living in some other part of the world, for himself and his daughter. He was going to need a lot of funding. Enough to take him across the great waters, to some place where the contract on his life would not follow him. It had been many seasons since he had come to Bonehaven, but he of all people knew that a price on a man's head lasted for as long as the man drew breath.

He needed more funding than what the mines

could provide. To get what he needed he went back to what he did best. There was no Assassin's Guild in Bonehaven. That did not mean there were no people that he could kill. People who had some coinage the assassin would be able to take for himself and his daughter. Not one person in all of Bonehaven would have the entire amount he would need, but enough of the citizens together would. He decided that over the next season, while he was waiting for the girl to turn five, the age when a woman could legally sell a child, he would go out at night, and kill again. This time it was not because it was his profession, but for his daughter.

The man followed his plan. Every morning he would go to work in the mines to pay for his provisions and lodging. When night came, he would go out and find his next victim. He always made sure he killed at least two times a moon-mark. He could not just start killing any citizen he came across because too many dead bodies would have what little law enforcement there was in Bonehaven to start looking for whoever was leaving bodies around; the man had to be cautious. If caught and sentenced to death for the killings, he would be no good to his daughter.

He would go out and watch the people that would go into the drinking houses and brothels. He was looking for the ones that visited the places on a regular basis. Since they attended them constantly then it would mean they had enough funds to do so. Those were the ones the man would take from.

When he had chosen his target, he would follow them to wherever they lodged. The next night he would sneak into their place and see if he could find any coin. He never took something that he would have to sell to get funds; he only wanted coins. Sometimes he would be able to find where the person kept their funds, but most of the time he came up empty. People kept their coin on them. Break-ins were common in Bonehaven, and there were no facilities where a person could place their earnings, until they needed them. If there were, they would have been owned by the same people who own the mines, and therefore, a person would end up giving the majority of their coinage to the people holding it for them.

If he found something, then the person was fortunate. They only lost their funds. They would have to work hard to get it back, but at least they were alive to work. If the man was not able to find what he was looking for, the next night he would follow the man again and wait for the right moment to pull him into an alley or darken doorway, then ask the man where he kept his currency. Coin was what kept a person alive in Bonehaven, so most people would not willingly hand over what they had on them. If they did not, the man had no problem searching the dead body, which his hesitant victim soon became. The assassin killed everyone he stole from. He could not leave anyone alive just in case they did go to the local authorities. He had to remain free and alive for his daughter.

The man did these assaults throughout the season. Once a moon-cycle he would take on a riskier mission, but with the risk, came a better payoff. He would sneak into one of the lodgings of the people overseeing the operations of the mines. He was an assassin, and he had no problem getting into any place that was his objective.

All transactions that took place in Bonehaven were with hard coin and paid the moment the transaction took place. There was no such thing as credit. If a person were to give someone a line of credit, they might not live long enough to pay the funds they owed. It was pay now; there was no later.

Because of this, the workers in the mines received their wages in coin. That meant the people overseeing the mines had to have the coins available to pay the workers. They might not have paid them much, but if they did not pay the workers at all, then there would be no ore coming out of the mines.

The man would make his way into a building that oversaw the operations of a mine. They kept their funds in a strong iron box with a lock. No one guarded the boxes. There were guards within the building, but it was nothing for the man to get by them. It was nothing for the man to pick the lock, or in some cases locks, so that he could get to the funds inside. Even though there were usually a lot of coins available for him to take, he only took about two or three of the gold pieces. The workers of the mines received their wages in copper, so the gold coins were for the company's overseers to purchase whatever they needed. He knew that if he had taken it all, the people overseeing the mines would have the security force search every place in the city to find the funds and the person who had taken them. Since he only removed a few pieces, then the people in charge of the funds would think they had miscounted. To increase that theory he never took from the same building more than once. There were over thirty different buildings that housed the operational aspects of the different mining companies. Since he only did this once a mooncycle, the man did not have to worry about someone reporting the missing coins.

After a season, he was ready to complete his plan. He had saved up some funds, but it was not enough for what he had planned. That would not stop him.

On the morning when the girl had turned five, he went to the brothel. When he knocked on the door, opened it, and saw his daughter staring at him with those deep eyes, he knew he was doing the right thing.

Before he left with the girl, he gave the child's mother a bag of coins that was more than what she would have received if she sold the child to someone else; much more. It was the man's way of settling anything between them. The child was the woman's as well, but the man had no feelings for her in any way. He understood that she was the one that gave birth to the child, but when he walked out of the room with the girl, she was his and his alone. The amount of coinage he had given the woman, made sure of that. If she spent it wisely, while still working in the brothel, then she would live a comfortable, if not a happy life.

That is, for the time, Bonehaven would still be standing.

The man took the girl back to his lodgings, gave her something to eat and drink, then prepared a spot for the child to sleep. Then he got some sleep himself. Even though he would work the morning shift in the mines, this day he did not. He needed to rest for what he had planned once the sun went down, and especially just before the sun came up.

When evening came, he told the girl not to leave the room. The mother said the child was good at following instructions, so he trusted that she would listen to him.

He left his lodgings and went out into the night. There were four buildings, which were close to where the man lived, which oversaw some of the mines. He was going to hit all four of them tonight. He was going to have to make sure he was extra cautious, to ensure no one would see him, especially since he was so close to leaving with his daughter.

He had no problem breaking into the buildings or the boxes where the company kept their funds. This time he took every bit of coin they had. He did this to four different buildings, and with what he had collected, he had enough to make a good life for himself and his daughter. The life he never had.

He would pay passage for a ship to take them to the other side of the world. He would find somewhere he could purchase some land and farm enough where they would not have to worry about food. He would get some milking cows as well, and even some chickens. Most of all he would get his daughter a dog for herself. When he was a child, he always wanted a dog of his own. He never had one. When he entered the Assassin's Guild at fifteen, he never thought about having a dog again. Not until the moment when he saw his daughter.

When he finished collecting the last of the funding he needed, and after he had buried it outside the city's gate with the rest of the coinage he had collected over the season, he made his way back to his room. He would dig up the coinage when he and his daughter left the city. They had to leave the city before anyone became aware of the missing funds to the mining companies or the guards would not let anyone leave, which was something that he would not allow.

As soon as he walked into the room, he noticed that the child was not in sight. Since there was only the one room, the only place the child could have been hiding was under the bed. But when he looked, she was not there.

He had only known that he had been a father for about a season. In that time, he had dreamed of what it would be like, but he never dreamt of what it would be like to find that his daughter was missing. For the first time in his life, the assassin, who had killed so many, knew what fear was. Not for himself, but for his daughter.

As he was standing there trying to decide what to do, he noticed the bag that he had packed with food for him and his daughter was gone, as well as the bag for water. He went over to the table but did not see them lying on the floor. Then he thought of what else he had in the room.

He went over to the bed and this time he did not have time to lift the mattress gently. He grabbed a hold of it and flipped it over so that it fell to the other side of the bed. Immediately he was able to tell which one of his weapons was missing. One of his knives.

He thought that maybe the woman he had bought the child from had double-crossed him. Had taken his coinage and then came back for the girl to leave Bonehaven on her own. The brothel where the woman lived was the next place he would be going. He did not even replace the mattress back on the bed. He just grabbed another of his knives to go with the one he already had at the small of his back. Someone was going to pay for taking his daughter.

When he reached the brothel, he headed straight up the stairs and to the room of the woman he was going to more than likely kill. When he broke down the door, he saw the woman. He did not see his daughter.

After he threatened the woman, with her life, and found out that she did not have the girl, he realized that someone else must have taken the child. He could only blame himself. He was the one who left her alone. Someone must have seen him bring her home and wanted the girl for themselves or wanted to sell her to someone else.

What was a surprise to both the man and the woman was that they were both concerned for the welfare of the child. They left the brothel and began searching Bonehaven. They searched for the entire day and into the evening. The man even went to some of the people he knew who dealt with the criminal elements of the city to find out any information. Since these people were not into giving information freely, the assassin had to threaten everyone he encountered to find out if they knew anything about his daughter or if someone had taken her. Three of those people ended up seeing just how easy it was for this man to take a person's life when they would not talk.

They searched the city for a day and evening, with no success. They would have continued their search if it were not for the rumbling noise they heard coming from over their heads.

Like everyone else in Bonehaven, when they heard the noise, they stopped whatever they were doing and looked up into the sky. The first thing they saw was that even though the sun had gone down not long ago, the moon was high in the sky as if it was the middle of the night. Once they were over the shock of the moon's position, they focused on what was making the rumbling noise. When the first rocks and boulders started falling from the mountains that rose up on the sides of the city, everyone knew that there was no escape. There was nowhere to run. There was no time.

The man and woman died not knowing what happened to their child. Like everyone in Bonehaven, the mountains had fallen on the city leaving everyone buried under stone. No one would know how the mountains crumbled and covered the city from the world. No one except for the little girl who had walked through the city gates the night before.

What the girl did not know was that the woman, her mother had loved her. What the girl did not know was the man that had taken her out of the room was her father and even though they had not known each other for long, he loved her. What the girl did not know was that the young woman who had taught her when she was two seasons old and was the one she watched from the other side of that door was her half-sister. What the girl did not know was that the woman who had struck her on the back of her head so hard that she wanted to kill the woman was her aunt, her mother's sister. What the girl did not know was that even though she did not know it, she did have a family, even if there was no love shone to her.

The girl did not know, but Moon did. However,

Moon did not want the child to know about a family or about love. Moon needed the child to think that the only one the girl could trust was Moon. Let her think the woman and the man did not care for her, it would only harden her heart and make her into what Moon needed. Maybe the time would come when Moon would tell the child about the family she had, but only if it made the child's heart even harder. Moon needed the child to be Moon's. And she was.

SEVEN

anna looked over the city of Maridian from the top of the building. She was on the roof, to hang out the wash, so it could dry in the sun, but whenever she went up there, she had to take some time for herself. To think about how her life had changed.

It had been five seasons since the Mountain Raiders had come to her village, which forced her and her family to leave Lorraine. If it were up to Hanna, she would have never left, but she did not have a say in what her parents decided to do. She may not have had a say, but it was because of her, they all had to find a new place to call home.

Even as Hanna was remembering, and even though she wanted to lift her head and look up in the sky to see the sun, she resisted the temptation. After the incident with the Mountain Raiders, she never looked at the sun again. Her life changed from that moment on.

Sun had told her that she would be the one to save the village and all the people living there would be happy with what she would do. Sun was wrong.

They might have been happy that the ones who came to destroy them did not kill them, but with what the child had done, they knew the Mountain Raiders were not the worst thing out on the field that day. The Raiders, even though destroyed, turned to ash right in front of the villagers' eyes, the one who had done the unexplainable act, was a child who had lived with them for those few seasons. The child, whom her parents and the leader of the village allowed back in through the gates of their village and looked at by the citizens differently from that day on. In their eyes, she was just as dangerous as the Raiders themselves.

Hanna noticed the way the villagers had changed towards her. Before they were always glad to see her. She was always smiling and so happy, and they enjoyed having her around. After she destroyed every last Raider, Hanna could tell, by the way the villagers stared at her, all they could think of was if she would do the same to them.

Even her parents looked at her differently. Of course, they still loved her, and her mother and father were the only ones who would even talk to her. They and the leader of the village asked her how she was able to do what they saw, but when she told them that it was not her, it was Sun, she could tell that they did not believe her.

Sun told her then, never to speak to anyone about Sun. They would not believe her, so there was no reason to tell them what the girl knew to be true. Hanna had even tried to convince Sun to tell her parents that she was telling the truth, but Sun had told her that no one would be able to hear Sun except for her. For the first time in her life, Hanna did not know if Sun was telling the truth or not.

Sun had told her, even before she knew it was Sun talking to her, that the people in the village would be happy with what she had done to the Raiders. When she saw the look on their faces while she was still standing outside the village gate, she knew Sun was wrong. She began to wonder if Sun was wrong or had lied about that, then maybe Sun was wrong or was lying about not being able to speak to others. Hanna did not know what to believe.

Sun told her that the villagers and her parents were acting differently because they did not expect to see such a marvelous miracle and that they would eventually see that she had saved them and they would soon be thankful for what she did. Sun was wrong or had lied to the child again.

After a cycle of the moon had passed, the villagers still looked upon her, as if she were something they did not want around. Darius had not even spoken to her since that day with the Raiders, and like the other children of the village, not only did they not talk to her, but every time Hanna looked at them and them at her, all she could see was the hate in their eyes. They even started calling her a name. Not to her face, no they would never do that because they were too afraid of her, but behind her back, she heard the name they had given her, Wicked Girl.

Soon Hanna did not associate with any of the children. To Hanna that was not so bad. Yes, she missed the fun they used to have together, but if they were going to be mean to her then she did not need them. Not even Darius. She was even glad he had stopped pulling her hair. At least a part of her was.

Hanna was ok with the children staying away from her, but what she did not realize was that in the same way, they kept their distance from her, the adults in the village kept their distance from her parents. In other places in the region that might have been ok, but for the people in the village of Lorraine, everyone depended on everyone else for their survival.

Hanna's father was a carpenter. He made his living by making things out of wood and either selling them to other people in the village or trading them for something his family needed. Food being the main item. Hanna and her mother worked in the garden but when they needed seeds to grow vegetables, no one in the village would trade with them. No one would even take coin from Hanna's parents, afraid that the child might have done something to the funds that would cause something bad to happen.

Her father and mother, even though they knew that what was happening to them was going to make their lives more difficult in Lorraine, they did not give up hope. They had lived in the village since the time they became husband and wife. They had come to Lorraine because it was a good, quiet place to raise a family, and since Hanna's father was a carpenter, and the woods surrounded Lorraine, he would always be able to make a living. Even after the villagers had distanced themselves.

It was the first time a trader came to the village that Hanna's parents realized they were going to have more problems than they thought. Before Hanna's father could get to the trader to barter his wares for coin or for seeds, the word had already reached the man on what the Wicked Girl had done. The villagers made sure of it.

It was the same way every time someone would come to the village. The trader would know what had happened. Even if they did not believe it, the person could see that if they did any business with the parents of the Wicked Girl, then none of the other villagers would do business with them. The traders had to think of their own welfare, and not of one family.

About a season and a half after the incident with the Mountain Raiders, just before Hanna's seventh Blessed Day, her parents told her that they would be leaving Lorraine, to head to another town or one of the bigger cities. Her father was a carpenter, and if he could not make his items, and sell them, he knew he would be able to find work somewhere even if he worked for someone else. To stay in Lorraine, meant that they would not survive another season.

Hanna was not sure how she felt about leaving. Lorraine was the only place she had known. And even though she no longer had any friends, she still had her mother and father; and as long as she had them, she would be ok. She decided that if she had to leave Lorraine, then she would still be happy.

Her father had a wagon, but no longer had a horse to pull it. He went to the village leader and asked to trade his home for a pair of horses so that he could take his family away. The man did not want to trade with Hanna's father. It was not because he was like the other villagers, at least not completely. Yes, he was a bit fearful of what he saw Hanna do, but he also knew that if she had not, none of the villagers, not even the village itself would exist. His reason for being cautious about associating with Hanna and her family was that he was the leader of the village. He had been, ever since his father passed away and he had taken over. His family has been leading the people of Lorraine ever since it existed for over one hundred seasons. The village, founded by one of his ancestors, named the village after his wife. The family line had held the position of leader since the beginning, but if he helped the man and his family then the other villagers might just decide that it was time to find a new leader. And he had to look out for his own family's welfare before the family of the Wicked Girl.

The leader of the village figured out a way to satisfy everyone. He would give the man the horses he needed. He would even give them supplies to make sure they had a chance to get far away from Lorraine. He would get the house of the man; something he could sell to someone else. But most of all, to make sure the other villagers did not see him as helping the family, he would tell them that he gave the horses to the Wicked Girl's father so that they could leave the village, which would be better off once the family took the child away. Yes, that was what he would tell them, and they would be happy that he had thought of a way to deal with the village's misfortune. To him, with his quick thinking and concern for the village, they would never try to remove him from the position of leader.

Hanna and her family left two sun-cycles after they received the horses. As they were riding through the village, heading for the front gate, the other villagers stood off to the sides watching them leave. The looks on their faces made Hanna start to think that she was going to be happy to leave Lorraine and live somewhere else.

She and her mother rode on the bench at the front of the wagon. Her father walked in front of the horses, holding onto their bridals to guide them. There was no room for him on the bench, and the back of the wagon had everything the family owned and could take with them. Their clothes, and some other household items, but mostly it held the items the man had made. They were something he would be able to sell so his family could start a new life. A life away from people that looked at his daughter and called her Wicked Girl.

Before the wagon made it to the front gate, Hanna turned her head to the right when she saw the one person she thought she would always be with. Even when she was older and ready to take a husband of her own. Darius stood on the front porch of his home, with his mother, father, and his little sister. As soon as the wagon was directly in front of the house, and while Hanna was still looking at him, he gave her one last stare that showed he was glad she was leaving. He then turned around and went back inside his house. Hanna would never forget how that one look made her feel. It was the first time she started to believe that maybe the citizens of Lorraine were right. Maybe she was the Wicked Girl everyone kept calling her.

Even though they passed a couple of small villages and a nice size town, Hanna's father wanted to get farther away before they thought about settling down. He knew news would travel, and since traders had come to Lorraine, and heard the story of what his daughter had done, he thought it would be best to make for the closest big city. There would be a better chance that no one would recognize him or his family. He was sure the story would have traveled, but to others, he was just another man trying to make a place for his family.

When they reached the first village, he was able to trade a couple of the items he had made for some supplies to help him and his family continue their journey. It was not the same when they reached the second village. Word of what had happened in Lorraine and an accurate description of Hanna had arrived before them, and the person he tried to trade with just so happened to know one or more of the traders who had come to Lorraine. They left that village before the sun had set.

Luck was with Hanna's family though. Just before they were about ready to stop traveling for the night, they saw a farm off in the distance. It just so happened that the elderly man and woman who lived there were generous enough to let Hanna and her family stay with them for a few days. They were so generous that they would not even accept payment, or any of the items her father made, for the meals and lodging they supplied. Hanna and her family did help the couple around the farm. Hanna and her mother in the garden and her father repaired the barn's roof, which was leaking.

They were happy while there but knew they could not stay. The elderly couple gave them some supplies and told them that the city of Maridian was just two sun-cycles from where they were and that Hanna's father would be able to find work there.

Hanna's mother and father thanked the couple for what they had done for them, and even though the elderly couple would not take any payment, it did not stop Hanna's father from leaving two of his best-made chairs in the barn the night before they left. He was a good man and always willing to part with something if it went to nice people. So nice that Hanna had asked her mother, why they could not stay with them. She told her that their life was somewhere else. Hanna understood what her mother had said, but she still wished they could have stayed at the farm.

She changed her mind when they reached Maridian. It was the biggest, noisiest, grandest, place Hanna had ever seen. She lived her entire life in Lorraine, and never knew a place like it could even exist. As they passed through the southern gate and made their way through the city, she saw the crowds of people who lived there. She saw that they wore a variety of clothes. She noticed all the shops lining the streets, and she was sure that out of a few of them, she could smell the aroma of food. Scents she had never smelled before.

Even though Hanna was trying to see everything she could, turning her head and even her body at times while sitting on the bench of the wagon, there was one thing she did see that she enjoyed more than anything, the smiles on the faces of her parents. Her father, who was walking next to the horses, would turn and look up at her mother. Hanna saw the smiles and knew that they might not have been happy to leave Lorraine, but they were happy with where they were now.

Luck was with them. Hanna's father found a shop where he not only was able to sell the last of the items he had made and brought with him, but the owner gave him a job to make more of those items. Her father was a very good carpenter. With the coinage, he received from selling his merchandise and what they received from selling the horses and wagon, Hanna and her family were able to rent a room in one of the boarding houses. They only had one room, and Hanna had to sleep on the floor, but to a child six seasons old, who was about to turn seven, it was part of the new adventure she and her parents were sharing. With everything that was happening, Hanna did not have time to think about Lorraine or even Darius.

After a few days, a normal routine began for Hanna and her family. Her father would go to work in the morning and come home in the evening. The coinage he received for the items he made was good, but to bring in more funds, her mother took a job working in the boarding house where they were staying. Since she did not want to leave Hanna alone to wander about the city on her own, she told the man and woman who own the boarding house that Hanna would also help with the cleaning and taking care of the place, and the couple would not have to pay her. How could they reject that arrangement?

The owners of the place were pleased with the way Hanna and her mother worked. They had lived in Lorraine for all of Hanna's life and were not afraid of any task given to them. Well, there was one, which Hanna was not too happy with. She was responsible for pulling out the ore drum in the relief shack and burning the contents. It stank, and most of the time Hanna did the task with one hand because she used the other to cover her nose and mouth to reduce the smell getting to her. It did not help much.

It was not long before the owners of the boarding house took a liking to Hanna and her family, especially Hanna. Once again, she was a child that brought a smile to anyone the moment they saw her. That was because Hanna was always smiling. With that smile and with the golden hair of hers, it was as if whenever she walked into any room, she brought sunshine with her. It was not long before the elderly couple told her that she could call them Papa and Mama. Names used to refer to mothers and fathers of a person's parents. Hanna was so happy that she had almost forgotten about her life in Lorraine and even the boy she had liked. Yes, Hanna was happy.

They had been in Maridian, for not even a season. Hanna was helping Mama with making the dinner she provided to the people staying in the boarding house. While they were in the kitchen, Papa came in and when Hanna looked up to see him, she could tell that there was something different about him. He made a gesture with his head for Mama to follow him. "You keep stirring that, and I will be back in a moment," Mama said to her, and then left leaving

Hanna to continue mixing the cake for dessert. She liked cake.

As she was stirring the mixture, she heard someone screaming from the other room. At first, she thought she recognized the voice, but she was not sure because she never heard her mother sound like that before.

Being a child and wanting to know what was happening in the other room, Hanna made her way over to the door and pushed it back enough so that she could look through the opening and see what was going on. When she could see into the outer room, she saw her mother sitting down on the floor; both Mama and Papa were sitting at her sides. It appeared that they were trying to hold her mother, as if they were to let go, she would fall apart. Hanna did not know what was going on but the way her mother was crying, she felt sad inside and confused. She had never seen her mother like this before and did not know what was wrong with her, or how she could help.

Hanna closed the door and went back into the kitchen. She knew that whatever was going on, the adults would take care of it. And if her mother and Mama and Papa could not, her father would be able to when he came home. It was then she looked out the small window in the kitchen and saw that the sun had already gone out of the sky. Her father had not come home yet. He always came home before it was dark out.

Hanna's confusion grew over the next few days. Her mother, and even Mama and Papa, were acting strange. Her mother stayed up in her room. Mama had moved Hanna into her own room the night her mother was crying on the floor. Mama told her that she was big enough now to sleep alone. Even though she liked that, she still wanted to see her mother, but Mama and Papa told her that her mother needed to be alone for right now.

Two sun-cycles after she had seen her mother sitting on the floor, her mother, and Mama went out. Her mother was still crying but she still left. Hanna asked Papa where her mother was going and that she wanted to go with her. All he said was that her mother would be back soon. That was when she asked him if her father would be coming back with her. Papa did not answer. He just took Hanna by the hand and led her into the kitchen to fix her midday meal.

Over the next few sun-cycles, Hanna decided that since her mother was not taking care of all the chores she normally did, then she would take care of them herself. After all, the adults were too busy to talk to her, and Hanna wanted something to do. To occupy her time, she cleaned the boarding house, washed the linen, and even took them to the roof to dry. Of course, since she was still only seven, she had to ask Mama to hang the linens up on the line.

One day, Hanna was in the kitchen cleaning and when she finished, she was going to go into the other room and find something else to do. Just before she left the kitchen, but had the door opened, she heard Papa talking to another man. Hanna stuck her head through the small opening to listen in, and she was also able to see whom Papa was talking to. It was the man her father had brought home a few times; the man her father worked for.

Since she found out who was in the other room, she did not have to keep looking. But she still wanted to hear what they were saying so she kept the door opened enough to listen. She had not heard the beginning of the conversation, but from what she could tell, they must be talking about her father. The man had said that he was the best carpenter he had ever seen, so Hanna knew it had to be her father. It just so happened the man in the room was talking about him.

Hanna heard the man say something about how someone had seen what had happened. They saw two men attack her father and had beaten him. When he was lying on the ground, they took from him the wages he received that very morning. Afterward, the witness saw them stab her father with a knife. That was why he had not come home that evening, nor any time after that.

Hanna understood what happened. Someone had killed her father. Murder was not something that ever happened in Lorraine, but when they came to the city, stories about people hurting other people, even to the point of death, were not an uncommon occurrence. Hanna came out of her thoughts in time to hear the last part of the conversation.

The man was telling Papa, that the two men who had committed this act had also worked for him. They had been carpenters as well, and they were not happy that Hanna's father had taken a good portion of their income from them when he came to work for this man. Everyone wanted to buy her father's items, so people stopped buying the ones the others made. And since the carpenters received a percentage of what the owner of the establishment made from selling the items, it left the two with a strong resentment toward Hanna's father.

The two killed him, took his coinage, and figured that with Hanna's father gone, they would be able to make the coinage he would have. Unfortunately, the two were more worried than brave, because they never went back to work. From what the city guard could determine, they were no longer even in the city. There would be a certificate of capture put out on them, but since it was only a carpenter murdered, there would not be much of a search for the two.

It was the words "only a carpenter," that bothered Hanna. He was not only a carpenter; he was also her father.

Hanna stepped back into the kitchen and began cleaning, even though she had finished cleaning the room before she opened the door and overheard the conversation about her father. But Hanna did not know what else to do. She now knew what happened to her father. She also knew why no one would tell her about it. To them, she was just a child, and if they did not tell her, then eventually she would just stop wondering when her father would be coming home. One thing was true. She stopped wondering because now she knew he would not.

At that thought, Hanna's thoughts returned to the present. She was no longer that girl of five seasons back in Lorraine. She was no longer that girl of seven seasons waiting for her father to walk through the door and grab her up in her arms. She was now ten, and she had responsibilities. She had to help Mama and Papa take care of the boarding house. Especially since her mother became ill and there were times when she could not even get out of bed, so she had to help take care of her mother as well. Something a child of ten seasons should not have to do, but Hanna did and never complained.

She stopped looking out over the city and turned around to start hanging up the linen. It was not quite midday yet, but she knew that with the way the sun was already shining, it would not take long for the linen to dry.

She did not look up into the sky to see just where the sun was. Even without looking, she could feel it. But that did not mean she wanted to have anything to do with it.

After the incident, back in her village with the Mountain Raiders, Hanna realized that Sun had not been true. She did not know if Sun had just been wrong or if Sun had lied to her, but either way, she never talked to Sun again.

Sun had tried to talk to her though, tried to tell her that it did not matter what humans thought about her, it did not matter what they called her. All that mattered was that Hanna listen and do what Sun told her to do.

Hanna did not. It was because she had listened to Sun that her life started to change. First, the villagers looked at her differently. Then they started calling her that name. Then she and her parents had to leave their home.

When they had come to Maridian, and even when Hanna once again started to be happy, she did not talk to Sun. She did not want what happened before to happen again. Listening to Sun caused her mother and father to take her away from the home she knew and loved. When they had come to Maridian, and life was starting to look bright again, Hanna still would not talk to Sun because she did not want to lose what she had gained.

Then her father died, killed by two men, but she even blamed Sun for that. If it were not for Sun, they would have never had to leave Lorraine and her father would still be alive. She blamed Sun for her mother becoming ill. If they had stayed in Lorraine, her father would be alive, and her mother would not have become sick. Hanna heard Mama and Papa talking about how her mother had slowly become ill immediately after the death of her father. It was because her heart broke, and that is why she does not have the strength to get better.

Hanna did not know if that were true or not, but she did know that everything that has happened in her life is because she listened to Sun. Something she swore she would never do again.

EIGHT

The girl looked out over the city of Faulkton; from the roof of the building, she was standing on. The moon was not full, but that did not interfere with her not being able to see in the darkness of the night. In fact, over the past five seasons, she had grown accustomed to spending the time that she was awake, outside, after the sun had set. For some reason, she just did not like the sun.

When she had left the city of Bonehaven, she traveled many nights before she even saw another person. It was not a city, town, or even a small village. It was a caravan traveling in the direction she had come from. Moon had warned her of the approaching people, so she had enough time to hide in the woods, but not so far away that she was not able to watch the multiple wagons go by. Moon did not even have to tell her, that if they were to see her, they would wonder why a child her age was out in the wilderness alone. More than likely, they would force her to go with them, and since they were heading toward the city she had left, she did not want to go back. Besides, there was no place to go back to, only the people of the caravan were probably not aware of that yet.

Bonehaven was so far away from any other settlement, that before she came upon one, the food she had brought with her had run out. Even a child of five seasons knew that without food and water, she would not be able to survive long. Moon was aware of her predicament, and the time had finally come when Moon could show the child, how Moon would always be able to help.

Water was never a problem for Moon. Moon controlled the tides, and since Moon always looked upon the world below at night, Moon could lead the girl to the water she would need. When Sun was in the sky, Moon would be on the other side of the world so Moon could not guide the child, since Moon would not be able to see the area she was in, so Moon always made sure the child was carrying enough water with her before Moon left the sky when Sun rose.

When it came to food for the child, Moon would not be able to help her as much, but Moon would still make sure the girl would not starve. Moon needed the child to survive.

Moon did not have any control over the creatures that roamed the world below. They were under the reign of whichever First gave them life. If the First known as Wolf, still existed, Moon could have told Wolf to send some of Wolf's children to hunt for the child. Even though the wolves living in the world still howl in the night when Moon is full and grand, they would not obey if Moon were to command them or even ask for assistance. They were still loyal to Wolf, even though Wolf has not been around and may never be again.

It did not mean that Moon could not help the child. Moon has existed just as long as the world, and just as long as Sun. Moon knows many things. Things Moon can teach the child.

To make sure she did not immediately starve, Moon informed the child, what berries and plants she could eat without becoming sick or even die. It was not just to make sure the child had food, but also so the child would understand that Moon would always be there for her. As the child ate the wild berries, which were something she had never had before, and tasted so good, the child could not help but feel exactly what Moon had wanted.

It was not long before Moon had another opportunity to show the girl how Moon could help her. It was just after the sun had gone down that Moon instructed her to sit down behind a tree with her legs under her so that she was on her knees. Moon told the child to remain absolutely still and quiet. The child trusted Moon, so she did as Moon had instructed her. The last thing Moon had told her was that she was to keep a hold of her knife so she sat behind the tree on her legs and knees; knife in hand and waited.

The girl noticed that she had sat there for so

long, Moon had risen higher in the sky. Moon could tell that the child was growing impatient and even understood. The child was five seasons old and was not accustomed to remaining so still, for so long of a time. Moon was old, and in the time Moon has been in existence, Moon knew that waiting was something that every creature in existence had to take part in, and Moon was good at it. Moon wanted the child to learn this lesson as well. With waiting comes great rewards. This is what Moon believes.

Moon had gone beyond the midpoint in the sky before Moon saw what was coming closer to the girl. *"Get ready,"* Moon thought to the child, *"But do not move until I tell you to."* The girl was so obedient in doing what Moon wanted her to, she did not even think an answer back to Moon.

It was not long before a small rabbit hopped around the tree where the child was sitting. She knew that this was something the cook, where she used to live, would fix sometimes in a stew. The one the cook had was dead but still had the skin and fur on it, so the child knew that what was in front of her was food. Only it was still moving.

"When I tell you, jump on the creature, and restrain it to the ground. Grab it just below the base of its head. If you do not, it could bite you and even though it is a small creature, it can cause you pain." The girl understood the word pain. She also understood that if she were able to get a hold of it, it would still be alive. Moon passed on to her what

she was to do. *"When you have it restrained to the ground, take your knife, and stab the creature in its neck. But when you do, make sure you keep a tight hold on it. The cut will not kill it immediately, and if you let go, it can run off."* Moon knew that if the rabbit did get away, Moon could see it clearly and would be able to lead the girl to wherever it fell dead, but Moon wanted the girl to make the kill without any error.

The girl sat there still not moving. The rabbit was now off to her right, just a little over an arm's reach away. She wanted to make a jump for it, but Moon told her that she could not move until Moon, said so. She would do what Moon wanted.

The girl continued to wait, and a moment later, the rabbit moved to be in front of her. It was facing to the child's left so she was looking at its side. *"Wait,"* Moon thought to make sure the child did not jump before Moon told her to. A moment later, the rabbit turned so that it was facing away from the girl. Even though Moon did not say anything, the girl knew that the time was close for her to make her move. Time to make the kill.

When the child had positioned herself behind the tree, she sat with her legs under her but made sure that her feet were placed on the ground with her toes and the balls of her feet pressed downward. She did not know why she had done this, but now she was glad she had. When Moon told her that she could move, she would push off the ground with her toes and the balls of her feet. It would give her the momentum to get to the rabbit with more speed. Now she would wait.

"Now," Moon thought to the child, and she did not hesitate. She sprung forward, and even though the rabbit was looking away from its attacker, it sensed the movement and started to jump away. The child was faster.

She sprung forth and landed directly on the back of the rabbit. She had the small knife in her right hand, but she still used it with her other one to pin the creature to the ground. Even though she had a firm hold on the back of the neck, the rabbit knew it was in danger and tried to free itself, by using the claws on its hind legs to strike at the girl. She accepted the deep slashes on her arms because she knew they were nothing compared to what she would end up with.

Even with the rabbit using its body to try to break free, the girl had enough of a hold to move her right hand and place her knife at the side of the creature's neck and force it inwards. The rabbit was small and so was the knife, but it went deep enough so that blood rushed out. The girl did not know it, or maybe deep down she did, but she made the cut so perfectly and cleanly that the rabbit took only five more breaths before it stopped struggling. After the sixth, it was over.

The child held her position until she was sure the rabbit was not going to run off. When she decided that the creature was dead, she sat back on her legs and lifted her kill so that she could see it better. She held it by its long ears and could not help the smile, which had come to her. She did not know it, but in Moon's own way, Moon was smiling also.

The child had made a perfect kill on her very first attempt. Moon could not ask more from her. At least not yet.

"What do I do now?" the girl thought to Moon.

Moon had seen many creatures eat their kill raw. Wolves, hawks, and other animals of the forest. There were also some who walked on two legs that did as well. Trolls and gnomes, especially. But Moon would not let the child be like the wild creatures of the forest or the stupid lesser creatures of the world. Moon had seen many humans and elves cook their kills over a fire, even the humans that live in the mountains, as savage as they are, did not eat raw meat. Dwarves on the other hand could either eat their meat raw or cooked, depending on what mood they were in. Moon had never started a fire before. With that thought, a bit of resentment Moon had for Sun came to the surface. Moon had to push it down, for now, Moon needed to guide the child in what she needed to do; and guide her Moon did.

Moon did not want the child to start a fire before she had made her kill. Even if the child had moved away from the fire, animals would be wary to come close to it, and the girl would have had a harder time catching something. Now that she had her food, she needed a fire to cook with.

Moon led her to a river nearby. Moon used the power Moon had over the water to pull it back away from the edge of the riverbank. Moon then told the girl to walk out into the riverbed and look for a black stone. One that would shine even once it was dry. There was enough light for the girl to see, especially since her eyesight at night had improved greatly since she left Bonehaven. Almost to the point where she did not need to use a torch at all on the darkest of nights. Since she did not have one anyways, her new gift from Moon came in handy.

She found the stone Moon told her about and then made her way back to the shore. Once there, Moon released the water so that it could continue to flow in its natural way. River did not like it when Moon controlled River, but since Moon was stronger, River could not stop Moon.

Moon instructed the girl to rub the stone on her dress so that it would dry. She did and when she finally had the stone ready, she held it up so that she could see it clearer. As Moon said, the stone still had a shine to it. *"The stone is called flint,"* Moon thought to the girl, *"You can strike your knife against it and it will create sparks that can start a fire, but first you must gather some dry branches and leaves that have fallen from the trees."*

The girl gathered the supplies and did not wait for Moon to tell her what to do next. She had seen a lot of fires start in the place where she lived. She made a pile of the branches so that some of them rose off the ground. She then took the leaves and placed them underneath some of the branches and placed some on top, then grabbed her knife and the stone. She held the stone in her right hand over the leaves and branches and struck it with her knife. The first hit brought forth sparks but did not allow the leaves to catch hold of them. She knew that it could take a couple of tries to get the fire going.

She only had to try four more times before the sparks took hold of one of the leaves and it started to burn. She placed the stone and knife down and moved closer to the pile of branches and leaves. She gently turned the leaf over so that the side burning would be in contact with the others. Within a few breaths, the leaves underneath caught fire as well. To entice it more, she gently blew on the leaves. Moon did not tell her to do this, but she had seen others do the same thing to get a fire going.

When the flames were burning, the girl sat back on her knees and looked at what she had accomplished. She then remembered that the fire was not the first thing she had done this night and turned to her left to look at the rabbit lying at her side. *"Do you think you will be able to clean the kill?"* Moon asked. *"It will be messy and it might make you sick."* Moon was giving the child a chance to come to a decision herself.

The girl reached over, pulled the rabbit up, and

held it by the ears once again to look at her kill. She then looked up to the sky to Moon, "Tell me what to do." She said and once again, Moon was pleased. Moon could never doubt that Moon had chosen well. Not that Moon would ever have any doubts when it came to Moon. To Moon, Moon was perfect.

Late in the night, the girl ate cooked rabbit for the first time. That is, for the first time where she had killed, cleaned, and cooked it herself. The rabbit was not very big, but there was enough meat on it for her to have a meal that night, and would have some left for about two more. Which was not a problem, because she knew that since she had killed one, she would be able to kill another.

Moon was pleased with what the girl had accomplished. More to the point, with what Moon had accomplished. Moon had thought about starting the girl with something a little easier, maybe a fish or two, and then move her to bigger game. But Moon wanted to know just what Moon's little chosen warrior could accomplish. Catching a rabbit, especially by hand, was a difficult thing for even an experienced hunter. That was why they use traps and bait. The girl had caught and killed on her very first attempt. It was the kill part, that Moon was most pleased with.

When the girl ate the last of her rabbit, Moon showed her how to catch fish in a stream. Rabbit was a good meal but they were creatures that were very wary of humans, and the girl would not always be able to find them so easily. Moon also showed her what a nest of a squirrel looked like, but the squirrels rarely stayed close to the entrance, and they would be harder to catch than even a rabbit.

In her travels, the girl stuck to mostly fish, and berries. She caught another rabbit the night before she saw a small town off in the distance. She was very hesitant about what she was going to do. So far, she had been able to survive on her own in the wilderness with the help of Moon. She thought that maybe she could live like this, but Moon told her that she was human and that she was going to need to find a more suitable environment to live in. But Moon did not push her at the moment. Moon allowed the child to decide for herself, and she decided that she was not ready to enter another place that might be like the one she had left some time ago.

Since she always traveled at night, because she did not like the sun, she had no problem slipping around, on the outskirts of the town. There was no wall circling the place, but even though she did not want to enter, she still wanted to see what it was like.

She saw buildings mostly; they were pretty much the same as the ones that were in the place she came from. What she did not see was any smoke coming out in large quantities into the sky. She remembered that when she was back in the city where she had grown up, someone had called the places with the black smoke coming out of it, the refinery. She took it that this place did not have one.

She did hear some noises. People talking mostly and there was music playing. Both of those things were common where she had come from, especially at night.

She lost interest in the place quickly enough and decided that she wanted to be away from the area before the night was over. She did not want anyone to see her and have them come after her. She even thought that maybe they would try to take her back to where she had come from. A smile came to her; remembering that the place was no longer there.

As she had wanted, before Moon was out of the sky and the sun had started to rise, the girl was so far away from the place, she could not even see it. She kept off the road that led to the town just in case someone would be traveling to it. She wanted to make sure no one saw her.

When Moon went out of the sky, and the sun rose, the girl would find a place to rest for a while. Normally she would just lie up against a tree and go to sleep. Since she was closer to a town, she decided that it would be better for her to climb a tree that had enough leaves to keep her hidden. The other good point about the tree she had chosen, was that not only would it hide her from any person, since people rarely look up into the trees, but the leaves were in enough abundance that they blocked out the light of the sun. Something the girl was starting to hate more and more.

After getting some sleep and as the sun was

leaving the sky, the child ate the last bit of rabbit she had and finished off the last of her water. She was about to ask Moon to lead her to a nearby river but did not. She had been out in the wilderness all this time, and yes, Moon had helped her. Moon taught her how to catch rabbits and fish, and to find berries. Moon would even tell her where water was. But something in her told her that she could do the same thing on her own. She was thankful for what Moon had done, but she decided that it was time for her to stop relying on Moon and start relying on herself.

Even though she did not plan to think those thoughts to Moon, Moon heard them but took no offense to the girl, in fact, Moon was happy that the child was taking the initiative to see to her own needs. Moon needed the child and knew that without Moon, she would have died just a few nights on her own. That did not mean Moon enjoyed watching and taking care of her. Yes, Moon wanted the child to be dependent on Moon, but Moon did not want the child to be useless. If the child learned to take care of her own needs, it would free Moon up to where Moon would not have to watch the child all the time. Moon also knew that for what Moon wanted the child for she was going to need her freedom. Freedom to live and make decisions for herself. Just as long as they align with Moon's desires as well. Moon remained silent and allowed the child a bit of freedom, just a bit.

The child stood up on the tree limb she had slept on and looked out. There were other trees as well and they blocked the child's sight. She knew that she would not be able to see anything while in the tree, so she climbed down to the ground.

Once there, she decided that she needed to find water first. She had just eaten, and that would last her until she could find either some berries or another rabbit. Also, she knew that if she could find water, a river, or even a small stream then she might find something to eat as well.

Since she could not see a source of water from up in the tree or even on the ground, she closed her eyes to concentrate on maybe hearing it. To her surprise, it was not her ears that picked up what she was looking for, it was her nose. She could smell the water.

She could tell that it was not close, but she also knew that since she could smell it, it was not too far away for her to find it. She opened her eyes and looked around. She then closed her eyes and moved her head around; trying to pick up the direction that she could best catch the scent of the water. When she made her choice, she opened her eyes to see where she needed to go.

She grabbed her bags and started walking. She knew she would come across the water eventually and as she was traveling to it, she would keep an eye out for any of the berries Moon had taught her about which she could eat.

Moon did not let the child know, but Moon was very proud. Of the girl, and of Moon.

The girl found the stream before Moon was even

close to reaching the highest point in the sky. What the girl found was a small brook. The water ran enough so that she was able to fill her water bag, but not enough to where any fish would be in it. That did not matter because the girl had found a plant with a lot of the red berries she enjoyed and picked enough to last her a couple of days and would eat from them until she found something else.

She thought about following the small stream back in the direction the water was coming from, to see if there was a bigger source, but she noticed that it came from the direction of the town she passed. Since she did not want to go near it again, she decided to follow the stream in the opposite direction. She would travel by it for a few nights so that she was close to the water in case she needed to refill her water bag. She also thought to herself that if she could find this source of water then maybe another animal would as well. One that she would be able to kill to add to her food. She was happy when she thought of that, and so was Moon. The girl was learning to survive.

Just before the sun rose, the girl did see an animal off in the distance drinking from the stream. Even though she was still a good distance away, she could tell that the animal was quite huge. Not only its body but also the things coming out of its head, which looked like branches. It was much bigger than a rabbit, but not as big as the horses the humans would ride or have pulling their carts. It was big, but the girl was confident that she could take it down with her knife.

Moon knew that the child was about to do something that would cause her great harm and possibly her death. Even though the big buck might flee before the child drew close to it, Moon could not take the chance. With the way the girl was performing, even better than what Moon had expected, she might be able to get to the buck before it got away. If she did, Moon knew that one strike from its hind legs, or from the dangerously sharp antlers, could severely hurt her. Moon could not allow that to happen.

At the same time, Moon did not want to impede the child's desire to attempt taking on bigger prey. That was part of what Moon needed her for anyways, but even Moon knew that the girl was not ready for the great buck.

Moon was not fond of this type of animal as it was. Yes, the buck and its kind would move about when Moon was in the sky, but they gave no respect to Moon. It might be because the creatures knew that Moon associated with Wolf when Wolf was in the world, and the buck at the stream, was no friend to Wolf. It belonged to Stag. One of Wolf's enemies. The story goes that it was Stag who had sent Wolf away. Those two had been battling almost as long as Moon and Sun. The only difference was that there had been a victor in the fight between Stag and Wolf. Moon and Sun were still battling on.

Moon saw the girl making her way to the buck.

She was still a distance away but she was moving quietly. Moon thought that maybe even more quietly than the way Moon had taught her. Right now, Moon needed to make sure the girl stayed alive.

The buck still had its head down drinking from the brook. Moon caused the water next to it to splash upwards and onto the creature. Since it was nervous to begin with, when the water touched it, it took off running. Thankfully, at least to Moon, in the opposite direction from where the girl was coming from.

When she saw the creature take off, a part of her felt deprived of something that should have been hers. Moon did not say anything to her, because Moon did not want the child to think that Moon caused the buck to flee. The girl lost this kill, and Moon hoped that she would not try for something as big as the buck again. At least not until she was older and bigger herself. Moon kept that thought to Moon.

One moon-mark, after the girl saw the deer, she came across another city. Only this one was bigger than the one she had last seen. It was more like the place where she lived for the first few seasons of her life. The city she was looking at now, from the safety of the trees, had a wall of stone surrounding it. She knew it was there for protection, but she thought that it did not give the city where she grew up much protection from the mountains which covered it completely.

The girl looked to her left and right and noticed that there were no mountains close to this place.

She had been by herself for quite some time now. She did not know how long, and it was not the presence of others that she was missing, it was something that she did not even know what it was. She still did not have any desire to talk to anyone, however, she was starting to think that there was something else for her to find, and it was not in the wilderness with the rabbits and fish.

She moved closer to the city staying just on the outskirts of the tree line running alongside the road, in case someone happened to come close, then she could head for the woods and take cover until they pass.

Since it was late, when she grew closer to the city wall, she noticed the gates closed for the night. If they had been open, she thought that there might have been humans standing guard just like the ones who had been standing at the gate in the city where she had lived. But with the gates closed, she was not sure how she would be able to get inside the city.

She thought about moving closer to the wall and going around it, then maybe she would find an opening she could sneak through. She did not want to take the chance that someone from the top of the wall might notice her before she could get inside.

Just as she was about to give up and ask Moon what she should do, she heard a noise coming from behind her. She quickly backed further into the tree line, and fell to the ground, lying on her stomach so that no one would see her, but still be able to see who was coming.

She waited quietly and soon saw a group of wagons coming down the road, heading for the city she had been watching. She could not help but smile. If they were heading for the city, then they would get in somehow. The gates would open for them and all she had to do was wait and run up to one of the wagons and climb inside, then jump out when the wagons were through the gate.

The child let the wagons pass by her, and she counted a total of six. When the last one passed her position, she did not run out to it. Instead, she stood up enough to where she was able to walk with speed while at the same time, she crouched down enough to the point that if she saw someone who might see her, she could fall to the ground quickly and hide.

She stayed inside the tree line until she ran out of trees. When that happened, she quickly sprung out and ran to the back of the last wagon in line. With her height, she would have to jump to reach the top of the wooden backing so that she could pull herself up. Just as she was about to make the move, she heard voices coming from the inside of the wagon. She knew that she would not be able to continue with her plan, without the risk of someone in the back of the wagon noticing her.

She did not run back to the woods. She decided that she would walk behind the wagon, and when it arrived at the gate, she would see if she would be able to sneak in on the side of it.

She received a second surprise when the wagon she was walking behind stopped. She thought that she would have to run because someone might look out the back of it. Just before she ran back the way she came, she looked down the left side of the wagon and saw a man talking to another man. The one doing the talking was in a uniform. Even though it was still night, she was able to see what the man was wearing, clearly enough.

She looked in the direction she needed to go, to take her back to the woods, but noticed that there was a lot of open space between her and the trees. The two men that were talking might see her, or someone else at the gate would. She could not go back and she could not climb up into the wagon. She would just have to wait and see what would happen.

As she was watching the two men talking at the wagon farthest to the front, she noticed another man in uniform starting to make his way down the line. The girl continued to watch him but stayed far enough behind the back of the wagon where the man would have a hard time seeing her. She came to realize that the man walking towards her was not going to stop, and soon he would be at the back of the wagon.

The girl moved from the left side of the wagon to the other side, and to her surprise, there were two men in uniform coming her way. She continued to watch them and when she was sure that they were not going to stop, she ducked her head back, wondering what she was going to do. She could not run now, one of the men would certainly see her. The voices were still coming from inside the wagon, so climbing inside was not an option either. The people inside would not know her, and they would know that she did not belong with the group; a detail of the whole situation the child realized.

The people would know that she was not part of the group traveling with the wagons, but maybe the men in the uniforms, probably the ones who guarded the gate, would not.

The girl had her food and water bag over her right shoulder. The food bag was hanging in the front, and she positioned her right hand so that she was holding onto it, but had her fingers curved around part of the cloth. Hidden in the folds of the cloth the girl was holding onto her small knife. If what she had planned did not work, she was going to make sure they did not try to take her. If it came down to it, she could strike as fast as she could and cause the men to pause long enough for her to make a run for the woods; and maybe they were not fast enough to catch her.

Now ready, she waited at the back of the wagon standing at the center of it. It just so happened that the one man from the left side of the row of wagons turned the corner at the same time the other two did. The girl looked at the two, then back to the one. All three of the men came to stand in front of the little girl, who just happened to be smiling at them. She had seen women smile at men, at the place where she used to live. Men seemed to like it.

She was not sure if these men did, but since they only gave her a quick look, and then all three of them walked back to the side of the wagon where the one man had come from, she did not care.

When she thought she waited long enough, she peeked around the side of the wagon and saw the men walking away from her. Not one of them turned around or even wondered what a little girl was doing standing on the outside of the wagon. The girl could not help but think that adults were not very clever if she could get away with what she just did.

She watched the three men head back to the front, and it was not long afterward, that the wagons started to move again. Soon the wagons passed through the gates, with one little black hair girl walking behind the last in line.

Just to see if she could do it and get away with it, when the girl was a few paces inside the city wall, she turned and waved to the men that were watching the wagons enter the city. It amazed the little girl, when the men that saw her, waved back. Yes, adults are not clever at all.

The girl had been in the city ever since. The girl asked Moon just the other night how long she had been there, and Moon told her that it had been just over five seasons since she had arrived. The girl has been in Faulkton all this time, but she still had not found what she was looking for. In fact, she did not even know what it was.

NINE

Hanna walked down the street of Maridian on her way to the bakery to pick up the bread that Mama would serve to the people staying at the boarding house. This bread would be for tomorrow; since there was enough to last until then.

Her mother was the one who would usually make the trip, and Hanna would come with her, if she had her morning chores done, which she always did when her mother had to go through the city to take care of some errands. Hanna enjoyed walking down the streets and seeing all the different buildings. Some supplied people with clothes. They even had fabric, people could purchase and make their own fancy outfits or have someone else make them for them. Hanna saw some people wearing those types and always wondered if she would ever be able to purchase something like what she saw or even have someone make it for her. Hanna loved the silk cuffs, and frills at the end of the sleeves on the dresses that some of the women wore. She liked them so much that she would dream of having a fancy dress of her own.

Hanna enjoyed these outings with her mother, except for the part where they would pass the building where her father had worked. Even though he had been gone for several seasons, it bothered Hanna when they came close to the building. One reason was that it reminded her of her father, and she felt sad that he was no longer with her. The second reason was that she saw the look on her mother's face as she looked upon the place herself. She knew her mother missed her father just as much as she did; maybe even more.

She asked Mama, why her mother would go by the place if it made her sad to see it, and Mama told her that sometimes adults do things just so they can feel something. Hanna did not understand and decided that it was an adult thing and did not bother to ask again.

Hanna enjoyed the outings she would take with her mother. But eventually, the outings grew further and further apart. At first, she and her mother would go out every three sun-cycles. When her mother started feeling ill, it was about only once per moon-mark. After a few moon-cycles, Hanna began to make the trip twice a moon-mark, alone.

Most of the time her mother was just well enough to get out of bed and take care of some of her chores in the morning before having to return to her room to get some rest. Now her mother does not even get out of bed at all, and even though Hanna still makes the trip to acquire whatever Mama and

Papa need and is not too much for Hanna to carry by herself, she does not enjoy the walks like she used to. Now she does it because it was part of her responsibilities. Not out of a reason to have a bit of happiness in a life that has changed so much.

She reached the bakery and once she took the usual order the baker had waiting for her, she stepped outside to head back home. As soon as she was out of the building, she saw the one person who was always there waiting for her.

Colton was a child who had become friends with Hanna. As much as Hanna would let him become her friend. She still remembered what happened back in the first place she lived. She used to play with some of the other children, and even a certain boy, although she could not remember his name. After the Mountain Raiders came, the children would not play with her again. She knows now that they had stopped being her friend because Hanna knew a friend would not call her Wicked Girl. A name, she would never forget.

Because of what happened all those seasons ago, Hanna decided that friends were not something she needed. Yes, she talked to Colton and even spent time with him, but she would never again let someone be nice to her, to the point where she would call them friends, but end up calling her a cruel name. She would not let someone hurt her again.

Colton liked Hanna. Not the way a man likes a

Paul W. Gibbs

woman, he was too young for that, but he did like Hanna. By the time they had met, Hanna's father had already passed away. Not long after they met, he asked her where her father was, and she told him that he was no longer with her and her mother. Colton knew what that meant, and the way Hanna looked at him when answering his question, he knew it bothered her and that he should not bring the subject up again, which he did not.

In a way, Colton was luckier than Hanna when it came to the topic of parents. He had none. At least none he knew of, and since he never knew them, he would never have to feel the loss of them leaving. Colton had grown up in the orphanage his entire life, although he does not spend much time there anymore. He only stops in long enough to say hello to some of the children still living there whom he had grown up with, or on days when he knows they are serving a type of food he enjoys. He did not like staying at the orphanage, but it was a nice place to visit especially when he wanted something to eat.

Colton and Hanna met when he was nine and she was ten. Of course, Colton did not know when his Blessed Day was because whoever was responsible for him, left him at the orphanage when he was just a baby, but the clerics who ran the place, counted his seasons starting with the day he ended up in their care. It did not matter to Colton that he did not know exactly how old he was. In fact, Colton did not have a care in the world.

158

When he was seven seasons old, the clerics at the orphanage told him that when he was fifteen, if no family had taken him in, then they would put him under the care of one of the many people who had a trade. He would study under a blacksmith, leatherworker, carpenter, or one of the other professionals in the city of Maridian. Over the next couple of seasons if he showed any signs of intelligence, which would make him stand out, then the clerics might be able to get him work in one of the higher trades, such as bookkeeping, scribe, or even an apprenticeship in one of the many tailors in the city. Colton did not like any of those choices.

Colton knew what his options were and he decided to make his own choice on how he would live. He would live on the streets of Maridian. And so, he began his training.

Colton did show great intelligence. He knew he had to learn from someone, so he found a group of older kids living on the streets who had not like living at the orphanage. He joined up with them and began his new life. They were happy to have him because they would use him to carry out most of the plans they came up with to get them food or on some occasions, some coin they could spend.

It did not take Colton long to realize that the reason the older children wanted him along was that they used him in the part of their plans when there was a risk they did not want to take. The children told him what to do, and with most plans, he succeeded in taking what he was after, but every now and then something would go wrong and Colton was the one caught. Since he was just a child, who seemed to be a product of an unkind world, most of the time the person would yell at him and send him on his way. However, twice he was too slow to get out of reach of his victim, and they grabbed him. Of course, none of his so-called friends ever came to his rescue. No, they got away.

When caught, they would turn Colton over to the city guard and they would take him to the orphanage. It was after the second time this happened that Colton decided it would be better if he struck out on his own and do things his way.

Colton never liked stealing. Although he could not deny the excitement of it, he knew it was wrong, so he decided to try a different approach.

After his capture a second time, he returned to the same street vendor he had tried to steal from the day before. As soon as the man saw him, he started yelling at Colton to get away or that he was going to call for the city guards. Colton just walked up to stand before the man's cart where he had a variety of fruits and vegetables. When the man finally stopped yelling, Colton said two words to him, "I'm sorry," and then walked away. He did not even turn around to see if the man was still watching him.

The next day, Colton returned to the same area. He saw the man with his cart again but did not go up to him. Instead, he walked by the cart but as he did, he called out to the man, "Good day sir." To add to the sincerity of the greeting, Colton moved his right hand to his head then away, as if he were tipping his hat to the man. He continued to walk by, not even taking an interest in any of the fruits or vegetables displayed on the cart.

Colton continued to do this. Since he could still go to the orphanage he did not have to worry about food, so he did not go hungry. If that were the case, he could not continue with what he was doing. Which was planning for his future.

Colton continued to greet the man every day. Same greeting as always, "Good day sir," and a salute with his hand. After about two moon-marks, the man would give him a smile and reply with his own "Good day." Colton knew then that it was time to put the second part of his plan to work.

He still greeted the man, and the man greeted him. Colton never said anything else to him. He would say hello to the man and then walk away. After the man had returned the greeting, when Colton was far enough away, he would turn around to watch and see how much business the man was doing. It was not much but it was enough that Colton knew he had to wait.

He continued to follow the same pattern. He would walk by the man and as he did, Colton would give his patent greeting. Then he would hide off in the distance and watch. Then came a day when Colton saw that the man had only one person stop to buy something from him. Colton knew it was time.

He made his way back to the man and his cart and stood in front of it. When the man saw him, the look he gave Colton, told him that the man did not know why the child was there. The child usually just said hello and went about his way. Now he was standing there looking at the man, and the vendor started to wonder if the child was about ready to try to take something from the cart.

Just as the man was going to say something, Colton turned around and started shouting at the crowd of people that were walking in the area. "Hey everyone. Come and get the best fruits and vegetables you have ever eaten." Colton then turned his head to look at the man standing on the other side of the cart. The man had no idea what to think. Colton turned back around and started yelling to the people walking by.

"Come on people, if you truly want the best fruits around, then you need to come and buy something from my father. He grows the best fruits and vegetables in the entire city." Colton once again turned his head to look at the man, who stood there, confused at what he was seeing and hearing. For he and Colton knew that they were not father and son, and the vendor knew that he was not the one who grew the food in the first place. He bought it from someone else in another part of the city, then brought it to the area to sell it at a slightly higher price. Colton did not know that, but it did not matter to him. He had a plan, and he was going to make it work.

Colton had been shouting for a few moments and all he received were stares from a lot of the people walking by. He knew he was going to have to up his charade. He searched the crowd for a particular person. Then he saw her. A woman who appeared to be not from this area. Her clothes were a bit too fancy and was probably only in the area to feel as if she did her part in spending some time with the more common people and purchasing some of their products. To her, it was a way to please Ourgós. Doing a good deed, by helping the less fortunate, would help her to have a better life when she left this world. She might have wanted a better afterlife, but Colton wanted a better life right now.

He ran over to the woman and stood in front of her. She was so surprised when he jumped in her path, she took a step back, and looked down at the small child, who before he reached her, reached down, and grabbed a bit of dirt to smear on his cheeks to make himself look a bit more, needy. "Good morning ma'am," Colton said and ended it with the biggest smile he could make. "Are you looking for some fruits or vegetables? If you are, my father has the best wares around," Colton said while extending his arm out to his left, to point at the man behind the cart.

The woman looked down at Colton, and smiled, "I'm afraid I am not looking to purchase any food at this time."

Colton heard her, but he was not ready to give

up just yet. "Oh, you don't have to eat it now. My father knows that people may want to keep the food they buy from him for later, so he makes sure he sells it at the best time, to allow it to last until you are ready to eat it." Colton could tell that he had not convinced the woman yet. Of course, he was just beginning. "Wait here," he said to the woman, and when he was sure she was not going to move, he ran back to the cart.

When he reached it, he placed his hand on one of the apples. Before he took it, he looked up to see the man watching him. Colton gave him a look asking the man if he could take it and the man gave him a nod. Mostly because he wanted to see what this child was going to do. When Colton saw the man give him the ok, he grabbed the apple, turned, and ran back to the woman who was still waiting where he had left her, but now she was facing Colton, watching him. When Colton saw that the woman was smiling, he was sure his plan was almost at its end.

"Here," Colton said and handed the apple to her, who took it without hesitation. "This one is free, and I guarantee that it is the best apple you have ever tasted." The woman looked down at the child and saw his dirty face, but she also saw the biggest smile she had ever seen on any child, as well as the biggest pair of eyes. Colton was trying hard to make it look as if he was the sweetest thing in the world. The woman could not turn down the offer to try the free apple.

As soon as she bit into it, Colton knew he had her. Like everyone else, Colton loved the taste of apples, and the thing about it was that usually once a person gets a taste of one, they want another right then and there, and maybe even one or two for later. The way the woman was smiling and the way the juice from the apple was running down her chin, Colton knew his plan had worked. "So, what will it be my dear lady? What do you say to buying another one for now, and one for later?" Colton did not wait for her to answer. He reached out, grabbed her hand, and pulled her behind him, back to the cart. "As you can see, my father's apples are redder and brighter than any around. And the redder they are the more juice they have."

The vendor behind the cart kept his mouth shut. He did not know what to say about the entire scene he had watched from the beginning. He definitely did not know how this child was going on about apples as if he was an expert on the fruit. Since the child had just brought over a potential customer, he was not going to interrupt the kid to ask him what he was doing.

"So, my good lady, what can we get for you this fine morning?" Colton asked, ending with a big smile.

The woman looked at him, took another bite of the apple she had in her hand, and then turned to look at the child's supposed father. When she finished chewing, she placed her order, "I will take twelve more of these delicious apples."

"OH! An excellent choice my dear lady," Colton said then turned his head to look at the man, "Father, please give her the best twelve apples we have." All the vendor could do was begin looking through the big baskets of apples and did his best to search for the best twelve. Of course, to him, they all looked the same.

The woman paid for the apples including the one given to her for free. She knew she was helping the man who was trying to make a living for him and his son, and she was sure Ourgós was very pleased with her today.

With business concluded the woman said her goodbyes to the child and the child's father then turned to walk away. Colton had one more thing to say, "Make sure you tell your friends about my father's most delicious fruits." The woman did not hesitate to yell back that she would.

Once they were alone, Colton turned to look at the man, who did not have any idea what to say. All he could do was smile and give Colton a nod of his head. With that motion, Colton turned around and went back to work. "My dear ladies, and good gentlemen, come and taste the best of the best. You will never taste anything as good as the fine foods that my father has to sell." He yelled out as loud as he could, and of course, people heard him and listened.

By the time the vendor closed for the day, Colton had convinced quite a few people to buy the biggest part of the produce. The man had a few figs, and berries left and some vegetables, but that was about it. The apples were the first to go, but the child promised others that had come when they heard about the most delicious apples, sold by this man and his son, that his father would have more in a day or two. A couple of the wealthier buyers even put in an order to have the products delivered to their houses. Like the woman who had made the first purchase, they only came to the area when they felt as if they needed to help some of the lesser citizens of the city. They were not planning to come back in a day or two. Colton told them that he would deliver their products personally, but of course, there was a delivery fee, which the customers agreed to pay. The vendor quickly came up with an amount to charge them for the personal service.

The vendor was happy with the outcome, for he had never almost sold his entire supply in one day. He had more than enough coinage to purchase more products to sell in a day or two. He would make sure he purchased the items the people had placed an order for first. What those people did not know was that they could have easily purchased the same items closer to the part of the city where they lived. The exact same items.

As Colton was heading off to find somewhere to sleep for the night, he started thinking about what else he could do to help someone other than the vendor. He knew he had found a way to make a living on the streets; he could tell by how full his hands were with items the vendor had given him. So much, that he could have used a couple more hands to help carry the food.

He decided that he would keep the fruits for himself. The vegetables he would take to the orphanage and turn them over to the woman who cooked the food. If she asked him where he got them, he would just tell her that he had earned them and did not steal them. It was the truth and in giving the vegetables to the orphanage, Colton felt as if he was truly helping others. Something Ourgós would want him to do.

The vendor did not come back for two sun-cycles, having to restock his entire supply. But when he did, Colton was waiting for him and used the first part of the morning to make the promised deliveries. Deliveries where on more than one occasion, he received a copper coin for himself as well as the payment he took back to Father. With the deliveries completed, he went back to drawing people who passed by the cart. They did not sell as much as they had the first time when Colton stepped in to help, but with the delivery charge added to the deliveries, the vendor walked away with a nice amount.

Even though Colton had made a couple of copper pieces for himself, the vendor was more than happy to give him some food to take with him at the end of the day. He even invited Colton to come back to his house to have dinner with him and his wife. Of course, Colton had to decline the offer; he had things to do. The vendor smiled and they went their own way. Colton went back to where he had been staying on the street, to eat his meal, setting the vegetables aside to take to the orphanage.

He did not really have anything to do like he said to the man, he just did not see a need to have dinner with the man and his wife. Colton knew that it might have been a different meal than what he normally would have, but to him, no meal was better than the one he was eating in the little hideaway he had made for himself a few streets over from the orphanage.

Colton enjoyed the freedom he had from living on the street, especially without an adult controlling him. Colton did not have any problems with any of the grownups he knew, he just did not want someone telling him what to do, how to do it, and when to do it. Colton was a child who knew that what was best for Colton, was what Colton thought it was. Now he just had to think of what he could do on the days Father did not need him.

There were other areas in the city where people would sell their goods. Colton had first thought that he could go to one of them and do the same thing he had done but with a different vendor. After going over the plan, he decided that it was too much of a risk. Even though the location would be different, there was the possibility that someone would recognize him, from the other area. A person would go to different areas in the city looking for items, and it would only take one person to realize that this was the same child they had seen previously; only he was now calling a different man Father.

For a moment, he thought about finding a female vendor and refer to her as Mother, but what if someone who had seen him before started asking questions. It might just get the woman in trouble and even the man he had pretended was his father. It did not sit well with Colton that the man might take the blame because Colton was trying to make a living. Colton might have tried to steal from the man at one time, but he had started helping him, and he did give him food, and if caught, then all of it would end.

Colton decided that he would continue to help the one man, but he still needed to come up with a plan to make up for the days when Father did not need him. He thought about it until the moon had risen, and then went to sleep. By the time he woke up the next morning, he had his plan.

He waited until the day he worked with Father. He had to because he needed to use some of the food the man always gave him at the end of the day. When he had his food this time, he made sure he had a couple of apples but did not eat them.

The next morning, he went to one of the upper-class areas of the city. He then found one of the shops that sold items to women, fancy clothes, and things of that nature, but he did not go inside. He waited down the street with two children that were only four seasons old and he promised to give an apple to each of them if they were to come with him and do what he said.

When he saw the woman that would work best in his plan, he gave the two young children the apples and had them commence with their part. They ran from where they had all been waiting, and right up to the woman who had just exited the shop. It was a shame that she had been carrying four boxes that were hard for her to hold onto when the two uncontrollable children bumped into her and caused her to drop her packages to the ground. The children were already out of sight before she even had a chance to look for them, but to her surprise, there was a nice young boy already reaching down to help her gather her items.

"I do apologize ma'am," Colton said as he started picking up the packages and handing them back to the woman. "I saw what those children did and thought that you could use some help with your items."

The woman looked down at the young child and saw that he appeared to be older than the ones who had so rudely knocked her packages from her hands. She noticed that the child had dirt on his face and must be one of the many children running wild on the streets, with little or no parental supervision. She realized that this one was now trying to help her. "Thank you," she said to the child as he handed her the last package.

"It's ok ma'am. I don't know who those two were, but if I see them again, I will make sure they know to be careful around adults."

The woman knew that many of the street children would only help grownups when they thought they would receive something in return. Now that she had her packages in her arms, she was sure the child would try to entice some type of payment for helping her. She even had her suspicions that he did know the two rude children and probably was in league with them, and they would all split the reward.

"Have a good day ma'am," Colton said and raised his right hand to his head then brought it back down as if tipping his hat. He then turned around and started walking away.

The woman felt bad that she had thought this child was behind the whole incident. So bad that Colton was not three paces away before she called to him, "Child!"

Colton had to make sure the smile was off his face before he turned around. "Yes ma'am," Colton said but wanted to play up to the woman a little more, "They did not hurt you, did they?" Colton asked with a concerned look on his face. It was so good and authentic, that the woman had to take a moment once again to berate herself for what she had thought about the child a moment ago.

"What is your name?" the woman asked.

"Colton ma'am."

They looked at each other and he waited for the

nice woman to speak. Colton was sure that is what a child with good upbringing would do, speak only when spoken to. "Would you mind helping me carry these few packages home?"

Colton made sure that he did not answer with too much enthusiasm. "It would be my pleasure ma'am." Colton then walked back to the woman, who happened to hand him the smallest package she was carrying. Colton would have been more than happy to carry a larger one, but since the woman did not offer, who was he to judge what an adult did.

The woman lived a few streets over, and during the walk, she asked him questions about who he was. Being the polite child, he told her that he was just a child who lived with his father in one of the other sections of the city. He did not say where, because he did not know where the vendor he had been helping lived. He did happen to mention where his father set his cart up to sell the fruits and vegetables, and that they just so happened to be the best in the entire city.

At one point, she asked him what he was doing in this part of the city if he lived in one of the poorer sections. When she said the word "poorer," she took a quick look at Colton who was walking to her left, to see if she had offended the child by reminding him that he did not have the wealth or the class she had. She decided the child must not have heard what she said or did not understand. Colton heard but made sure he did not react to it. He did not want the lady to feel too bad for insulting him.

Colton told her that he would come to this area when his father did not need his help so that he could see all the beautiful houses and shops that were here because they were not like the ones in the part of the city where he lived. He even mentioned how the temple of Ourgós was even more extravagant than the one close to where he lives. It was the truth after all, and when he just happened to look up to his right, he saw the woman looking at him, and the pity she was feeling for the child, showed on her face. Colton had to turn his head to make sure he did not smile. He would hate to let the woman think that she was acting exactly the way he wanted her to.

When they made it to the lady's dwelling, Colton walked her up to the front door, handed her back the small package, and was about to leave. "Wait a moment," she said and started to open the door, but Colton reached it first since he noticed that the sweet woman had her hands full. When she stepped inside, Colton waited on the front porch. She had not invited him in, and a well-behaved child would not dare enter someone's home without an invitation.

When the woman returned, she extended her arm out and Colton positioned his so that it was under her closed hand. She then dropped two copper pieces into his hand. He looked up at her and made sure the look on his face let her know that he did not understand, even though he did. "For helping me with the packages," the woman said.

Colton looked from her to what he was holding. He knew what he had to do, and looked back to the woman, "Oh I did not help you for any reward." He even went so far as to take the woman's hand, turn it palm up, and drop the two copper pieces back into it. "It was my pleasure." He then smiled at the woman, turned around, and started walking away. As he reached the first step to the porch, he turned around to face the woman whom he knew would still be there watching him. The look on her face told him that she did not understand the child. "I had better get back home. I will be busy tomorrow helping my father sell his fruits and vegetables." He then gave the woman his standard salute with his right hand, turned around, and started running away, but before he got too far, he yelled, "It was nice to meet you." He was not surprised to hear her reply.

"It was nice to meet you as well!"

The next day, while he was helping Father sell his wares, as Colton thought, one of the first customers was the woman he helped carry her packages to her home. He knew she would; there was no doubt in his mind. He just thought it would take longer than it had before she started feeling sorry for the poor helpless child who had been so kind to her, and was so courteous, that he would not even accept the two copper pieces she had offered him.

That was the reason Colton had declined the payment. He knew, if he had, the woman would have felt that she had done her part and compensated the child for what he had done for her. By turning down the offer, Colton knew the guilt she felt inside would eat away at her until she had to do something to balance out the generosity. That was why he made sure he told her about his father's cart, where he sold fruits and vegetables, and where it was located.

Before she even reached where he was, Colton could see the smile she had on her face. Of course, he returned the smile, interrupting his calling out to the people passing by; long enough to make sure the woman knew he had seen her.

"Hello Colton," she said when she came up to him.

"Hello, it is good to see you again," Colton said in a tone that made the woman think her showing up was a surprise to him. He then took her by the hand and led her over to the cart Father was standing behind, taking care of yet another customer.

When he was free, Colton introduced the woman, "Father this is the woman I told you about. The one I met yesterday, that the two children knocked her packages out of her arms, and I helped her to carry them home." Colton summed up the entire story in just a few words. He never told the man about what he had done and realized that if the woman started talking to him, then he might give something away to make the woman think that Colton had arranged the entire situation. Thankfully, the man was a man of few words so after Colton relayed the story, all the man did was smile and nod his head to the woman.

They stood there chatting; mostly the woman was doing the talking, while the man packaged up the items she had chosen to purchase. Since one reason she had come was to compensate Colton for what he had done, and since he would not take the coinage, she was more than happy to purchase some of the products his father was selling. More than two copper pieces worth.

Colton was ok with what was happening. He did not want coinage from this woman. He needed something else and taking payment from her would only make her think that was all he wanted and even her pity for the underprivileged had its limit.

Before she walked away, she had one last reason for coming that day which she explained to the man she believed was Colton's father. "Sir, since your son was so helpful to me yesterday, and if he is not busy tomorrow, I was wondering if I could borrow him to help me once again to carry some of the packages I will be acquiring tomorrow."

It was now time for Colton to say something, "Oh please Father, may I? I love to see the fancy buildings and shops that are close to where she lives. Please, may I?" Colton made it appear, at least to the woman, that he wanted to help because he enjoyed going to the area. All the man could do was, give the woman a smile, and nod his head. Colton made sure he continued with his part, "Oh thank you Father," he said ending with a big smile, which the woman thought he had because she had granted him something he would enjoy doing. Colton was able to show a real smile because he could not believe how well his plan was working.

They said their goodbyes and the woman told him to meet her just before midday in front of the same store where they had met. It was an appointment he was not going to miss.

Colton made sure he arrived at the proper time. He even made sure he had no dirt on his face and that his hair was combed. Well, at least more than what it usually was. He still had to present himself as a child who did not have much in life.

The woman met him and since they were already in front of the store, she decided that she would start with it. When she went inside, Colton waited until she had gestured for him to follow her. She did receive some glares from a couple of the other women in the shop but soon she was in a discussion with them, and one of the other ladies brought up the concern as to why the child was with her. The woman simply said that the child was helping her carry any packages she may purchase today. Colton took this moment to act as if he was not paying attention to the conversation, which of course he was.

The woman started telling the other two, about how the child had assisted her, and that his father was just a man who sold fruits and vegetables in the poorer section of the city. Out of the corner of his eye, he could see the other two women looking at him with pity. He then heard the woman he was with, tell the other two that it only seems right that she helps the poor child and his father any way she could and that she was sure it was what Ourgós would want her to do. Colton heard the two women speaking concerned agreement with the other one.

As they were about to leave, the lady said her goodbyes to the other two and turned, making sure she informed Colton that it was time for them to go. Colton decided that it was time for him to leave a bit of an impression on the two women. He turned to face them and when they were looking at him, he gave them a slight bow, and said, "It was nice to meet you, ladies. Please have a lovely day." Of course, the women thought Ourgós had blessed them to have such a fine young child treat them with so much respect.

Colton traveled with the woman for a good part of the day, going from shop to shop. In fact, they had gone into so many that Colton had grown tired and started to reconsider what he was doing, but only for a moment because he knew that what he was suffering through now, would eventually bring great rewards. They would go into one of the many stores and of course, the woman he was with, always met someone she knew, and of course, she just had to tell them how she was more than happy to help someone of Colton's stature. Of course, the people she talked to, men and women both, looked at him with pity in their eyes.

When the woman had finished her shopping, having only bought one item that was in a small box, Colton carried it home for her. Before she went inside, she reached into her handbag, brought out two copper pieces, and held them in the palm of her hand so Colton could see. Of course, he did not take them. "It's ok, you earned them," she said with a smile.

Colton had not planned on taking any coinage from the woman. He needed her for other reasons, but at the same time, he was starting to feel bad at turning down coinage offered to him, for doing pretty much nothing. So, he made a compromise with himself and the woman. Instead of taking both coins, he only took one. When she looked at him, he could tell that she wanted to know why he only took the one, and he gave her an answer. "As not to offend your generosity." All the woman could do was smile. Returning the last coin to her bag.

Colton said goodbye to her, and even gave her a slight bow as he had done with the women in the first store, then turned and headed down the pathway. "I will contact you when I require your assistance again," the woman said just before he reached the end of the path.

He turned around, to say one more thing, "It would be my pleasure." Then turned and left, heading back to the section of the city where he slept.

The next day he was back helping Father sell his fruits and vegetables. Throughout the day, he saw a total of four women he had met just yesterday and one man; all happy to purchase products from his father, as well as asking for his son's assistants. He was able to accept the offer from the first two women, but when the third woman asked for his help, he had to politely decline, because he would be busy the next day, and the day afterward he had to help his father with the cart. Of course, the woman knew the child had to do whatever he could to help make the funds he and his father needed to live their lot in life, so she was more than happy to postpone her plans for three sun-cycles, until the child would be able to help her. Colton agreed to assist her in any way he could, and he would.

On the days, Colton did not work with Father, he would always have work to do for one of the generous women or men in the upper-class part of the city. Most of the time, all he did was travel with them from store to store and carry any packages they might purchase. At least the ones that were not too big for him to carry. And if there were too many, then sometimes the person he was with would pay the fare to take them home in a carriage.

When they arrived at their destination, the person would offer him some coins. No matter what they had in their hands, Colton would only take half, and of course, he gave his patent reply, "As not to offend your generosity." He even made them feel as if he was doing them a favor for accepting the small offering.

Colton knew that if he took all the coinage then there would be a greater chance they would start seeing him as being greedy. He wanted to be able to continue with his plan for as long as he could. If so, Colton would have a very nice life living on the streets of Maridian. Which is what he wanted.

TEN

Colton fell into step next to Hanna as she walked away from him to head back home. Hanna was the quiet one of the two, and Colton knew that he would have to be the one to start the conversation. "Would you like to come with me to the auction circle today?" It was where the citizens of Maridian would go to auction off anything they wanted to sell. Cattle, horses, wagons, land, and of course slaves. Even though she did not mind going to the auction circle it was the last item that Hanna did not like to see.

The auction circle was not a place Hanna would go to make her happy, it was more to the point that it took her mind off the life she had, at least for a while. "No, I need to get home and do the rest of my chores," Hanna said without looking at Colton.

The reply she gave was a typical one. Most of the time when Colton asked her if she wanted to go somewhere with him, she would tell him that she had chores to do. He thought that maybe she would want to go to the auction circle, because he had not taken her there in a while, and he knew she would not go by herself.

He liked the excitement the people at the auction created. The auctioneers yelled out to the crowd what was up for barter, and the people yelled back their offer. It would go on until someone would purchase the item, and then it would start over again. It reminded Colton of the time when he used to help Father sell his fruits and vegetables. Something Colton no longer needed to do.

He had started helping the man when he was seven. Not long after Colton had turned nine, the man had made so much coinage, with the help of Colton of course, that he was able to purchase a shop in one of the nicer sections of the city where he could sell his produce and other items. When the man opened the shop, Colton knew his time with Father had come to an end. He was happy to help the man while he had his cart, out in the open, under the sky, but Colton did not want to spend every day inside. His life was on the street and was where he needed to be.

Even though the man had offered to take Colton in, as his real son, and even adopt him, Colton declined the offer. They had worked together for two seasons, and Colton had come to feel something for him, and even with what the man was offering to do, Colton could not see himself living in a home and working inside a store, let alone having parents. Since he did feel something for the man, he did not want to leave him without any help. Colton decided he would find the man some.

He still visited the orphanage now and then, when he knew they were serving some type of food he liked. He had also continued to stay in contact with some of the children there. One boy, in particular, was very nice and polite and was only seven seasons old. The same age Colton had begun to work with Father.

After the man had opened his shop, Colton took the young boy to it and began to teach him what he needed to do to assist the man. Colton never even asked the man if it was ok. He just walked in and began showing the boy how to clean and how to make sure that the items on the shelves were nice and neat. The main thing he taught the boy was that in the morning, just before the shop opened for business, he had to take some water and splash it across the fruits and vegetables. Not only did it help keep them fresh, but it would make the items look more enticing to the customers.

From the very first day that Colton had begun to train the young boy the man who owned the shop did not even ask what he was doing. It was because of Colton he had been able to make more coinage than he ever had in his life, and if Colton was up to something, the man knew he would benefit from it.

After a moon-cycle, Colton stopped training the boy. In fact, Colton stopped coming to the shop every day. Now and then, he would stop by and see how the man and his new adopted son were doing. If he was not busy, Colton would even go with the young boy to make some of the deliveries the shop continued to perform. For Colton, his time with Father had played out its course. The man now had a boy he could call his son, and the boy had a mother and father.

There was a small part of Colton that felt maybe he would have enjoyed that type of life, but he made his decision and with everything he had accomplished, a lot of people were better off. The man had his shop and made a very good living. He and his wife had the son they always wanted, and the boy had parents. Colton, well he had all the coinage he saved up from the time he started helping the man sell the best apples in the city. That same phrase was on the sign in front of the store, "Best Apples in the City," and they were.

Every time Colton would leave the shop after one of his visits, he would always look at the sign on his way back to one of the many places he had claimed as his own. Whenever he saw the phrase, he could not stop the smile from appearing on his face, or the tear in his eye.

Now Colton is eleven, and he wanted to do something with Hanna. She may have been a season older than him, but it seemed as if he was the one who always had to remind her, that they were still children and had to have some fun, and to Colton, going to the auction circle was fun.

He knew Hanna did not like it when they auctioned off the slaves. The truth was he did not like it either. He thought that it was cruel, the way people would bring the elves up on the platform and make them stand there, usually with no clothes on at all, while people would inspect them as if they were cattle. Maybe not exactly like cattle, humans gave more respect to the creatures than they did to the elves.

Not only were most of them without clothing, but all of them, men, women, and children had their heads shaved so that there was not a single bit of hair left. Colton knew the reason for this. It was to let everyone know that this was an elf and was not even worth the coinage that someone would pay for them. Without hair, everyone would be able to see their pointed ears. The elves, the ones who were not slaves, had long hair, which they never cut in their entire life. At least that is what Colton heard. He had never seen one with hair or one that was not a slave. The elves live far, far away, in lands across the great waters to the south. Since no humans would go there, the only way humans could capture the elves sold into slavery, was by a few slave companies that used ships to go out into the great waters and capture any elven ship they came across.

No, Colton did not like to see the elves used as slaves. All he had to do was think of what it would be like if someone forced him to do whatever they wanted him to do, and if he did not, they would beat him, even to the point of death if it came to it. Colton hated slavery, maybe even more than Hanna did.

"If you don't want to go to the auction circle, I found a skeleton that looks like it was a dog when it was alive. We can go and look at it," Colton said and stopped walking when Hanna did so that she could turn and give him a look to tell him that she definitely did not want to see a skeleton of a dog. When she was sure Colton knew her answer, to what he had suggested, she turned and continued on her way. Colton took a moment to wonder why someone would not want to see a skeleton of anything but decided that Hanna was just not into skeletons.

He had to run a bit to catch up to her. "Hey, will you be going to the festival coming up?" Colton said to continue the conversation.

"I don't know. Maybe, if my mother is feeling better."

Colton did not give a response to Hanna's answer. He knew that Hanna's mother was sick. Hanna's mother was always sick. It was because of that, Hanna was always doing chores, and that was why Colton thought Hanna always seemed to be, not sad, just not happy. Colton knew that if all he had to look forward to, every day he woke up was to do chores, then he would not be happy either. No, Colton did not know what it was like to worry about a mother, or to go through life without a father he had known, so the only reason he could come up with as to the way Hanna was, is that she is always doing chores.

The day the two met, she was doing chores. It

was on a day when Colton had nothing to do. He had stopped by Father's shop and there were no deliveries to make. No one had asked for his help to carry any packages while they went shopping, or for help with anything else. It happens. Being a nine-seasons-old boy, when he had nothing to do, the only thing to do was to get up to something that would be fun, and maybe even a little risky.

Colton did not like stealing, but at the same time, he could not deny the excitement he felt when he would acquire something he did not have to pay for. On this day when he could not take the boredom any longer, he decided to find something to eat, something that was not his.

Colton did not like to steal, and the truth is, he did not need to. He was still more than welcomed in Father's shop, where he knew he would always have something to eat. He even knew some of the vendors who sold their goods on the streets. He did not have a relationship with them the way he had with the man that he had started with, but he was nice enough to them that he was sure that after a few polite words and a charming smile, he would be able to acquire something to his liking.

Another reason Colton did not need to steal food or anything else was because he had coinage. Since people always supplied him with food, he never needed to buy any. In fact, Colton hardly bought anything.

When his clothes wore out, and he needed new

ones, one of the women that he would help was more than happy to purchase him a new shirt, new trousers, or even new shoes. A couple of them had bought him all those items at once. They were nice clothes and when he went to help one of the women, he would make sure that he would wear something, the individual purchased for him. He did not do it because he liked the clothes, he did it because he knew they would appreciate seeing him in whatever they had given the poor child. Of course, that meant they just wanted to buy him more clothes. It would make them very happy to be helping the child, and the most important thing to them was that it would make Ourgós happy.

The truth was that Colton did not like the clothes the wealthy women bought him. They were too tight and too stiff, and he only wore them when he was with them. When he needed clothes, he was more comfortable with, he would go to the orphanage and rummage through the donation of clothes others would give to the orphanage. Most of the items were old and worn out, and would not last long, but they allowed Colton the mobility and comfort he enjoyed.

Ever since he had been earning his funds, Colton very seldom used any of it to buy himself anything. He just did not see value in buying something when he knew someone would either buy it for him or would just give it to him.

On this day, he was in the mood for a little risk.

Since many of the street vendors knew him, he had to make sure no one recognized him when he did his bit of thievery, so he disguised himself before he went on his little crime excursion. He tied a piece of cloth over his head to make sure none of his hair was showing. Then he climbed up to the roof of one of the many homes in the city, and reached down into the chimney, bringing out handfuls of soot. He then spread the contents completely over his face, and across his clothes. On these occasions, he made sure he wore some of the clothes the women had bought him but had already seen him wear. For what he was doing, he did not want to mess up his street clothes. They were the ones he liked.

When he arrived at his chosen destination, he waited until one of the vendors was not paying attention and had their back turned, then he would run out and grab whatever he had set his eyes on. Usually, it was an apple, or two. There was something about them that just pulled at him to take.

Most of the time he would be able to snatch the produce without anyone taking notice of him, but if someone did, he had already dashed off and was far out of the reach of the vendor. If by chance they got a look at him to report him to the city guard, the only description would be of a young boy with a scarf on his head, and filth covering his face and clothes. That would describe half the children living on the street. All except for Colton, who very seldom had filth on him. That is unless the occasion called for it.

Once the heist was over and Colton came down from the rush, he would feel bad about stealing the item. Every time he did this, he would go back the next day, not in disguise of course, and tell the vendor that he had heard about the theft and offer to pay for the produce stolen by one of his fellow street urchins. He would even hand the coinage over. Sometimes the vendor would take it, but then there were others who would just tell him to keep his coinage and that they understood that not all children could be like Colton.

It did not matter if they took the coinage or not, his sincerity pleased every vendor and they would give him an apple for being such a concerned and upright child. One that all children should be like. Of course, they did not charge him for it. As for the coinage, the ones who did accept his offer, well he still only paid for the apples he had taken, but still got one for free, so in the end, Colton came out ahead every time.

It was on one of these days that Colton met Hanna. A day of boredom, not one where he was going to pay for the produce he had taken.

He had just made his theft, but it just so happened that on this day, there were two city guards in the area. When the vendor yelled for the child to stop, and yelled out "Thief," the guards took off running after Colton. Usually, the city guards did not bother going after a child who had stolen something to eat, even if they were in the area. A couple of apples were not worth the sweat and trouble they would have to put up with in capturing the child. However, on this day, the guards must have been in a bad mood, or they were just as bored as Colton was because they took off running after him.

Colton did not worry when he turned his head and saw the two guards were not far behind him and closing the distance. The guards had on their standard uniforms, and even though it was a warm day, part of that consisted of armor. Colton knew that it would not be long before they gave up the chase because neither the child, the apples, nor the vendor, was worth the effort. If the guards just happened to be in the mood to trouble the thief, then Colton would make sure that if they wanted him, they would have to work for it.

Colton stuffed the two apples down his shirt, which he had the end tucked into his trousers. Now he had his hands free and did not have to worry about tossing the apples away. He made a left down one street and then a right when he reached the corner of the next street he came to. He had lived in this area for his entire life, and to Colton, only the rats knew every nook and cranny better than he did.

He reached the place he was heading to, but instead of running to the door, he ran down the side of the building. That was where a hole was, just big enough for him to crawl through. He knew he would be able to fit, because he was the one who had made the hole, just in case he had a need to get into the abandoned building, which had been for a number of seasons. If the guards happened to see where he had made his way inside, they would have to either knock the bricks away to make the hole bigger or go back to the front of the building and pry away the wood beams someone had placed over the door to keep the local vagrants and children out. All but one.

As soon as Colton was in the building, he made his way to the stairs that would take him to the upper floor, once there, he went to the hatch leading outside, onto the roof. When he had made the hole in the wall and found the little opening to the roof, he saw the entrance sealed with an iron lock. It took him over a moon-mark to cut through the wood around the latch, with a sharp stone, so that he would be able to remove it and the lock together, to allow him access to the roof.

Once on top of the building, he immediately ran to the side the hole was on and looked out over the edge. He did not see anyone below, so he ran to the side overlooking the front entrance. Once again, there was no sign of anyone following him and he knew he had reached the roof in enough time to see if the guards were going to try to break away the brick around the hole or remove the wood beams. Colton saw that they had chosen neither of those options because they never saw him enter the building in the first place.

When he saw the vicinity below was clear, Colton

looked down the street to his right, to see if he could tell where the guards were. He did not see them, but when he turned his head and looked to the left, he saw that they were still running. Only now, they were running away from him.

At the second street, Colton had turned right, but when the guards had made it to the intersection, they had turned and gone left. Of course, Colton had figured they would and that was why he had chosen to go right, and even chosen this building as part of his escape route. He figured that if he had to elude the city guards or a vendor, adamant about getting their property back, once they saw the child turn left the first time, then more than likely the child would make another left at the intersection, taking the culprit back in the direction where he had committed the crime in the first place. Colton figured that the person chasing him, would think that a normal criminal would run away from the crime scene, but to throw off the guards, they would head back the way they came, thinking the guards would head the other way. The only difference was that Colton knew how people thought, especially adults, so the guards would think that they knew the criminal was trying to outsmart them by double-thinking the plan. Colton was too smart for the guards and did what a normal criminal would do, which was go in the direction away from the crime. Even Colton had to pat himself on the back for what he had come up with, and he did; literally.

He was smart enough to know that he could not risk going back onto the street right away in case the guards came back. He also knew he could not stay in this particular building because he was still too close to the area where he acquired his lunch. Like many of the children living on the streets, he used the closeness of the buildings to make his way across the city.

Most of the time, he could stand on the edge of one building and jump over to the next. Sometimes he had to get a running start, but he still cleared the distance with no problem. Of course, there were some buildings, which had too wide of a gap between them, but that problem was taken care of as well.

This was not something Colton had come up with, though he was thankful for whoever did. Someone, more than likely a child using the rooftops long before he had, placed wooden planks across the buildings that had too big of a gap to jump safely. There were some places the gap was so wide that someone secured two boards together, either by nails or rope, so they would cover the distance. Every now and then, the people living in the buildings would remove the boards, but every child who used these routes knew that it was in their best interest to replace the missing boards. Colton figured that over time, most of the adults who removed the boards grew tired of doing it, so they just left them in place. In Colton's opinion, adults always gave up too easily.

As Colton made his way across the rooftops, he pulled the two apples from inside his shirt and carried them in his hands. Yes, he loved to eat apples, but he would wait until later. Right now, he enjoyed the feeling of holding his reward for a job well done.

As he continued his stroll, savoring his victory, he saw across the way, a girl on top of a building hanging up linen. He had never seen her before and since he thought he had come across every child in the nearby part of the city, he thought that maybe she had just recently arrived. He did not know that the girl had been in the city for a few seasons, but ever since her father passed away, she was always busy with chores, and very seldom got out of the house, and only when her mother took her to pick up any items they needed.

Being the courteous child, Colton decided it was only polite to introduce himself. Maybe even show the girl with the golden hair around the city, because Colton knew every bit of it.

He knew that he would have to make a good impression because the first was always the most important.

He made his way to the building next to the one where the girl was working. When he came to the edge closets to the building across the way, he called out to get the girl's attention, "Beautiful day isn't it!"

Since the girl did not notice the boy until he spoke up, it startled her when she heard him, causing her to flinch a bit. To Colton's surprise, he was sorry he had surprised the girl with the golden hair, who was still looking at him. Colton knew that this was his chance.

The distance between the two buildings was nothing for Colton to jump across from where he was standing. Since he wanted to make a grander appearance, he turned around and walked five paces away from the edge of the building. When he turned back, he was happy to see that the girl was still watching him.

Since he needed his hands free to do what he had planned, Colton once again placed the two apples inside his shirt, so they would not fall out, then he took off running toward the edge of the building. When he reached it, he jumped out and upwards to clear the gap, but also to make sure he made it over the edge of the second building which was higher than the roof. As he landed on the building with the girl, he tumbled forward and did a somersault, but came out of it perfectly, standing just a few paces from the girl. Even though the girl did not say anything, he could tell that he had made an impression. At least that is what Colton thought to himself.

With the initial contact made, he did not want to push too hard in getting to know the girl. So instead of saying something to her, he just walked around her and went to the opposite side of the roof. When he reached it, he jumped up on the ledge and turned around. He saw that the girl had turned to face him, and he was sure that even though he did not see it, she never took her eyes off him, as he walked away from her.

Now that they were facing each other, Colton had a couple more feats to perform to make an impression. The first was that he reached into his shirt and pulled out both the apples. He tossed the one he had in his right hand to the girl. Not too hard, because he wanted her to catch the gift he was offering her. Once she had it and was still looking at him, he placed the second apple in his mouth, holding it there with his teeth. Then he placed his left arm behind his back, bending it at the elbow, and placed his right arm across his stomach, bending it the same way. He then bowed to the girl, with the apple in his mouth, but made sure he never took his eyes off her.

He thought with all he had done, the tumbling routine, the gift he gave her, and the respect he showed her by bowing, he would have at least brought a smile to the girl's face. She just stood there looking at him. Colton did not give it much thought, because he still had one more act to perform.

He stood up out of his bow and turned to face the side of the building. Without looking back, he jumped over.

The girl seeing the unknown boy jump, ran to the side of the building expecting to see that the boy had fallen to his death. When she looked, his body was not on the ground below, and when she raised her eyes a bit, she saw that the young boy was already running to the other side of the street.

When Colton had jumped, he had enough practice and skill that he grabbed onto the small ledge extended from one of the windows on the second floor of the building, allowing him to stop his fall completely and then let go to continue down to the ground. He had done this on a number of occasions and knew how to land, without causing himself any injuries.

When he made it across the street, he turned around and looked up at the building where he had last been. As he suspected, the girl was standing at the edge of the roof, looking at him. From the look on her face, his little stunt had not left an impression on the girl, but Colton had one final act to finish with.

They held eye contact for only a brief moment before Colton raised his right hand to the top of his head and brought it down in his patent salute. He held his hand away from his head and he did not have to wait long before he saw the young girl with the golden hair smile. He knew that his introduction had come to an end. At least for now.

He turned and walked away, making sure he restrained himself from turning around to see if the girl was still watching him. He did not even care that he had to surrender one of his apples to get the girl to smile. It was worth it.

He decided that he would return to see if the girl would be there in a couple of days. Maybe even bring another apple, only one, but he would be more than happy to share it with her. Of course, he would probably have to remind the girl that he was the one she had met because Colton still had the rag on his head, and the soot on his face and clothes, but the next time he visited her he would wear better clothes. Maybe even some of the clothes that one of the many women had bought for him.

That was the day he met the golden hair girl named Hanna.

Colton was true to his word to himself and found Hanna a couple of days later. He even brought an apple to share with her, even though she declined his offer. He did not wear any of the fancy clothes though, to him she was only a girl.

Over time, Colton had done as much as he could to make Hanna smile. Every now and then, he might say something that would cause the corner of the girl's mouth to rise as if she was about ready to smile but then forced herself to stop. Even when he found out that she had lost her father, he thought that if the girl would just smile more, she would come to accept what happened, and she would feel better.

Until this day, with him being eleven and her twelve, he still could not get Hanna to smile. But Colton was never one to give up.

He began to focus on being there with Hanna now, walking back to her home, and figured he would try one more time to get her to do something fun, "Maybe tomorrow, we can go to the upper city and look at all the fancy shops," Colton said. Doing that always made him happy.

Hanna did not even look at him when she gave her reply, "I'll be busy tomorrow." Hanna gave her typical answer. It was not that she did not want to do something with Colton, but she knew that tomorrow would be just like today. She would have to take care of the chores; hers, and her mother's.

Colton knew that he would not have any luck today with Hanna, so he decided that he would at least walk her back to her place and open the door for her since she was carrying the bag she had. He still was not going to give up on showing Hanna that she could have some fun in her life. He would stop for the day, but there was always tomorrow, or the next day, or the next day. He smiled as he continued to say, "or the next day or the next day," to himself.

Just as they were walking up the pathway to the place where Hanna lived, Colton suddenly felt cold. He had never felt like this before, and for some reason, it scared him. So much so that he stopped walking towards the building. When he looked at it, he knew that whatever was making him feel this way was coming from inside, the same place where Hanna was about to enter.

"Hanna!" Colton yelled so loud she turned around to look at him, just as she was about to open the door. She thought he had called her because he wanted to open the door for her. He usually did when she was carrying something, and she was even a little surprised that he had waited this long to do so. Colton walked forward even though he did not want to, but he did not want his friend to go inside. "I think it might be better if you don't go in there."

Hanna gave him her usual puzzling look when Colton said something she thought was strange. Just like when he asked her if she wanted to go see the skeleton he had found. "Goodbye Colton," Hanna said, opened the door herself, and stepped inside, closing the door behind her.

Colton stood there for a moment but with what he was feeling, he wanted to get away, and fast. When he was halfway back to the street, he heard someone screaming. He had never heard it before, but he knew the scream came from Hanna.

When he had first arrived, he was so nervous he did not want to step anywhere near the house, but now, he thought Hanna was in trouble, and whatever was in there that made him feel this way, could be after her, Colton ran back to the house and through the front door.

He heard someone shouting and he could tell that it was Hanna. He ran in the direction he heard her, and it led him to the stairs, to the second level. When he was halfway up them, he saw Hanna coming down towards him. She was crying. "Hanna what is it?" he said and tried to grab a hold of her by her arms, but she pushed him away, and he fell back against the wall. Hanna ran down the rest of the stairs and ran off further into the house.

Colton wanted to go after her, but something made him look to the level above. Whatever he had felt coming from this place, was coming from that direction.

Colton was always one for a small adventure. However, at that moment, he thought it would be wisest for him to turn around and leave. The only reason he did not, was because a part of him needed to know what was up there.

He climbed the rest of the way to the second floor. Whatever was happening up there, Colton had no problem with sensing it in a certain room. When he came upon it, the door was open. There were four adults in the room. Two were the ones who help take care of Hanna, the ones she called Mama, and Papa. The other two adults he did not know. What he did realize was that he did not see the person the room belonged to. That was when he looked at the bed and saw that there was something under the covers. Then he thought that it was not something, it was someone. The person the room belonged to, was Hanna's mother. She was lying on the bed, but someone had pulled the covers up over her head. Colton knew the reason; it was for people who have gone to meet Ourgós. Now he knew why Hanna had screamed.

He looked down and saw the bag Hanna had been carrying lying on the floor in front of him. A loaf of bread had fallen a little out of the bag, but the sweet cake in there as well had cleared the bag completely. He had seen Hanna with one of the treats before and even asked her if he could have a bite of it. She told him no because it was for her mother who loved the treat. He figured that she had bought it for her today and had come up here to give it to her. That was when she saw what was in the room.

Colton picked the items up, placed them back in the bag, and headed back downstairs. He made his way to the kitchen, where he placed the bag on the table. He had been in this room before because Mama would give him a drink of water when he would stop by and see Hanna. He thought Mama was happy that Hanna had at least one friend, even though Hanna might not think of him as one.

Colton left the house and went to his nearby hideaway. The one he had found when he decided that he needed to have a place close to Hanna in case he wanted to stop by and visit. He slept there that night but rose early the next morning. He had an errand to do, and since it was in the upper part of the city, he needed to be about it as soon as possible.

Once done, he returned to Hanna's house and Mama told him she was up on the roof, and that right now, Hanna could use a friend like him.

Colton made his way to the roof, and this was one of the few times he reached it by going through the house. When he walked out into the midday sun, he looked around and saw Hanna, only this time she was not hanging out the linen to dry.

He walked over to where she was, sitting on the roof with her back up against the part of the building that made up the ledge. The same part he jumped up on, the first day he met her, and dropped to the ground below.

She had her legs pulled up to her chest and her head resting on her knees. For the first time in his life, Colton did not know what to say. He just stood there, and when Hanna realized she was not alone, she raised her head and looked up at Colton. He saw the tears in her eyes, and it appeared that she had not stopped crying from the time she ran down the stairs past him yesterday. Colton still did not know what to say, so all he did was hold out the bouquet of flowers he had bought for her that morning. He had gone to the better part of the city because he wanted the nicest ones he could find. He paid quite a bit for them, and since he was buying them for Hanna, he did not even try to get the woman who sold them, to lower the price.

Hanna did not take the flowers from him; she just lowered her head back to her knees and continued to cry.

Colton turned around and was about ready to walk back into the house, but something inside him told him that he should stay. He turned back to look at Hanna who still had her face hidden. Colton knew that she wanted to be alone, but Colton also knew that sometimes, people do not really know what they want.

He walked over and sat down next to Hanna. She did not move, so he sat the flowers down on the roof at his left, then took his right arm and placed it over Hanna's shoulders. He did not even have to pull her towards him; she did it on her own, and now she was crying into his shoulder, which he did not mind.

Colton never had any parents. He never had someone he loved or knew so much, that if what happened to Hanna's mother had happened to them, he would feel the loss she was feeling. He did know that the golden hair girl, whom he had known since he was nine and she was ten, was going through something he did not know how to fix. Usually, Colton could fix any problem he would come across. Usually, but not this time.

ELEVEN

The girl arrived in the city of Faulkton when she was five seasons old. She had decided that the life she had now, was better than the one she had where she first lived, but for some reason, she never seemed to be content in what she was doing. To her, there had to be more than just waking up in the evening, providing for her daily needs, then go back to sleep while the sun was in the sky, so she could start over when she awoke again. She knew there had to be something more; she just did not know what it was.

When she arrived in the city, she had to learn to survive. After the first few days in her new environment, she thought that maybe it would be better for her if she were to go back out into the wilderness and live there. Moon told her that it would be best if she stayed in the city, because there are things in the wilderness that could do her harm, and Moon would not be able to protect her. The girl listened to Moon because she knew she could trust Moon.

Moon had not lied to the child. Creatures like

the big buck were some of the timid animals living in the woods. There were wolves, bears, and even the wild boars roaming the area, would not hesitate to attack the child, and Moon needed her to live. Besides the animals, there were the humans living in the mountains that would come down and attack anyone they came across. In the city, the girl would be safe from them, but out in the wild, she would be defenseless to them as well as gnomes and trolls which seemed to be increasing in numbers every full turn of a season. Moon did not know why that was, but Moon did not want to take a chance that the child would find an end before Moon could begin to use her.

The night she entered through the city gate, she spent the remaining time before the sun came up exploring. Since it was night, when she had made her way farther into the city, she saw many dwellings that reminded her of the place where she had lived before. Only the women she saw inside seemed to have redder cheeks and whiter faces. She did not think that was their natural look but decided it was not important. The girl had never seen women paint their faces to make them look prettier to entice the men they were associating with. In Bonehaven, makeup was a luxury and the women who worked in the brothels would not waste what little coinage they had.

When the girl took a chance and stuck her head inside the doors to a couple of the places, someone, usually a very big, ugly, looking man would yell at her to get out. The girl would quickly do as instructed, as always, but she did not understand why they would not allow her to go inside. She had lived in a place just like what she was seeing, so she thought she would be able to find a similar place to stay when the sun came up. Even though she did not want to, in fact, she had thought about going back out into the woods and climbing a tree to sleep in until the sun went down. She knew she would have a problem getting back through the gate. One of the adults would wonder why she was heading out of the city, at night, all alone.

By the time the sun was coming up, the girl had traveled halfway into the city but still had not decided what she was going to do. With the rising of the sun, she wanted to get under cover and sleep until it left the sky. Since she had not found a place to stay, she walked down an alleyway between two buildings and when she was near the center, she crouched down on the ground. The sun had not risen high enough to cast a strong amount of light where the child was, so she decided she would just wait there until she wanted to continue her exploration of the city.

While still crouching down, with her knees up to her chest and her arms wrapped around them, the child was able to get some sleep. Of course, being in a new environment, one the girl did not know well, she kept her knife in her right hand, just in case.

Every now and then, she would hear a noise, usually, someone speaking off in the distance, and she would open her eyes to see if they were coming towards her. When she was sure she was still safe, she would lower her head and close her eyes to go back to sleep, until the next noise she heard caused her to make sure she was in no danger. If anyone saw the child, they would have thought that she was an animal being cautious of its surroundings, and in some ways, the child was.

Before the sun was high in the sky, the child felt the warmth from it and when she raised her head, she happened to look up and the sight of the sun's glare bothered her eyes. She immediately stood and raised her right arm up to block out the light. With the sun rising higher and higher, she would not be able to stay where she was.

She picked up the two bags she had and hung them over her shoulder. The water bag had a bit left in it, but the other one only had a small amount of the last rabbit she had caught and a few berries. At that thought, the child's stomach made a noise and she realized with all the exploring she had done last night, she had forgotten to eat, nor did she eat when she settled to rest. More than likely, it was because she was too tense to eat, being in a new place, and always making sure she was not going to encounter anyone who would cause her problems.

The child made her way to the opening of the alleyway, where she had entered. When she reached it, she stayed at the edge and looked out. With what she saw, she quickly took a step backwards. When her courage returned, she looked back out to the area before her. She saw what appeared to her to be a good portion of the city's inhabitants walking about. Not only that, but the sun was even brighter, now that the two buildings were not blocking her view.

She decided that heading out into the crowd and the light was not something she wanted to do, so she turned around, and headed back into the alley, continuing past the section where she had been waiting.

When she made it to the other end, she saw that even though there were some people still moving about, there were not as many as there were at the other end, and the light was not as bright either. She stepped out of the alley and began to continue to explore the city.

By the time it was midday, the child had not eaten and had only a bit of rest, so she was growing tired. Moon could tell and decided to speak to the child, to guide her. *"You will need to find shelter,"* Moon thought to her.

"There are no trees for me to climb," the girl thought.

"You will need to find a house or some other type of dwelling where there are no other humans. Someplace where you can rest and eat."

The child knew she had to eat, and sleep, but to her, all the buildings she had seen always had someone in them. Last night she had thought she would be ok with staying in one of the places like the one where she had first lived, but since they would not let her enter, as well as all the noise and the people inside, she wanted to find somewhere she could be by herself. While traveling to this city, the child had come to enjoy being on her own. She did not see any need to stay with others, and since Moon had told her to find somewhere with no one else then she knew that was what she had to do.

The sun was up, so Moon could not see the city she was in, nor could Moon guide her. All she could do was continue to walk about the city. When she would come to a place where she had to decide on which way to go, she always chose the direction that had the fewest people in the area. She continued to do this until the sun was way past its midpoint in the sky, and by now, the child's eyes were hurting her, as well as her skin was starting to itch. It was making her uncomfortable, and even a bit angry.

What she did not realize was that by choosing to go in the direction where there were fewer people, she eventually came to the worst part of the city. The part where there were more mouths to feed than there was food. Even though the sun was still in the sky, there was something about the surroundings which made the area a little darker than it actually was. For some reason, just entering this part of the city made the girl feel better. Even maybe a little homesick for the place where she used to live. The place, now covered by the debris of the mountains.

She continued farther into the part of the city she had come to. After turning down a couple of streets, she saw a building that looked as if it was what Moon had told her about. The doors and windows had wood over them, so she figured that no other human would be inside, or else they would not be able to get out. Unless they had already left and placed the wood back over the door until they returned.

The girl was growing tired, and her stomach was making noises more than before. She knew she would have to find a place to rest soon, and the one she was looking at would be just as good as anything else she would find. She decided that if someone was in there, or came in after she was inside, she always had her knife.

The girl made her way to the building, making sure no one was watching her. Since this was the worst part of the city, it was not something she had to worry about. The people living in the area kept to themselves, and if anyone had noticed the child, they would think that she was just one more of the street urchins who ran wild in the city. One little child was no different from any other.

Even before the girl made it to the front entrance, she knew the wood across the door would be too difficult for her to move. Whoever had put it there wanted to make sure it stayed.

She walked to the left side of the building and saw the windows boarded up as well. Even if they were not, the child was too short to grab hold of the ledge and pull herself up.

She continued to walk around the building and was about ready to give up and look for some other place, but when she reached the back, she saw another door. Unlike the one in the front, the boards placed across it only covered the top half. But like the ones on the front, these were too big and secured enough to the door, that the child would not be able to remove them.

Since the boards ended near the middle of the door, the girl noticed that the bottom half was visible, as well as the small hole which seemed to be rotting through. She moved closer to the door, and when she was sure that the plan she came up with might work, she sat the bags down on the ground to her right. She then sat down next to them.

She positioned herself so her feet were towards the door. She extended her right leg out and noticed that she was still a little too far away so without standing she moved closer to the door. When she thought that she was in the best position, she pulled back her right leg, and with it raised off the ground, she slammed it forward, causing her foot to strike against the door, just to the right of the small hole. It did not surprise her that she did not increase the size of the hole. She pulled her leg back again, then forced it forward once more. This time, even though she did not do any damage to the door, she did feel the wood give a little. Once again, she pulled back her foot and then sent it forward. This time the wood did not give completely but she saw that it was set in further than it was before the last strike.

It took her about another twenty hits to the door to get the wood to break apart for her to be able to squeeze through the hole. When she did enter, the hole was still too small for her to carry her bags over her shoulder and crawl through the opening, so she had to slide her bags through first and then follow them.

Once inside, she welcomed the darkness that came with the place. With the windows boarded up, what little sun that did shine down in the area did not get through. She then looked behind her at the hole she had made. Someone else might find it and decide to come in as well. Maybe she could find something to block it, but for right now, she would leave it alone. Her first thought was to seek out a place to sleep.

In her travels to the city, on most days she just slept on the ground, but when she realized she would be safer up in the trees, she decided that the higher she went the better she would be. It was the same in the house she was exploring.

She walked through the building and saw stairs leading up to the next level. As she was climbing them, she could tell that like the door she had crawled through, the steps were old, and if someone placed too much pressure on them, they would probably crumble. The girl liked that idea. Since she was small and did not weigh much, she would be able to use them, but someone bigger, who might want to do her harm, would have trouble making it to the next level.

When she reached the next floor, she found another set of stairs leading to the level above. She took them as well, still believing that the higher she was, the safer she would be. As with the set of stairs before, these were in the same condition, worn down by time or by termites feeding on the wood. There was even a step, the fourth one from the bottom with a hole in it. The girl stepped to the side of the hole, not wanting to jump to the step above because her weight might break the wood.

When she reached the top level, she walked down the hallway until she came to the last room she could find. The door was already open and when she looked inside, she saw that it was empty, not even a single piece of furniture occupied the room. Which was ok with her, she had not sat in a chair in the time she had been on her own, and even when she lived with the woman, she always had to sleep on the floor. This would not be any different. Then again maybe it was, the child thought, maybe this was better.

The girl entered the room, and to make sure she was as safe as possible, she closed the door behind her; making a screeching noise, since it had been a long time since anyone used it.

There was no light coming into the room at all. There was a window, but like the front door, it had boards placed across it, but the child had no problems with seeing in the dark. She was used to traveling at night, and even though there was no moon or even stars in the room, the child was able to see clearly.

She walked across to where the two far walls came together to form one of the corners of the room and sat down with her back to one of them. She had slept on the ground, so the dust on the floor did not bother her. She opened the bag that had her food in it and ate the last of the rabbit and almost all the berries. She drank some of the water and then curled up on the floor to get some sleep. Which she did, all the while she kept a hold of her knife in her right hand, just in case.

The girl slept until something woke her. It was not Moon; it was the small pain she was feeling on her legs. When she heard a squeaking noise, she realized what it was. She had to deal with rats when she lived in the place with the woman. Since she had to sleep on the floor, if they came out to her and started chewing on her arms, legs, and feet, she had to kick and slap them away. Now and then, the woman who ran the place would pay someone to get rid of the troublesome pest, but it was mainly because the rats got into whatever food the place had stored. It did not matter to anyone that they would chew on the limbs of a child.

Before, the girl had no defense against the rats except for swatting them away and hoping they would eventually give up. Sometimes they did, but then there were times when she would spend the majority of the night, awake, defending herself. Now it was different.

The girl had fallen asleep lying on her right side using her arm to rest her head on. She knew that was not the best position for what she had planned. She slowly turned over on her back, as if she were still asleep and was just getting more comfortable. The rats scurried away when she started to move, but when the girl was in the position she wanted to be, she made sure that she remained completely motionless. It was not long before the rats returned, hoping to continue with the meal they had chosen.

Even when the rats began nibbling on her again, the child did not move. She waited until she knew the rats were back to feeding and were concentrating on what they were doing. When she was ready, she made sure she had a good hold on her knife, which she had adjusted so that she had the handle in her hand, but the blade was pointing downwards.

With the way she was lying on her back, she could not see the rats at her legs. The only thing she could go by was the feel of where they were chewing on her. That was what she focused on, so when she made her move, she quickly sat up, bringing the knife up, forward, and then directly down on the spot where she had felt one of the rats biting her. She was fast. Faster than the rat.

As the knife plunged into their lost nest member, the other rats took off running, knowing that the one they had chosen that night to dine on, was fast enough to take out one of their brothers. They would not come back tonight, it was too dangerous, but they would return later to get at the meal nesting in their domain.

When the girl was sure the remaining rats had scattered, she raised the knife up to see her prize. She had brought the small knife down, on the back of the rat, directly through its spine. If the child had observed it sooner, she would have been able to see the few short spasms the rat went through before it stopped moving and breathing entirely.

The girl smiled at what she had done, but then she remembered that the reason rats came around humans was to find food. The girl, while still holding onto the rat, reached over and grabbed her water bag; glad to feel the weight of the water inside. After inspecting it further, she saw that the rats had not gotten into it. Even if they chewed the outer cover, she would not have been able to use it.

She then lifted the other bag, but since it hardly had any food left in it, she stuck her hand inside to see if the few berries she had were there. They were not. The rats had probably smelled them first and ate them before they decided to dine on the bigger meal.

That was the last of the food the child had. That was what she first thought when she found the berries missing. She then looked at the rat still impaled on the knife in her hands. She then looked back to the bag she carried her food in, then back to the rat, and stated to it, and to any of its fellow creatures, within the sound of her voice, her intentions. "You eat my food, you become my food."

Later that night the child dined on rat cooked over a fire that she was able to start with some of the wood she had broken off from the door where she had entered. There was not much meat on the creature, but it would hold her until she was able to get some more berries or maybe a rabbit or fish. Or maybe she just needed to catch more than one rat to make up for their size.

She stayed in the place for the remainder of the night and into the next evening. She caught two more rats that were down on the first level and hiding in one of the cupboards in the kitchen. From their size, she realized that rat might keep her from starving to death but just barely. And even though they did not taste bad, there just was not enough meat on them.

The child went out as soon as the sun had almost set. She took the water bag with her and knew that she only had enough to last maybe one more day, even though she did not drink as much as an adult might. She remembered seeing the fountain in the middle of the city the first night she arrived, so she knew where to fill it. She would also keep a lookout for someplace closer to where she was staying so that she would not have to travel all the way back toward the front of the city.

In her travels, she did find a couple of troughs used for watering horses, but from what she saw in them, she decided that it might make her sick. She had no problem with eating rats, but the water that smelled strange she avoided. She even found a couple of wooden barrels that appeared to be sitting out to collect any rainwater that fell, but they smelled just as bad as the water from the troughs. The girl decided she would still go about exploring, but when she was ready to return to where she had slept, she would stop by the fountain and fill the water bag to last as long as possible. It might be heavier than it normally was since she usually did not fill it all the way, but at least she would not have to travel the distance every night.

She continued her search through the city but did not move too fast because she wanted to make sure she could find her way back to where she was staying. If she had not needed to fill the water bag, she would have stayed closer to the house.

Since the evening was turning to night, the crowds were not as big as in the day, but what she did notice was that the people were making about the same amount of noise. In fact, some of the crowds were louder than the ones who were out when the sun was.

By the time she made it to the fountain in the middle of the city, the streets were quiet, and there were hardly any people around. The ones that were out at night, stuck to the areas of the city where the drinking houses, brothels, gaming rooms, and all the other types of depravity were located, which many of the people in the world enjoyed.

The girl filled her water bag and since the moon was past its midpoint in the sky, she decided to head back to where she slept. She wanted to make sure she was inside before the sun came up, and maybe even have time to catch a rat or two and cook them before she laid down to sleep.

As she was making her way through the city, she saw other people when she drew closer to the less respectable areas of the city. Even on the first night she arrived, the places she explored seemed more welcoming than the places she was seeing now, lined up on both sides of the street. When she passed through this area the other morning, the places here had closed their doors for the day, so she had not seen just how much activity took place when the sky grew dark. Now that it was night, she saw what the places really looked like, and it might have looked gloomy in the daytime, but the atmosphere now caused the girl to grab a tighter hold on her knife, which she always kept in her right hand.

She held it by the handle but had the blade positioned so that it rested against her wrist. She kept her right arm down at her side but had her left hand lifted, up and across to her right shoulder to help support the water bag and the extra weight it had.

To her surprise, no one was paying any attention to her. The adults' only concerns were on whatever they were doing or were too drunk to even care. Now and then, someone would look her way, but when they saw that it was only a little girl, they turned away and went about their business.

She continued to walk through the city, and when she happened to walk close to one of the many places that had lights inside, and noise coming into the street, she saw a man turn to look at her, and even though he saw that she was only a little girl, he did not turn away. As the child walked by him, she made sure she kept her eyes off him and continued on her way.

It was not long after she passed the man, that she felt as if someone was not only watching her but following her as well. When this feeling came over her, she first thought that she was just being nervous, but the feeling would not go away. She resisted the urge to look behind her to see if someone was following her, because she did not want the person, if there was one, to know she had sensed them. But she did not have to look.

"Moon?" she thought to Moon.

"Yes child," Moon replied.

"Is there someone following me?"

Moon answered her question, "Yes."

Now the girl was sure someone was behind her, and for whatever reason they were, the child did not want them to follow her back to where she slept. Since she had been doing so much on her own recently, without Moon's help, she did not even ask Moon what she should do. She turned down the next alley she came to so that whoever was behind her, if they decided to follow her in, would catch up to her because she slowed her pace. Not enough to where she was standing still but enough to make the person think that she would be an easy catch. To increase the success of her charade, she continued to adjust the water bag on her shoulder with her left hand to make it appear as if she was having trouble with the item. She kept her right hand, down at her side, with the knife blade resting against her wrist. She did not know how she knew, but she thought it would be best to keep the shiny blade, hidden until the last moment so that it would go unnoticed.

Before she was halfway down the alley, someone placed their hand on the child's left shoulder and spun her around. She let them guide her so that their focus was on her, and not on the hand she had the knife in. As she spun, she flipped the knife in her hand so that she was still holding it by its handle, but the blade was now pointing outward.

As soon as she turned around, she saw the person who had followed her and had put his hand on her. It was the man she had passed who had not taken his eyes off her as he was doing now. When he first spun the girl around and saw her eyes and black hair, he thought the girl would fetch him a fair price in one of the more sordid brothels that catered to men who liked their women young like this one. That was where he would take her after he had some fun of his own. It was when he realized that he was feeling a sharp pain in his stomach that he looked at the girl and saw just how deep the child's eyes were. Even though the light from the moon was minimal, the look in her eyes told him he had made a mistake.

When he looked down, he saw the girl holding onto the handle of a knife. He could not see the blade since it was in him. While he still had his eyes on the child's right hand, she pulled it out of him. That caused him to look up and back at the child's face. He did not know what was more of a surprise, the look in her eyes, or the smile on her face.

Before the man fell to the ground, the child turned around and started walking away as if she had no worries about the man following her or anyone else for that matter.

The man fell to the ground and was able to position himself against the wall of the building so that he was sitting up. He placed his hand over the wound to try to stop the blood from seeping out, although that was not what he was most concerned about. He could feel the fluids from his stomach flowing out and could feel the burning it was causing. He knew he had to get some help or he would not be alive much longer.

He thought back to what had just happened and remembered that he had seen that the blade was not that long, but he was not that big of a man, with little meat on his bones. Because of that, the small blade had been long enough to cut into him, deeply, causing him a lot of pain. When the girl stabbed him in his stomach, she pulled the blade across his middle causing the wound to increase.

He forced himself to stand because he did not want to die in the alley, in fact, he did not want to die at all. As he was making his way to the entrance, he could not help but think about what the child had done. It did not matter to him that he had something nasty planned for the girl. She should not have done this to him. Before he reached the entrance to the alley, he thought to himself that when he healed, he would find the child and show her just who he is. Yes, he would find the child with those deep eyes, and he would do more to her than he had planned to do when he first saw her. All he had to do was get out of the alley and get some help.

He did not make it out of the alley before he fell over onto the ground; face lying in the dirt thinking that the girl with the deep eyes did this to him. It was the last thought he ever had.

The only one that saw what happened in the alley was Moon, and Moon was incredibly pleased.

The girl made it back to where she was staying with no further incidents. When she went exploring the next night, she went back through the same area where the man had been and even went into the alleyway. When she passed through it, she did see some red dirt near the entrance, but she never saw the man again.

She had been in the city for about two moon-marks, and with the exception of the first day, she had always gone out at night. She knew that if she were going to see anything besides the people and places that were active after the sun had gone down, she would have to go out while the sun was up.

She had been living off rats and water for the entire time and knew she would not be able to for the rest of her life. Surprisingly, the rat population in the place where she was staying had decreased, and the rats that did remain learned that it was best for them to stay away from the big creature with the sharp object which a good portion of their siblings had died upon.

The girl waited until there was a day when the sun was behind the clouds. The light did not bother her as much, and she still preferred to go out at night, but she had to find a way to get a different selection of food. If she could not, she would have to travel out of the city and into the woods close by to find some rabbits and berries. She figured if it came to that, she could kill one or two rabbits and that would last her for at least one moon-mark.

As she was walking through the area of the city where she had found a lot of different shops, she looked inside a few of them but since she did not have any coin, she would not be able to buy anything. She may only be five, but the woman who had taken care of her, taught her about coinage before she could even count to twenty.

She came across a man standing in front of a shop and saw something she recognized. She walked over to where the man was standing on the other side of a high counter. He was wearing a white smock, or it might have been red with white spots. The girl decided that the color of the clothing had started out as white, but with the blood that had soaked into it, it now took on a reddish tint.

The man was not very tall, but he was broad around his midsection. His hair was greasy and slicked back on his head. The girl did notice that even though the man was heavy set, his arms were very solid, especially the one he was using to cut into the rabbit lying on the table in front of him.

The girl, not saying a word, stood and watched the man. When he happened to look up from working on the rabbit and reached over to grab the next carcass, he noticed the girl staring at him. At first, he thought she was just one of the many children that ran wild in the streets. He went back to working the carcass but happened to raise his eyes enough to see that the child was still staring at him. He did not know the child, but with the way she was looking at him, and with those deep eyes of hers, it was making him feel uncomfortable.

"Go on, I ain't got nothin' for ya," the man said, waving the cleaver in his hand as if that would shoo the child away. He was able to make two more cuts on the rabbit before the staring got to him again. "What do ya want brat?" he asked when he looked at her again.

The girl looked at what was lying on the table, "Where did you get that?" she asked.

The man took his eyes off the girl and looked at the animal lying on the table, then back to the girl, "What the rabbit?" the man asked, and the girl nodded her head. When she had seen the rabbit, she thought that there might be more like them in the city and if that were so then she would not have to go out to the woods to find any. "I bought it, now be on y'ur way before I take my hand to y'ur bottom." The man said and went back to his work.

"Where?" the girl asked.

The man looked up, letting out a sigh because the child was interfering with his work. He looked at the girl and asked his question, "Where what?"

The girl explained what she meant, "Where did you buy the rabbit?"

The man went back to working the carcass but continued his conversation with the child since it appeared that she was not going away any time soon. "I bought'em from some trappers. They catch'em and I buy'em for the fur and meat."

The child understood now. The man gave coin to others that brought him rabbits. He would pay for their services. To the girl, it was just like what the women did back in the place where she had lived for those seasons. The men would give the women coin, and the women would give them what they wanted.

The girl thought back to the night she had seen the girl with the man and quickly pushed the image out of her head, but she did have an idea. "How much do you pay for the rabbit?"

"What?" the man asked not knowing why the child would even care.

The girl repeated the question, "How much do you pay for the rabbit?"

The man went back to cutting into the now skinned rabbit but gave the child an answer. "Five copper," he said then slammed the cleaver down onto the carcass removing its head. "Five copper for rabbit, ten copper for coon, twenty copper for beaver, and two silver for deer." When the man looked up again the girl was no longer there. He looked down the street to the left and then to his right but saw no sign of her.

Three sun-cycles later the child showed up in front of the man again as he was working on cutting up another carcass. This time the girl was standing closer to the counter, so he only saw the top of her head down to her nose. "Ya back again? What is it now?"

As soon as he finished the question, the girl moved her left arm and brought it up over her head, so that she could toss the three rabbit carcasses onto the counter. The man looked at them and then back to the girl, "Fifteen copper," she said, and all the man could do was look at the child not knowing what to say.

The girl walked away with fifteen copper pieces. Yes, it took a while to capture the rabbits, but Moon guided the child to each of the kills. When the girl told Moon that she wanted to catch rabbits and sell them for coinage, it pleased Moon that the child had found a way to earn a living. She caught one the first night and two more the second night she was out in the woods.

Now that she had coin, the girl went to one of the street vendors and bought some fruits that she had seen, and even though she did not know what they were, she wanted to try one. The man who sold her the red fruit told her they were apples, and since she liked them and they only cost one copper piece for two apples, she bought four. She would have to figure out a way to keep the rats away from them if she did not eat them all by the time she got to where she was staying, but if it came to that, she could always eat the rats that got too close to her apples.

As she was walking down the street, thinking about what else she could buy with the thirteen pieces of copper she had, she thought a question to Moon. *"Can you show me what a beaver looks like?"*

"Yes," Moon said, pleased with what the child had done, with only a bit of assistants from Moon. She had learned to kill rabbits, and now she wanted to go after a larger animal. Maybe soon she would be able to take down a deer. Why wouldn't she? She killed the man with no trouble. Yes, the child was becoming very efficient at killing. Moon could not be more pleased.

TWELVE

The child was now twelve and had made a living by trapping animals and selling them. She still remembers when she was only five, the first time she walked through the gates of Faulkton that afternoon to search for rabbits to sell to the man. When she started out of the city, one of the guards on duty asked her where she was going. The girl simply told him, she was going into the woods to pick some berries. The guard, being a little concerned for the child, suggested that she should wait until her mother or father could go with her. The child replied with the truth, "I have no mother or father." With that, the guard did not know what to say, so when the child walked by him and out the gate, he went back to performing his duties. He could not worry about one child.

She had stayed out in the woods that night and Moon had led her to a rabbit. Before the sun had come up into the sky on the third day, she came across another two and was able to catch, kill, and clean those as well. Even though she was not going to eat them, by removing the parts from the insides that were not good to eat, the three rabbits were lighter and easier to carry.

By the time she made it back to the gate, it was not quite midday, but she wanted to hurry to get her kills to the man and get home before the sun was high in the sky. When she approached the city, she recognized the guard who had talked to her when she passed through the other day. When he saw her, walking towards the gate, he remembered that she was the child who had gone out to pick berries but had not even thought about the child since then. As she passed through the gate and walked by the guard, she did not look at him. He could not take his eyes off her. Not like the man she had come across in the alley, no the guard just did not know what to think. He did have a question for her, which he yelled to her after she had gone a ways, "I thought you were going to pick berries?"

The child did not turn to look at the guard when she gave him her answer, "I did." She walked away and the guard did not say anything else to her. She had not lied, she did find berries, and she ate them during her time in the woods. Any rabbits she was going to catch, she wanted to save for coin. She could live off berries for the time she would be out in the woods; she had before.

Two sun-cycles after she had sold the rabbits, she walked through the city gates again. The same guard was on duty, and when he saw her, he asked her, "More berries?"

She did not look at him but still gave an answer, "Yes," she was a child of very few words.

She spent the remainder of the day resting in a tree. Moon was not visible yet, so the child had to wait until Moon rose, so Moon could lead her to the creatures she was after.

As soon as Moon was high enough, Moon began to lead her to the closest creature. It was another rabbit, and even though the girl was happy to make the kill, she knew it was only going to bring her five copper pieces. She wanted to find bigger creatures so she would be able to get more coin. She decided that she would cook this rabbit for herself and use it for her own food. With it, she could stay out in the woods longer, maybe even until she found a coon, which would bring her ten copper pieces, or maybe a beaver that was worth twenty.

Moon told her that beavers live near water, and she would have to wait until one of the creatures left their home they made in the streams and lakes. The girl did not understand what Moon was telling her, but she trusted Moon. She cooked the rabbit, and when morning came, she once again climbed a tree and rested.

As soon as the sun was almost out of the sky, she took some of the rabbit meat and berries and ate a small meal, while she waited for Moon. Once in the sky, Moon led her through the woods. *"Follow the stream and you will come to see a mound close to the center of the water. That is where beavers make their homes."*

The child did as Moon had instructed, and after a while, she saw what Moon had described. The mound was a big pile of sticks and branches. She also noticed that there were three of these in the area. "Where are the beavers?" she asked Moon.

"They live inside."

"Where is the opening to get in?" the child asked.

"Under the water. But you should not try to catch one of them in their home. They will defend their lodgings and they have very sharp teeth and claws, which they will use. You will have to catch one when it comes to feed or to search for material to add to its shelter. Look to your right." The girl did. *"They come onto the land and chew down the trees."*

The girl walked over to where she saw the stubs of many trees. She looked back into the woods and saw more. "They have used up all the ones close to the river," the child said to herself, more than to Moon. She then looked back to the water's edge. She realized that if she tried to kill one of the creatures close to the water, it would have a chance to make its way back into its home, and she would either lose the kill or would have to go in after it. Not that she would not if it came to that, but she knew it would be better if she could capture the creature before it retreated to the water.

She looked at the mounds of wood where the beavers lived. She then turned around and walked further into the woods. When she saw where the beavers had not cut down any of the trees, she knew that this was as far as the beavers had traveled inland. This was where the beavers had ended their search.

She looked around and saw the trees were of different sizes. The smaller trees were the ones the creatures were using for their homes, but there were also others, large enough for her to climb.

She found one she thought would suit her needs and walked over to climb it. Since there were no lower branches for her to grab a hold of, she had to take her time and use her arms and legs to make it up the tree. After two unsuccessful tries, she realized that the dress she was wearing ever since she had been on her own was too confining when she wrapped her legs around the tree. That was an easy problem to fix. She removed her dress and tied it around her waist. She still had on her undergarments which would keep most of her skin from scraping against the tree.

After two more tries, she was able to get high enough to reach the closest branch and pull herself up to rest on it. The branch was not thick or sturdy, but she was not going to use it to sleep on like she would in the other trees. She had to be as close to the ground as possible to do what she was planning.

Moon had moved across the sky but still was not at Moon's highest point. While waiting, the child had grown thirsty. Even though she had brought both her water and food bag with her, she did not bring them with her up into the tree. She had found a smaller tree where she placed the two items in, high enough off the ground, but that tree was not in the path of the way it appeared the beavers travel in the area.

The girl did not want to climb down and retrieve the water, because she would have to climb back up and did not want to go through the trouble again. In addition, if there was a beaver close by, it might hear her and not come to where she was. She stayed in the tree, thirsty, but determined she could follow through with her plan.

After Moon was beyond the midpoint in the sky, Moon called to the child, *"One is making its way towards you."*

The girl heard in her mind what Moon said but did not make a move. She remained still, and even reduced the number of breaths she was taking; even though she did not realize she had.

The girl soon heard something making its way along the ground below. Moon was high in the sky, but not full, yet the girl still had no problem seeing the creature coming towards her. When she climbed the tree, she made sure she positioned herself so that she was facing the direction the creature would be traveling towards her, the direction leading back to the water.

When the beaver passed by the tree, Moon thought to the girl, *"Now, jump down and make the kill."* The girl did not move. She kept her eyes on the creature as it walked by the tree and was soon behind her. *"You missed your chance,"* Moon thought, and the girl thought Moon was angry because she did not do as Moon had said. The child did not respond. Even though she could think what she wanted to say to Moon, and no one would hear her, she did not. She knew she had to wait and be patient. She had to keep still and remain quiet. The time was not right.

She heard the beaver chewing on a tree behind her, but she did not turn to look. Not even so much as to glance over her shoulder. She remained absolutely still. When she heard the tree make a creaking noise as it was falling, she knew the beaver had cut through the base and soon she heard the rustling of the tree and leaves on the ground. Without looking, she knew when the beaver was making its return trip. It was at this time the child stopped breathing completely.

Moon had not said anything else to the child. Moon was not happy that the child had disobeyed, so when Moon saw the creature walking back to the girl, Moon did not speak to the child. The girl would learn that if she did not listen to what Moon told her to do; she would have to suffer the consequences.

The girl kept her eyes focused on the ground below. When she had first climbed into the tree and taken up the position she was in now, she had pulled out the knife she had placed at her back, in her dress that she had strapped around her. She held the knife in her right hand with the blade facing upwards.

When the beaver made the trek back to the

river and passed by her tree, the girl saw that it was a little farther to her left, and not directly under her; she would have to adjust her plan. Instead of dropping directly down below, she used her right foot, the one against the tree, to help her push off, out of the tree. This gave her the momentum she needed to place herself over the top of the beaver's back, which she did perfectly.

The child dropped down and landed so that her feet were at the end of the beaver's long flat tail, but at the same time, she fell forward and caused her body to lie across the animal's back. She had seen how long the creature was, so when she fell forward, she made sure her left hand came down on the top of the animal's head, close to its neck. As her left hand made contact, her right hand, the one she held the knife with, slid into the side of the creature's neck.

The child held the position, including holding the weight of her body, against the creature to reduce the amount of struggling the animal was doing. It did fight but not enough, and with its blood flowing from the killing strike, it did not struggle for long. Even after it had stopped moving, the child waited a bit longer, before she removed the knife from the animal's neck. When she was sure the creature was dead, she stood up and looked down at her kill. She then looked up into the night sky to face Moon, "I never miss," she said to respond to the last thing Moon had said to her.

Moon did not reply. What could Moon say? Even

Moon thought the child was not going to be able to make the kill. Moon's pride would not allow Moon to admit that Moon had been wrong.

When the beaver had made its way toward the girl, she remembered what Moon had told her about the creature's teeth. She had seen animals carry items they had, and they always placed them in their mouths. The girl reasoned that if the beaver had to take the tree back to the water it would have to carry it between its teeth. With something in its mouth, it would be less likely that the creature would be able to bite down on the girl when she made the kill.

As she looked down at the dead animal, she saw that the creature still had the part of the tree it had been holding onto in its mouth. The child was so quick when she placed her hand on the back of the creature's head that it was not able to let go of the tree and use its sharp teeth to defend itself.

The girl undid her dress and placed it back on. She then bent over and with much effort, she lifted the beaver up and strung it across her shoulders behind her neck. The creature's weight caused the girl to stumble back a bit, but she soon adjusted her stance and leaned a little forward to balance herself. She then looked behind her and saw where she had placed the water and the bag of food. She would have to come back for them later after she was through with the kill.

She had to clean the animal, but she wanted

to do that further away. The smell of the innards, especially if she were to leave them lying in the area, might make others like this creature not come around, and the girl wanted to make sure she would be able to catch another one.

Once she had the kill cleaned, she carried the carcass back to where she had left her bags and secured them around her shoulders to carry them as well, then turned to head back to the city. She did not even have to ask Moon, what direction to go. Somehow, she knew.

It was already past midday when she reached the city, and when the guard who had spoken to her before saw the girl coming towards the gate, with the beaver carcass over her shoulders, he could not even bring himself to speak. He just stood there watching the girl as she walked by him with what was definitely not berries. That particular guard was not the only one speechless when they saw the child. The other guards who stood watch with him did not know what to think after seeing the girl. There was no doubt in their minds that she was the one who had killed the animal she was carrying; even though she was only a small child.

When she reached the man, she had sold the rabbits to, he was busy with a customer, but both he and the man he was talking to stopped when they saw the child walking towards the shop. Other people on the street stopped what they were doing when they saw the small child walking with the dead animal across the back of her neck and shoulders.

When she reached the counter, she had to struggle a bit as she positioned the carcass so that it was only across her right shoulder. She placed her left hand on the part of the animal that was in front of her and used her right hand to push the top of the carcass up so that it landed on the counter. She then used both hands to push more on the animal to get it to rest on the counter without falling. She then turned and looked at the two men who were staring at her, with their mouths open. "Twenty copper," was all the child said. When the man gave her the coin, she did not say a word to him. To her, the transaction was complete. The man received what he wanted and the child got what she was after.

She now had a total of thirty coins. She had spent three of the previous amount to purchase six more apples. Before she bought more food, the girl decided to obtain something else.

She went to the different shops in the area, and finally came across a shirt, a pair of trousers, and a pair of shoes she could wear, that would make it easier to travel through the woods and make her kills. She still had fifteen copper pieces left, and she was going to buy some apples or maybe try a different type of food, but she would make sure she saved some coins just in case she needed them.

Over the next few seasons, the child became efficient at making kills, which not only supplied her with food, that she did not have to pay for, but also it brought in the coin she needed to buy items such as clothes when the ones she had wore out. After one of her beaver kills, she bought a small whetstone, which she could use to keep her knife sharpened. No one told her she had to, not even Moon. No one told her how to use it to make sure the knife was equally sharp on both sides, she just knew.

When the cold weather came to the area, the child had a harder time catching the animals she had come to make her living on. Moon told her that they stayed in their burrows and rarely came out, or maybe not at all because they would have stored up what little food they use during this time inside with them.

Since the child always saved a bit of the coin she made from each kill, she was able to purchase food when she could not find any in the woods. Even the berries did not grow during this time, so the child had to rely on food from the shops in the city. Not that she did not like it, but she did not want to have to spend all the coinage she had saved. When she lived in the first city, and the woman taught her about coinage, she told the girl, that if she was just able to save some of the coin she made, she would not be so bad off when times grew tough.

The girl did not understand what the woman had meant then, but now she did. If she used up all her coins before the end of the cold season, she might not be able to obtain something to eat. Unless it was rats, but the child had been eating well for a while and did not want to go back to them as the only source of food. Even though she would if it came to it.

One day when she was out in the woods trying to find a rabbit or anything to kill, to eat, or trade, she heard a noise off in the distance. It was something she had never heard before. The sun was out but like on so many days during the cold season, the clouds were always in front of it, so it did not shine as bright. That was one of the good things to come with the cold season.

The girl followed the sound and came upon one of the lakes in the area. She saw what was making the noise but did not know what they were. She had seen something like it; Moon had said they were ducks. They live near the water and feed on the grass and plants that grow beneath the surface. The girl never tried to kill one of the ducks because when she saw the young ones, something inside her, made her take a liking to them and she decided to leave them alone.

Moon was not in the sky, but the girl could ask Moon her question. *"Moon?"* she thought.

"Yes, child."

"I see creatures that look like ducks but are bigger. They have long necks that are black, but their wings and bodies are grey and black."

Moon could not see what the child was looking at since Moon was on the other side of the world but knew what the child was seeing. *"They are called geese. They are like ducks. They have come to the area, to nest for the season while it is cold in the place where they normally live."*

"Do they ever come out of the water?" the child asked.

"Sometimes." As soon as she heard that word in her thoughts, the girl had a plan.

She slowly and quietly made her way, away from the lake, and back to where the stream and the lake met. She followed the stream a ways and then waded out into the water. It was cold but the child needed to find what she was looking for and knew that it would be easier to spot the item away from the shore.

When she found it, she picked up the small stone and tossed it in her hand. It had weight to it and was exactly what she was looking for, but she continued her search until she found four more like the one she had. With the five stones in hand, she left the stream and made her way back to where she had seen the creatures Moon had called geese.

When they came into sight, she crouched down so they would not see her, and moved quietly toward them. As she grew closer to the lake and the geese, she went down onto her hands and knees. With the amount of noise, the creatures were making, she did not think that they would hear her, but if they saw her moving towards them, they might take off flying, the same way the ducks did when she tried to get close to them.

She crawled on her hands and knees, only moving one or the other, every so often. She moved as slowly as she could, not wanting to scare the creatures away. When she was close to the edge of the water, the geese still had not left. She slowly positioned herself so that she was sitting on her knees with her legs under her.

In the time she had left to find the stones, more geese had arrived and now they completely covered the lake. As she looked out across the water, she doubted that she would even be able to count them all.

As she made her way toward the lake, she placed three of the stones in her left hand and two in her right. It was the two she was going to use first. She positioned one of the stones in her right hand so that she was holding it between her thumb and the two fingers next to it. The second stone she held against her palm with her last two fingers.

She then quickly pulled back her right arm and brought it forward releasing the stone she was holding with her thumb and two fingers. Many things happened at that moment. The motion she had made alerted the geese to her presence and they immediately took to the air. Just as fast as the girl had thrown her first stone, she used her other two fingers to flick the second stone in her hand up to her thumb and first two fingers, and she let it fly just as the geese rose out of the water.

With all the geese in the air and circling above, she could not make out where one creature ended and another began, but as soon as the second stone left her hand, the child stood up and walked over to the edge of the water, now free from almost all the geese.

She reached down and picked up the bird that had not flown away with the others. She then had to take a few steps into the cold water to retrieve the second bird she had struck with the second stone. Since the motion from her first throw alerted it, it took to the air before the stone made contact, causing it to land further away from the first kill.

The geese were heavy, more than a rabbit but both of them together were less than the beavers she would catch, so she had no problem with carrying them off into the woods. *"Moon, I need you to tell me how to clean a geese."*

It pleased Moon with what the child had said. Moon did not even correct her about how just one of the creatures is a goose, not a geese. Moon told the child how to clean the kill. The child removed the innards but left the meaty portions as well as the feathers. When she killed rabbits or beavers, the man she sold them to, sold the meat and the fur. The geese did not have fur, but she did not remove the feathers in case the man, she would sell them to, would buy the geese, and wanted the feathers as well.

As she was working on the ones, she had killed, she heard the other geese off in the distance, and it sounded as if they were returning to the lake. By the time, she finished cleaning her two kills, and by the time she had made it back to a different spot close to the lake, the geese had settled down as if nothing had happened.

The girl walked out of the forest that day with four geese. She decided she would take three and see if the man she sold her other kills to, would pay for these as well. If he did not, then she would be able to eat all four, because Moon told her that humans did eat them.

When she made it to the gates of the city, the guards, now use to her coming and going, could only stare at the child. After she had first started to go hunting, the guards would place bets on what creatures she would come back with and how many. When the cold weather came around, they started betting on whether or not she would come back with anything at all. The betting had stopped for a while because the child would return too many times empty-handed. When they saw the child walk through the gates with the four geese, they knew that when the child left the next time, the betting would once again continue.

When the girl arrived at the shop where the man would pay for her kills, she had to go inside because that was where he would be since it was the cold season. When she entered, he saw the child and could not believe what she had. It was very seldom someone would bring in geese for him to purchase because a person had to be particularly good with a bow, or a sling, to bring one of the birds down. If someone was going to do it, he knew the girl would be the one.

She placed the dead geese on the counter one by one. "What about that one?" the man asked when he saw the girl still holding onto one.

"It is for me," she said then asked the question she needed to know the answer to, "How much?"

The man looked from the girl to the kills and could not even remember the price he had paid for the birds, since it had been so long since someone had brought him any. They did not have much meat on them, but with what they had, cooks in the better part of the city would pay for it, and the feathers he could sell to one of the shops that used them for stuffing cloths, for the rich people that liked to lay their heads down at night on a soft pillow. He knew he would be able to make some coinage off the kills, which would come in handy since this was the season when his business slowed down, and so did his earnings. "I'll give ya fifteen copper a piece."

The child agreed, not knowing if that was a fair price or not. Even though she knew she needed coinage to live in the city, she did not put a value on the coin the way others did. With fifteen copper pieces for each of the kills that would give her forty-five, and with the number of geese she had seen, she knew she would be able to make coin during the cold season.

The man gave her the coins, but as he was counting them out and placing them in her hands, he asked, "How did ya kill them?" The child waited until she had all of her coins then she reached into the front pocket of her trousers and showed the man the last stone she had from the stream. The man thought he knew how she had brought down the four birds. "Ya used a sling and stone?"

The girl looked at the man for a moment then asked him a question, "What is a sling?" He explained to the child what a sling was, thinking she had used one but she did not know the name of it.

When he finished explaining to the girl, she just turned and walked out of the shop. To her anyone who wasted time putting a stone in a piece of cloth with a string attached to it, then swing it round and round over their head, then letting the stone fly forward, was putting too much effort into killing geese. All she needed was a stone or two, or four.

When the girl left his shop, the man still took a moment to look at the three geese before he started preparing them for sale. He had given the girl a fair price for the birds. She had been bringing him her kills for almost a full season and in his heart, he had a soft spot for her. He had even thought about offering her a place to stay with him, but every time he tried to talk to the girl about something other than whatever kill she brought to him, she would always turn and walk away. The one personal question she did give an answer to was when he asked her what her name was. Her answer was one he had not expected. She simply said, "I don't have one," then turned and walked away.

As he was working with the carcasses, he decided that when he did sell the meat and feathers and found out how much he could get for them, if it was more than what he had thought, then he would increase the amount he paid the girl. He would even give her enough to make up the difference for the ones he had just purchased. With what the child was bringing him, he was making a good living. She was even better than some of the other older trappers, who always mutilate their kills before they even brought them in to sell.

Yes, the man had a soft spot for the small girl with no name. She was different from other children. That was the word he used to describe the girl. Except when he thought about her eyes, different did not cover what they looked like. Every time he looked into the eyes of the child, all he could think of, was how deep they were.

THIRTEEN

S he had been in Faulkton for two seasons when some other children had stumbled onto the hole in the back of the building where the child had made her home.

When she heard noises coming from one of the levels below, she quietly made her way to the door of the room she occupied, which was the only room in the entire place she used. When she opened it, she could tell that whoever was in the house was coming up the first set of stairs. Not only could she hear the creaking every time someone placed their foot on one of the steps, the children, and she knew that there was more than one, were talking about how they could make the place their new living quarters. The girl was not sure if she liked that idea. She figured that it was best if the children, who were about to stake their claim to the place, might want to check with the one who had lived here for the past seasons.

Before the two children made it to the stairs that would bring them to her level, the girl moved to the end of the hall. Even if the two had not been talking, they would not have heard the girl above them, opening the door closest to the top of the stairs, stepping inside the room, then hiding behind the door, leaving it open.

The girl heard the children coming up the second set of stairs and she prepared herself. She had her knife, as usual, in her right hand with the blade facing out. She had left the door open for a couple of reasons. One was that if they decided to inspect the room she was in, they would not see her, and she would be able to make her move as they stepped inside. The other was if they just looked into the room, and then move farther down the hallway, they still would not be able to see her hiding behind the door, and she would be able to come up behind them as they moved away from the room.

Being children, and since they were snooping around the house, when they saw the door opened, they stepped inside to see what they could find. They only entered enough to where they were standing just inside the doorway, so the girl did not do anything, yet. She would wait and see what the two intruders were going to do.

When they had said a couple of things about the house and the room, they turned around and walked out the door. The girl heard their steps out in the hallway and could tell that they were traveling toward the room she had made her own. That was when she knew she could not let them get any further. Not only was it her room, but it was where she kept her water bag, her bag of food, and the few things she had acquired during her time in the city. Even more important, that was where she had hidden the coin she had saved from her hunting, and in the two seasons she has been in the city, it had become a nice sum.

She waited until they were a few steps away from the room, so she could get around the door and come up behind them. When she glanced out into the hallway, she saw that both children were taller than her, but that did not bother her, she belonged here, they were the intruders.

When she was sure they were not going to turn around and were talking to each other, she made her way into the hallway, and even though the wood beneath their feet creaked every time the boys took a step, the child made each of her steps without noise. It was something she had practiced since she had come to this place. She was glad she had because the two boys did not hear her come up behind them.

When she was close enough, she pushed the boy on the right side of the hall forward, and as he was stumbling away, the other boy turned to see what happened to his friend. Out of the corner of his eye, he saw an object coming toward him, in the air. He was not fast enough to get out of the way, so when the girl jumped at him, he fell to the ground, landing on his back. When he looked up, he could barely see the person that was on top of him, but he could definitely feel the knife pressing against his throat. In all the commotion, the other boy positioned himself so that his back was against the wall closest to him. He did not try to help his friend. All he saw was him lying on his back, and he was not even sure if he was still alive.

The eyes of the boy lying on the floor had adjusted enough to the dark so that he was able to make out that whoever was on top of him, was only a child, but since he felt the cold metal on his skin, he did not speak. In fact, he just laid there, thinking that he wished he had found a different place to enter.

"What are you doing here?" the child lying on top of him asked. When he did not reply, he felt the blade press more against his throat, then heard the same question, "What are you doing here?"

The boy thought it was in his best interest to answer the question. "We just came in to explore. We wanted to see what was in here." The boy thought that his answer was good enough, but the person on top of him must have thought differently because the knife pressed a little bit harder against his throat. He knew that if it were to move forward anymore, it would be in his throat and not just against it. "Honest that is why we came in here."

The way the boy said his last statement made his friend speak up. "It's true; we found the hole in the back entrance and came inside."

The girl remembered that the boys were taller and bigger than she was. And even though she had to make the hole a little bigger for her since she had grown some, she knew the hole was too small for the two to get through. "You lie; you could not fit through the opening."

The boy whose throat she had her knife to, knew he had to say something, and did not hesitate, "We kicked more of the wood away to widen the hole."

"He's telling the truth!" the other boy said, trying to do what he could to help save his friend's life because if his friend died, he knew he would probably be next.

The girl believed they had not come in to cause her harm. For some reason, she could sense the two were frightened, and she had nothing to fear from them. Not that she would be. She sat on top of the boy for just a moment longer, then quickly and effortlessly, pushed herself up so that she was standing. The boy who had been beneath her quickly jumped to his feet; just not as eloquent as the girl had. Now that he was standing, the boy who came in with him stood as well and they both came together in the middle of the hallway.

All three stood there looking at each other, and it was the taller of the boys who spoke, "We just came here to look for a place to relocate. The place we had been staying in was taken over by some adults, so we had to leave."

"Can we stay here with you?" the smaller boy asked.

The girl did not look at them, she just walked to

the left of the two, and when she was close to them, they moved over to the other side of the hall. Before she reached her room, she turned back to face the two boys. "This level is mine. Stay off it," she said and started to head back to her room.

"There are other kids that are with us, just not here right now," the bigger of the two said.

The girl did not turn around to look at them but gave her reply to what they said, "They are not to come up here either." She then went back to her room and closed the door behind her. She heard the two boys running down the hall and down the creaking stairs. She was not sure if they would be back or not. She had been in this place for a while, and even though she did not need the company, she understood that if other children were here, then they would be the first warning if someone enters the building who did not belong. She did not have anything against the children who roam the city streets, she just did not have any use for them; until now.

Over the next few nights, eight kids had taken up lodging in the house. One evening as she was coming down the first flight of stairs leading from her floor, she saw the smaller boy she had met the first time, sitting at the foot of the stairs. He heard her coming closer and when she reached him, he stood up to look at her. She stopped long enough and the look on her face told the child that she wanted to know what he was doing. "Randolph, he is the one you were lying on the other day, told me that I was to sit here and make sure no one tried to come up to where you are. He said that if anyone did, I was to get him before you killed them." The girl did not give a reply, she just turned and headed out of the house. From what the boy had said, she was sure she had gotten her message across.

One night just before she was about ready to make her way to her room, she heard some of the children talking. She never really paid much attention to what they would be talking about, but this time she heard part of the conversation, and it sounded interesting. When she reached the top of the stairs, she sat down and continued to listen to the children on the first floor.

"...But if they let me join then I will be set for life," one of the boys said.

"Tat, you can't even kill the lice that live in your hair. What makes you think you can become an assassin, and kill a person?" It was Olivia who had asked Tat the question. She was the only girl who had moved in with the other children.

"Because they will teach me. That is what they do. They take you in and train you to become an assassin. Then when they have taught you everything you need to know, they send you out to kill people and you get coin for doing it."

"But killing isn't right," Randolph said, always being the one to keep everyone else out of trouble. "And besides, the Assassin's Guild is in Sarzanac and you don't have any coinage to make the journey, and you definitely can't walk there."

"Can to," the one called Tat said.

"Cannot," Olivia replied.

They went back and forth, and only stopped when they noticed the girl who lived on the third floor, by herself, was standing in the room with them. Since she never came into any of the rooms the children used, or even talked to them, it surprised them, to see her now.

The children had made a small fire and were sitting around it, but not one big enough to draw attention from anyone outside. It was big enough to light the room so that all the children saw the girl's face, and with the way the light reflected off her deep eyes, they each jumped a little in their seats when she asked her question, "Where is Sarzanac?"

None of the children spoke, but when Randolph saw that the girl was not going to leave or do anything else until she got her answer, he pointed off to his right. The girl then left the room.

That night she packed up her things and left the house, and the city of Faulkton behind. She had heard what the child had said about the Assassin's Guild. She was not completely sure what it was, but from what she heard, something inside her had awakened, and she knew that what she was missing in her life, she would find in Sarzanac.

FOURTEEN

When the girl left for Sarzanac, she did not even know how far away it was. Only the direction she needed to travel and for her, that was enough. She left the city where she had lived since she was five and did not look back as she exited the southern gate. There was nothing for her in the city, and everything she had, she took with her. Her blanket that she would cover up with when it was cold. The clothes she was wearing and one extra set. Her water bag and the bag she used to carry food, the bag of coins that she had saved over the seasons, and of course, she had her knife. Which she had taken up the habit of flipping it in her hand and passing it through her fingers as she walked. She did not know when she started this, but it was something she did.

She left the city at night, and just before the sun rose, she stopped traveling on the road and went into the woods to find a tree to climb to sleep. The trees in the area did not have a lot of leaves for cover, so when she had chosen the one that would suit her best, she used her blanket to cover up from the sun.

It continued to bother her, and the girl noticed that with every passing season, her agitation to the sun grew worse.

When the sun had gone out of the sky, she climbed out of the tree and continued her journey. Instead of going back to the road, she stuck to the woods and kept a lookout for any berries or animals that she could kill to replenish her supplies. She did not know how long it would take to get to Sarzanac, so she wanted to make sure she kept enough food on hand to survive.

After a few days, she came across a small village. Logs, with the tops cut into sharp points, made up the wall surrounding it, to help keep out anyone who tried to get over it. If she wanted to, the child knew she would be able to find a way to get over the top, but first, she would head to the gate and see if they would allow her to enter, even though it was late at night.

Before she came within twenty paces of the gate, someone yelled out to her, "Stay where you are and state your business!" The girl looked up and saw a man standing at the top of the wall. Next to him, at each of his sides, were two other men with their bows raised, and arrows ready, pointing at the girl.

"Is this Sarzanac?" the girl yelled back.

"No, you have come to Bidsbury," the man yelled back to her.

The girl then turned to her left and started walking away. The men at the top of the wall kept their eyes on her, all the way to the point where the small girl, which they could tell by her voice, walked out of their sight and into the woods. They then looked at each other but did not say anything, yet all of them were wondering what a young girl was doing out in the wilderness all by herself, especially at night.

When the man told her the name of the place, and since it was not the one she wanted, the girl knew that her journey was not over, and there was no need to stop in the city she had just walked away from. She still had enough food to last for about a half a moon-mark, and unless she ran out and could not replenish it in the wild, then she would not need to enter any city other than Sarzanac.

Three sun-cycles later she had not come across any other villages, towns, or cities. She had found some berries, and even caught a rabbit and had time to clean and cook it before she went to sleep. Her water supply was getting low, and she had not sensed any nearby, so if she did not find a source soon, she would ask Moon to lead her to some.

As she was resting in the tree, she heard a noise coming from behind her. She had her blanket over her head, but since she wanted to remain out of sight, she did not remove it. As she listened to the noise, she could tell that it was coming closer. She waited until the sound was almost directly under her, then she slowly moved the blanket enough so that she could look down at the ground below.

All the while, she had her knife in her hand, just in case whatever was coming towards her would be a problem.

She soon saw a deer. She had seen them a few times since the first time she saw the buck by the river, and she knew the one below was a doe. As it passed the tree, another two came behind the first. Then another one, but this one was less than half the size of the others, a fawn of one of the does that had just passed by. She watched the group as they walked away and when they were out of view, she replaced the blanket over her head to go back to sleep.

She had just closed her eyes when she heard another sound coming from behind her. She figured that it was another deer, but she still moved the blanket slowly so that she could see it. When the creature came walking past the tree, the girl saw that it was not a doe, but a buck. A very big buck.

Ever since she had seen the one that night and it had run off, the girl always wanted to see another one. She had seen a lot of does, but the bucks she came across were never as big as the first one she saw. This one, the one that had just passed beneath her was even bigger. A smile came to the child's face.

As much as she wanted to go after the buck, she did not want to walk out in the open. Even with the trees blocking part of the sun's light, it still bothered her. She positioned the blanket over her head and went back to sleep, dreaming of what it would be like to kill one of the creatures.

She waited until Moon appeared in the sky, and then climbed down to the ground. When she landed, she faced the direction the buck had gone. *"Moon?"* she thought.

"Yes," Moon thought to her.

"Can you lead me to the buck that is in the area?"

Moon did not respond to the child's question immediately. Moon knew the child was able to take down rabbits, beavers, coons, and even geese. Going after a buck was something Moon thought the child was not ready for. Or was she?

Moon decided that maybe it was time for the child to go after bigger prey. She had killed that man those seasons ago, but she was only able to do so because she surprised the pitiful human. If Moon led her to the buck then Moon would be able to see what she was capable of, now that she is older. Somehow, if the child fails, then perhaps it will teach her that she needs to have patience, just like Moon. Moon also knew the risk of letting the child hunt the buck. They could be dangerous creatures, but after thinking it over, Moon concluded, so was the child. *"Continue in the direction you are facing, and I will lead you to the creature,"* Moon thought to the child so she could begin to track the buck.

"I need you to get me in front of it," the child thought to Moon as she started running through the woods.

Moon did not know what the child's plan was, but Moon was curious. *"I will guide you."* Moon thought to the child. Moon had not been disappointed with the way the child had performed since she has been on her own, and Moon did not doubt that the girl would not disappoint Moon on this night.

Moon led the child on a route that took her around the herd of deer; wide enough so the animals would not hear her. With the amount of time the child had spent in the wilderness hunting, she had learned to walk in a manner where she made no more sound than the small fawn she had seen earlier. She had also spent so much time in the woods, that her clothes, and even herself, had the scent of the surroundings.

Moon led her to the area where the deer were and the child saw the does but did not see the buck with them. *"Look to the left of the creatures,"* Moon thought to the child.

The girl turned her head until she saw the buck standing some distance away from the others. As if, it was keeping guard over the herd while they ate. The buck was looking in the direction away from the child, and she knew the buck was too late in what it was doing because whatever danger it was looking for, was already in front of it.

The child had a plan but it was going to be difficult to make it work. She watched the group of deer for a while and every so often, they would walk off in search of another grazing area. As the females moved, so did the buck, but it always stayed off in the distance. She noticed that it did follow when the does moved further away.

As the does and the buck moved, so did the girl. She waited until the deer started walking so that their steps on the leaves and twigs on the forest floor would cover up any sound the child would make, which was not much at all. As she moved with the herd, she also moved closer to them, but when she saw that they stopped, so did she. She kept her eyes on the herd because she knew the buck would not be far behind them.

Moon was beyond the midpoint in the sky before the child was close enough to the group to put the next part of her plan into action. When she was halfway between the does, and the buck, she made her way to a tree, and very quietly climbed up into it. Usually, when she climbs a tree to rest, she gets to the highest branches that she can. Now she only climbed high enough to where she was no more than three times her own height from the ground. When she reached the branch, she had chosen, she positioned herself so that the does were to her right and the buck was to her left. Then she waited.

At first, she thought about pulling one of the stones she kept in the pocket of her trousers and using it to cause the deer to take off running by throwing it towards them, but she could not be certain that when they took off running, the buck would follow the path the does went.

When she was moving with the herd, she noticed that the buck always walked the same path the does traveled. That was why she chose the tree where she was waiting. The deer had just passed it before they settled to continue their feeding.

As she stayed in the tree, she made sure she did not move any part of her body except for her eyes. She would alternate between looking in the direction of the does and the buck. She was not always able to see either of them, but she knew the does were still in the same area which meant the buck was as well.

Moon had now entered the part in the sky where Moon would be, just before the sun rose. It was at that time when the does started walking away from where they had been grazing for a good portion of the night.

When the girl noticed the herd start to move, she slowly and slightly turned her head in the direction of the buck. It had not start moving, but the girl knew it would wait until the does were away from the area they had been grazing before the buck followed them. The girl waited and soon thought to herself, *"Now it will start making its way."* The girl had just finished the thought, and the buck did exactly what she knew it would. She had watched the buck follow the does and had picked up its pattern. She knew exactly what the buck would do and she also knew it would pass by the tree where she was waiting.

The girl was not high in the tree, so when the buck started walking toward her, she did not move her head but kept her eyes on it. She did not want it to see her make any motion, and she only looked down when she heard it directly below her. That was when she jumped from the branch she had been waiting on and landed directly on the back of the buck.

She had to turn her body, so when she landed, she had one leg on each of the buck's sides. She made sure she positioned herself so that her upper body was leaning forward, which allowed her to stab the buck in the side of its neck with the knife she had been holding onto ever since she climbed into the tree.

This was the first time she attempted to take down an animal as big as the buck. This was also the first time, that after she had stabbed an animal in the neck, cutting into the veins that supplied blood to the creature's body, where the animal did not die after a few more breaths. Not only did the buck not die, but it also took off running, with the child straddling its back.

The child used her legs and squeezed them tight as soon as the buck rushed forward. She knew she would fall off if she did not hang on, and what was more important to her than her own safety, was that if she did fall, the creature would get away, something she would not allow.

As the buck ran through the woods, the child was not able to see what was happening. She had seen deer take off running before and knew that they were fast and could leap a good distance. This one, the one she was riding, was moving so fast that all she could hear was its feet striking the ground, and the sound of branches striking the buck's antlers as the beast collided with them. Some of those branches struck the girl, scratching her face, and even the skin through the shirt sleeves covering her arms.

She now understood that the buck was not like the other animals she had taken down. She did not know if the knife was not long enough to get into the thickness of the creature's neck to do any damage, or if the creature was just too stubborn to realize its part in the girl's plan. Either way, the child knew it would give out before she gave up, or the creature would somehow cause her death. The child learned at an early age, that it was always her will against someone else's and she always won.

As the buck continued to run, the girl pulled the knife out of its neck, and thrust it in again, in the same spot. When she had killed animals before, she would leave the knife in the wound until the creature died. She had a feeling that if she did the same with the buck, she would be in for a long ride.

She continued to thrust the knife in and out of the neck of the creature. She was not sure how many times she removed it and thrust it back into the exact same spot, but the buck tumbled forward, either from the loss of blood, most covering the side of its neck and the girl's hand and arm, or from something that had tripped it. As its rump came up and over, the girl tumbled through the air, away from the buck because of the speed the animal had been running.

When she flew free of the creature's back and went over its head and antlers, her hand never let go of the knife so it came along with her. As soon as she hit the ground, she rolled over three times and only stopped when she collided with a tree. She did not hesitate to jump to her feet and turn in the direction where she thought the buck was. About five paces away from the girl, the buck was lying on its side. Its antlers were so big and wide that they did not allow the buck to lay its head on the ground.

The girl noticed its side moving up and down and knew it was still alive, which was not what she wanted. Without fear, she walked over to the creature; its back was to her, with its head to her right.

She positioned herself so that she was standing at its neck and knelt on the ground next to the buck. She then leaned forward and spoke to the creature, "You were good. I was better." She then stabbed the buck on the left side of its neck pushing it deep enough so that half the handle of the knife and her fist went below the creature's fur and skin. The buck did not live long afterwards.

Moon had enough time to tell the child how to clean the creature before Moon had to leave the sky and was not able to see her. The child had pleased Moon this night, and Moon was sure it would not be the last time.

With the meat the child was able to cut from the animal, she had enough to last for some time. She had to leave a big portion of the creature where she had made the kill because it was too big for her to carry, especially since she had to travel some ways back before she came to the area where she had left her belongings. She did not worry that the remaining meat would go to waste, other predators in the woods would take care of it. There may be others, but to the girl, and even to Moon, there were none better than her.

Five sun-cycles later, as she was walking through the woods, she saw fires burning in the night. She made her way closer to them and saw a group of travelers who had made camp. Normally she would stay away from anyone she came across, but she decided that she would see if someone within the group knew where Sarzanac was to confirm that she was still heading in the right direction.

As she stepped into the camp, she stood at the edge for a moment before someone noticed her. It was a habit she had learned as a child. Adults always seemed angered when a child would speak before being spoken to. Since the child did not care if they spoke first or not, then she would wait.

One of the women, sitting around the fire saw her first. When she did, she placed her hand on the man to her left to get him to stop talking to the man sitting next to him. Soon everyone was quiet and all eyes were on the little girl standing at the edge of the clearing the travelers had chosen as their campsite.

It was the man, next to the woman, who spoke to the child. "What are you doing over there child?"

Since the adult had spoken, then the child decided it was her turn. Even though she was not going to answer the man's question. "Where is Sarzanac?"

The people around the campfire all looked at each other wondering what to make of the child. Even though a few children were traveling with the caravan, they all knew the child before them was not one of their group. "Where are your parents?" one of the women asked her.

They had not answered the question she had asked and figured they would not unless she told them something. "I have none," the child said, knowing what parents are, but did not know who hers were. Since she answered one of their questions, it was time for them to answer hers, "Where is Sarzanac?"

The adults looked at each other, then back to the girl. Now intrigued by the child, they stood up and faced her. The girl saw all eight of the adults in front of her, but she did not move. Not out of fear, but because she had not received her answer. If they did try something, she could quickly run back into the woods, and if anyone came close to her...well she still had her knife, which she was holding in her right hand, behind the bag hanging from her right shoulder.

"Child, are you out here by yourself?" one of the men asked.

"Yes." She decided she would answer the question, but if they did not tell her what she wanted to know after she asked her own, she would turn and walk away, and wait until she came across someone else who could answer her question. "Where is Sarzanac?"

By asking the question for a third time, the people thought the girl might not be right in the head. Because any child old enough to speak would surely be more concerned about being out in the wilderness alone, instead of asking about a city a great distance away. The man who had spoken first finally gave the girl an answer to her question. "Sarzanac is many sun-cycles away. We will be reaching it but will make a town or two before we do."

"But you will be heading there?" the child asked.

The adults looked at each other again then back to the girl. "Yes," the man who had given her an answer replied.

The child then turned around and walked away. Before she made it to the tree line behind her, she heard one of the women yell to her, "Child you cannot be out in the wild by yourself. Come back to the camp."

The child did not respond. She was not going to go to the camp again, and she had no problem with being in the wild by herself.

The next day, as the caravan of ten wagons, continued its journey, every now and then some of the people thought they saw something moving in the woods that ran alongside the road. When they brought the concern to the man in charge of the group, the same man who had spoken to the girl last night, he told them to keep an eye out for any bandits and if anyone saw something, they were to pass the word immediately.

Before midday, the people were saying that they noticed a child running just inside the tree line, and it appeared that she was holding a blanket over her head. When the headmaster heard this, he took one of the loose horses, and rode up and down the caravan. Sure enough, every now and then he saw what everyone was talking about. Since he saw her last night, he recognized the child, even though he did not know her name.

For the remainder of the day, as the wagons moved along the road, the girl ran alongside it within the trees. Far enough in, so that if someone should try to get to her, she would be able to take off running, but not so far where she could not keep an eye on the caravan that was traveling and would eventually make it to Sarzanac.

When the wagons stopped for the night, the adults who had spoken to the child the previous night, made sure they kept a watch in case the child made another appearance. The only thing they saw was a fire off in the distance. Every now and then when the wind blew towards them, some of the adults thought they could smell deer cooking.

The child followed the caravan for the entire time that it was on the move, and even though the sun was up and she was used to traveling at night, she knew that if she kept the wagons in sight eventually they would lead her to Sarzanac.

When the caravan had stopped for the night, the child, who was tired, especially after traveling during the day, and having to keep her blanket over her head to block out some of the sun's light, decided that she should resupply her food and water. Water was something she would be able to come by easier so she focused on food. Moon was able to lead her to a herd of deer, and she was able to make another kill. It was only a doe, but it was big enough to replenish her supplies.

After days on the road, the caravan arrived at the next city they were making for. This one did not have a wall around it, but there were guards positioned at the entrance to which the road led. This caused the wagons to stop so the headmaster could relate to the guards of the city the business of the caravan.

After the headmaster of the caravan had spoken to the guards, the wagons started moving again and entered the city. He took to riding a horse instead of in the lead wagon and waited on the side of the road to watch the wagons enter the city and to watch for the tagalong who had attached itself to the caravan.

As the last wagon was entering the town, he saw the girl coming up towards him. He knew that if he were to try to go to her, to talk, she would just turn and walk away. He had tried this before, so he knew she would do the same thing this time. Since she was coming his way, he stayed where he was, sitting on his horse, waiting for the girl to make her way to him.

"Is this Sarzanac?" the girl asked when she was still a good ten paces away.

The man turned his head to look at the girl, "No this is Koston. Sarzanac is still a good ways off." He then turned his head to look towards the town, and then back to the girl. "It is in that direction," he said pointing towards the city, "But there are certain turns you will have to make when you come to some crossroads, and some of them are not marked." The girl turned to her right, and the man knew that she was planning to go around the city, instead of inside it, to continue to her destination, which the man knew, the girl had her mind set to reach.

She started walking but before she was too far away, the man yelled to her, "Hey!" The girl looked over her shoulder to see the man, "We will be leaving here in two sun-cycles. By the entrance on the other side of the city. I know if I ask, you won't join us in our travels, even though it would be safer for you, but if you can wait, then you can continue to follow us. At least to the next place we come to. If you stay with us, you will get to where you want to go."

They held their stares for a moment, until the girl turned her head, and headed off back into the woods. The man stayed there and watched her leave, then turned his horse to take him into the city. He had made the offer to the child and was sincere about it. There was nothing else he could do.

Two sun-cycles later, after the caravan had left Koston, it did not take long for word to travel through the caravan, that the child was once again in the woods, shadowing the wagons. When the leader of the group heard this, he told everyone to go about their business, and leave the child to herself. Maybe others thought the child would not survive on her own for much longer, but when the man had talked to the girl before he had entered Koston, there was something in her eyes that told him, she would reach the city of Sarzanac, even if everyone traveling with the caravan did not. There was something about her eyes, and all the man could think of was that they were deep. He was sincere with his offer to the girl, but after he stared into her eyes, he thought that it might be best if the child stayed alongside the caravan, instead of joining it.

For two moon-marks the caravan traveled during the day, and the child stuck to the woods, making sure she could see it. Just before the sun left the sky, the wagons would stop someplace and the people would make camp for the night. On some of those nights, the people would look out into the woods for a campfire. Sometimes there would be one but on the mornings after they had not spotted one, the majority of the people wondered if they would see the girl when the wagons would start moving.

Each day it was not long before they saw the child shadowing the caravan.

A few of the men began making bets between themselves on the nights there was no fire. It consisted of whether or not the child would survive until the next morning or did a wolf or one of the other predators living in the wilderness eat her. The words gnomes and trolls came up a couple of times as well but when the caravan started moving, the child was soon following it, and the couple of men who always wagered against the girl had to pay up. Once the leader of the caravan heard about what some of the men were doing, he put a stop to it immediately. He may not have wanted the child to take him up on his offer to travel with them, but he did not want her to come to any harm, and making wagers on if she would or would not survive the night, did not sit well with him.

After the sixth settlement that the caravan passed through, the girl came upon something she had never seen before. Or it was a lack of what she saw that caused her to take concern. The caravan had entered a part of the region where people have lived for a longer period of time than where the child had come from, and with that, there were no trees any longer, or they never grew there in the first place.

When the child came to the end of the woods, she stopped, but the caravan did not. She saw it continue to move away from her out into the openness of the land. Ever since the child had been on her own, she always had the woods to travel through, now all she saw was open space, covered with green grass. There were no trees to climb or to sleep in, and what bothered her the most, was that the sun shined on all the land she was seeing before her.

She stood at the edge of the woods, as the caravan drew farther and farther away. She thought that maybe she could wait where she was, and travel at night, asking Moon to lead her to where the caravan had stopped to make camp. She then realized that if the rest of the land was like this, it did not matter, when the sun came up, she would not have any cover to keep its light off her.

She looked behind her and saw the security of the woods. She then turned and stepped out into the open space, making sure she had her blanket over her head to protect her as much as possible. Going back was not an option. She needed to travel forward to get to where she needed to be.

Since she did not have the trees to keep her hidden, she traveled behind the caravan, keeping a good distance away from it. When they stopped, as the sun was lowering in the sky, the child did as well.

Even though there were no trees around, there was enough green grass and rabbits were plenty in the area. Even more abundant than in the woods. Since she did not have any trees to hide behind and wait for them to come close to her, she changed her tactics to where she would lie down on the ground and slowly crawl in the direction Moon would lead her. She might not have been in the woods and did not have access to the berries she would eat, but she did not go hungry.

After a moon-mark had gone by, the caravan reached another city. When the girl looked at it from the small hill she was standing on, she thought that it was the biggest city she had ever seen.

The caravan was making for it, and when it reached the gates, it had to wait in line for its turn to enter. Before it did, the girl walked up to the leader of the caravan, coming closer to him than she had since the first night she walked into their camp. "Is this Sarzanac?" she asked, thinking that she had finally found the city she was searching for and determined to reach.

The man answered her. "No this is Yorkington. Sarzanac is still a moon-mark away. We will be here for that amount of time ourselves then we will be heading out a different gate. The next city we reach will be Sarzanac." The girl then did something he had never seen her do. She walked through the gates and entered the city.

When she saw the buildings, she could not help but notice how big the place was. She was only twelve and still not as tall as most people, but in this place, she seemed even smaller. She was staring at all the people but still knew when the man in charge of the caravan stepped up beside her. To his surprise, the child did not run away even though he was within an arm's reach of her. From that, the man realized the child did not stay away from him and the other people he traveled with because she was afraid of them, the girl just did not want to be around them.

"Which way is the gate leading to Sarzanac?" the child asked.

The man took a few steps away from the girl, then turned to face her. He knew he would be wasting his time trying to talk to the child about anything other than what she had asked, so he stuck his arm out and pointed to the left. "You go in that direction and keep heading for the wall surrounding the city. Since the wall is high enough, you will always be able to see it. There will be signs that will lead you to the east gate; the one that leads to the road which leads to Sarzanac." He then thought of something else to ask the child, "Can you read?"

The child looked from the direction the man had pointed and back to him, then gave her answer, "No." She then looked back in the direction that would take her to the east gate. "Where can I purchase some clothes?"

The question surprised the man more than when she answered his question about if she could read or not. Even though they had exchanged very few words, he would have never taken her as someone that would be thinking about what she was wearing. To answer the child, he told her what direction the mercantile district was located then made another offer. "I'll be heading that way myself, as soon as I make sure the wagons and everyone is settled in, if you want to wait for me to go with you?"

The child heard the man but did not give him a reply. All she did was start walking in the direction he had told her where she would be able to buy some clothes. It was the last time he would ever see the child again.

Before the sun set that day, the child exited the city through the eastern gate. She took with her the bag of water she had filled in one of the city's fountains. She had her bag of food, in which she had placed the four apples and loaf of bread she purchased in the city. She had her bag of coins, and even though she had to spend some, she had plenty remaining. She had her blanket and of course her knife.

There was one more item the child had when she walked out through the gates of Yorkington. She now wore a black cloak, which she purchased from one of the shops. It had been hanging in a window, and as soon as she saw it, she knew she would have a use for it. Since she was still only twelve, to anyone else of her size, it would be too large, but for her it was perfect.

When she entered the shop and told the woman that she wanted the cloak in the window, the woman politely told her that it would be too big for her. If she was going to purchase the item for her mother, then it was more than likely the child would not be able to pay for it, seeing how it cost three silver pieces. It was the child's appearance, and odor, that the woman had based her opinion on. When the child opened her bag of coins and brought out the three silver coins, the woman did not know whether to sell the child the cloak or call the city guards to see where this child had stolen the bag of coins.

When the woman looked into the child's eyes, she decided that it was best to take the coins and send the child on her way. The woman would receive the coinage for the item, and she would not have to try to keep the child there while she waited for the guards. It was something about the girl's eyes, which made the woman decide that since the bag of coins was not hers, it did not matter.

Away from the city, the child continued to make her way toward her destination traveling by night. A couple of times she came across a tree and climbed it to get out of the sun. The cloak she had purchased was big enough on her, that the hood fell over her face, and with her bending her head downwards, it kept the sun out of her eyes.

She kept the front of the cloak pulled together, and her arms and hands inside it, unless she needed to do something. The length of the cloak was so long that it went to the ground and even drug along it as the child walked.

Since it was black, on the inside and out, when

the child confined her body to it, she felt as if the dark of night surrounded her, even while the sun was up.

One night she had been walking down a road when she saw off in the distance a city. Even from where she was, she could tell that it was bigger than the city where she had purchased the cloak.

When she reached the front gate, she saw that even though it was night, the gates were open and people were entering. It appeared that whatever place this was, they allowed people to go through the gates at all times.

She walked closer to the gates but kept her distance from the man she saw. Usually, the child would wait until an adult would say something to her before she spoke, but since the man had his back to her, he had not seen her approach. For some reason, the thought came to the child that since this man was a guard, which she could tell by the armor he was wearing, then he should have been more aware of who was coming up behind him. The girl knew she would have been able to make her way over to him and put her knife in the man's back before he even knew she was there.

She pushed the thought from her mind and asked her question, "Is this Sarzanac?"

The guard turned around and saw the only person standing behind him who could have asked the question. He saw the child in a black cloak, one which was too big for her, but other than that, he did not think anything else about her. He had seen more than enough people pass through the city gates, and one more child was just like any other child, but he did answer her question, "Yes, this is the city of Sarzanac."

Hearing the answer, the child walked around and entered the city. Thinking to herself, she had finally arrived.

FIFTEEN

She came to Sarzanac when she was twelve. On the first night in the city, she knew that this was where she belonged. It was not the city itself or even the people; there was just something inside her that when she heard the boy Tat talk about it, she knew she had to get to Sarzanac. When she arrived, she realized that it was not the city that was calling to her, but the other topic Tat mentioned, the Assassin's Guild.

What Tat had been telling the other children, was something most people did not talk about. Even the child knew that killing people was against the laws of most places, but for some reason, which the child did not know, she needed to do what felt right to her, and not what others thought.

She wanted to ask someone where the Assassin's Guild was, but since most people were against the killing of other humans; the child decided she would see what she could find out on her own. If it came to a point where she could not find the place, then she would see if Moon knew, though she would only ask if she needed to.

When she began to hunt for her food and to earn coin, the girl started to rely on herself more than she did on Moon. She would ask Moon to lead her to water, or an animal when she was hunting, but she preferred to depend on herself. The child did not know it, but Moon preferred it that way as well.

For her first night in Sarzanac, she spent some time walking the streets; observing the city and people. Even at night, there were citizens who continued to take care of whatever business they were out doing. To the girl's surprise, they did not appear to be going in and out of any drinking houses or brothels like the girl saw in the first two cities where she had lived. She had no doubt that there were some of those places in this city, but since she was still close to the front gate, then the businesses in the area, were the more respectable ones.

The child continued to walk around until Moon was past the midpoint in the sky. The child knew the sun would be coming up soon, and even though she had her cloak, she did not want to walk through the city when the sun shined its light. After she had left the caravan behind, she had once again started traveling at night, and took shelter in the daytime wherever she could, even if it were just to curl up on the ground and cover up with her cloak. She preferred the night and that was when she felt more comfortable.

She stopped looking around at what was going on in the area she was in and decided to find a place where she could rest until the sun had gone down. She did the same as she did in the first city she had come to when she was on her own and decided to stay. She walked through the streets and turned in the direction where she saw fewer people. Eventually, she came to the area of the city which had the types of establishments she had seen and even lived in for the first few seasons of her life.

There were drinking houses, brothels, gaming houses, and other places that supplied the citizens of the city with whatever they needed to take their minds off whatever they wanted to forget. She continued through that part of the city but did not look for a place to rest. She knew the people in this area were more likely to bother her, for a number of reasons. It was because of that; the child had taken a tighter grip on the handle of her knife and was more alert to anyone she might pass by or look at her for too long. She also kept a lookout for any alley she could use to lure anyone who decided to trail her. She never forgot about the man who had followed her that night into the alley. Even though she never saw him again.

The girl continued to walk through the streets, making the turns she felt would lead her to what she was looking for and before Moon left the sky, the child found it.

Every city has its sections where the desolate people could go. There were even people lying on the streets. Some were probably trying to get whatever sleep they could, but the child had a feeling that more than one of the citizens would not be waking when the sun rose, and she was correct.

At least in Sarzanac, the ones who ran the city would have people come through places like what the child had found and remove any of the citizens who were no longer living. They would even get a burial in one of the cemeteries on the outside of the city walls. Of course, to save time and space, the daily grave dug was big enough to hold all the bodies collected on that day.

As the child continued to make her way through the area, she looked for a place where she felt she would be able to make her own. With the ones she saw, there were always adults standing in front of the buildings and the child did not want to be around them. As she made her way further into the section of the city, she came across a building where there were a group of children in front of it. Most of them were standing around talking to each other, but there were some running around as if they were trying to catch their companions.

She stopped at the end of the pathway leading up to the building. The children looked as if some of them were younger than she was but most of them were bigger. Some may have even been her age, but the child had never known what her Blessed Day was, so even she did not know her own age. She knew she was older because she grew, but even though she was twelve, she did not know how many seasons she had been alive.

The sun would be up soon, and she wanted to be somewhere inside before the first of its light came into the sky. She was fine sleeping in a tree, or even out in the open, but since she was now in a city with other people, she wanted to rest in a place where she would have more protection.

Since the sun was close to rising, the girl decided about the place she was looking at, with all the children. As she walked down the pathway, she had her hood pushed back off her head but kept the front of the cloak pulled together, with her left hand on the inside. On the inside of her cloak, she had her bag of coins tied to one of the loops of her trousers. Within her cloak, she had her blanket slung over her right shoulder, and over it, she had the water bag hanging at her back, with the other bag hanging over the front of her shoulder. She had her right arm bent in front of this bag to keep it from falling but held the knife in her right hand. With the cloak closed around her, no one would be able to tell what she had on her. That is unless they tried something the girl did not like, then the first thing the person would find would be the knife.

When she made her way to the steps of the building, she saw four boys sitting there watching her walk toward them. They all appeared to be older, but since they were still only children, the girl did not hesitate to speak first, "What is this place?" she asked.

Three of the boys looked towards the last one as

if they were waiting to see if he would be the one to speak, which he did. "It's ours, if that is what you are asking." The boy, even though he was only fourteen, was the leader of the group of youngsters residing in the building. The building they had claimed as their own and defended it to make sure it remained theirs. "I'm Selby, you looking for a place to stay?"

The girl nodded. She did not like being around others, but she also knew the benefit of having them around. If she were by herself then she would have to be more watchful in making sure no one tried to sneak up on her while she slept. It was easier when she would sleep in the woods in a tree because there was less of a chance that someone would notice her. Within a city, there was always the possibility that someone might be looking to do her harm.

Since the girl did not say anything, the boy gave her his well-rehearsed speech. "We don't let any adults come in here that are looking to take this building from us. If they try, then all of us and that includes you, if you stay, are to fight them off until they leave or they are dead." The girl did not say it, but she did not have a problem with that. Selby continued, "Any food you snatch or get is to be brought to me or one of my lieutenants." When he said the last word, Selby glanced at the other three boys sitting on the steps, just below where he was. "Don't worry, each night we divide up whatever we all gather so everyone gets something. But we share it all. Is that understood?"

The girl nodded.

Selby waited to see if she was going to say anything, but when she remained silent, he continued. "If we find out that you have been holding food from us, then we will not only take it, but beat you until you can barely walk then toss you out of here. Is that understood?"

The girl nodded, but to herself, she thought that they would have a difficult task in following through with the last part of what the boy had said.

"So, you want to stay here or not?"

The girl did not say anything, but she did respect the way the boy and the others with him kept this place for themselves. The girl thought that they would be good for ensuring no one bothered her while she was resting. To answer the last question the boy had asked, the girl, while keeping her arms hidden inside her cloak, pulled the bag of water and food off her shoulder with her left hand then walked over and placed them both on the step just below where one of Selby's lieutenants were sitting.

The boy grabbed the bags, and since he could tell what was in the water bag, he opened the other one and looked inside. It was night and there was not enough light for him to be able to see the contents of the bag, but when he opened it, he could definitely smell some type of meat. He stood up, climbed the steps to Selby, and handed him the bag, who reached in and pulled out a piece of the cooked meat. He looked at it, then at the girl who was still standing at the first step. "What is it?" Selby asked.

"Rabbit, and some deer," the girl said not showing any expression to tell the boys how she came about it, even though the looks on their faces were asking that question.

The boy put the bit of meat he had taken out of the bag back inside then his lieutenant closed it and returned to his position on the step below Selby. "Ok you can stay," Selby said, with a smile. He would always allow any of the children who wandered the streets to remain in the house. He had grown up on the streets himself and knew it was not only difficult but also dangerous to be alone. Children came up missing all the time, at least the ones that live in the worst part of Sarzanac. "You got a name?" Selby asked.

"No," the girl said.

"Then what do we call you?" one of the lieutenants asked. The girl did not give him an answer. She only turned her head and when they stared into each other's eyes, the boy turned away first. All four of the boys understood that the child's lack of a name was no concern of theirs.

Selby was the one to break the silence, "Find a place inside that doesn't have a blanket on it. Wherever there is one, someone has staked that place as their own, so leave it alone, and don't touch anything on the blanket. It is their property.

I'm sure you don't want anyone messing with your stuff, so it's only right you leave others alone." The girl did not say it, but she thought Selby made sure everyone followed the rules he had recited to her.

The girl walked up the steps, staying to the left so that the four boys did not hinder her climb. Before she made it to the door, she heard Selby call to her, "Hey," The girl stopped walking and looked over her left shoulder down the steps, "You might want to stay out of the top loft. Whoever owned this place before we took it over, must have kept something in there that brought every rat in the city to it. They don't come down to the lower levels much, but you will get used to the ones that do." Selby waited for the girl to say something but all she did was turn her head and walk inside.

She climbed the stairs as far as she could, and when she made it to the fifth floor, she saw a ladder positioned underneath a hatch. She climbed the ladder, and when she opened the cover to the loft's entrance, she heard the rustling of hundreds of feet moving around inside. She climbed up the rest of the way and closed the cover behind her. She then moved her cloak to position it at her back and began to reduce the rat population of the building. The girl thought that at least with this many rats, she would replace the bit of food she had given away.

She had spent a good portion of the morning removing the previous tenants. After the first twenty-five met their death by the sharp knife the child had, the remaining rats had not only left the highest room in the building; they left the building altogether. It was the same when she had begun killing the rats in the first city she had come to and took up residence in the abandoned building. The child thought that they had just decided to seek shelter somewhere else, but the real reason the rats had left, was because Rat told them to.

Rat, the one who watched over all rats, knew the child was Moon's and Rat did not want any of the rats, to have anything to do with the girl. Rat knew Moon was up to something, and Rat wanted nothing to do with it. Rat figured that if Moon was involved then it had something to do with Sun, and since those two were always battling one another, it was best for Rat and everyone else to get out of their way. Rat had lost quite a few rats to Moon's child; Rat did not want to lose anymore.

The child slept the rest of the day, in a rat free environment, except for the ones she had killed and cooked before she turned in. When she gave her bags over to Selby, she had the flint stone tucked in one of the pockets on the inside of her cloak. She would go to Selby later and get her bags back. They could have the food and any of the water, but the girl would need to keep the bags to use them again.

Since she had spent so much time killing and cooking the rats, she did not wake up until Moon was already in the sky. When she climbed down the ladder from the loft, she placed one of the small stones she kept on the last step. She positioned it so that no one would notice it unless they bent down to the floor. She balanced the stone on the edge of the bottom step and if anyone touched the step in the slightest way, the stone would fall. If it were on the floor, when she came back, she would know someone had tried to enter the area she had claimed as her own.

She went downstairs and when she exited the front entrance, she saw Selby and his lieutenants in the same places as when she arrived. She walked down the steps on the same side she had climbed them, and even though she did not look, she knew all four of the boys were watching her. When she reached the bottom, she turned around and moved to stand in front of the boy she had given her bags to. She then removed her arms from inside the cloak and brought them out handing the boy what she had. The boy took it, and turned his head to look up at Selby, since he did not ask, the lieutenant did, "What is this?" The boy could tell it was some type of meat but did not know what kind.

"Rat," the girl said and looked up at Selby who had a smile on his face because of the girl's reply. "I will need my bags back." Selby stopped looking at the boy, and what he had in his hands, and focused on the girl. He nodded to let her know she would get what she asked for.

The girl turned around and started walking away. "Hey," Selby yelled to the girl to get her attention since she did not have a name. When she turned around, he continued, "We already divided the food for the day, I made sure some was saved for you." The girl did not say anything. She was not hungry, and the thought that someone would make sure she had something to eat did not even register with her. Since she has been on her own, she has always taken care of getting her own food, and she always would. She did not have a problem with sharing the food she had, if that was the price to stay, she would abide by the rule.

She turned around and started walking away, back into the city to start her search for the Assassin's Guild.

Before the sun had risen, the girl returned to the place she had taken up residence, since she had no luck in finding what she went looking for. Selby and his lieutenants were still on the steps, but she did not say anything to them. As she reached the step Selby was sitting on, she noticed her bags were next to him. She stopped and turned to look at her items. It did not take Selby long to understand what she wanted even though she did not say anything. He handed her the bags then she went inside.

When she reached the ladder leading to the upper loft, before she placed her foot on it, she bent over and picked up the stone that was in the same position where she had left it. She then went up the ladder, opened the hatch, and climbed through the opening, closing the hatch when she was through.

The first thing she did was go over to her blanket and unfold it. She then took the remaining rat meat and placed it inside the bag. She had given the majority of the meat to the boys, but she kept more than enough for herself. She remembered what Selby had said about holding food back from them, but since she was the one who had killed the rats, cleaned them, and cooked them, she was going to keep what she wanted. If they found out about it and said something to her, then they could always learn what a rat felt as a knife entered its spine.

There was one window in the loft, but it was not on a side that allowed the sun's light to enter in too much. The girl had to open the window last night when she cooked the rats to let the smoke leave the confining room but closed it and the shutters that were on the inside to keep the morning sun from shining in. Even with the sun in the sky, the room was dark, but the child had no problem seeing, and no problem sleeping.

The next night after the girl rose and ate some rat, she went downstairs and found Selby. He, and his lieutenants, were in their usual spots, on the front steps. When she reached the one their leader was on, she stopped and looked at him. Since he was sitting and she was standing, he had to raise his head to see her face. When he did, she asked her question, "Where is the Assassin's Guild?" Selby did not say anything because the girl's question surprised him, but after a moment one of the other boys on the lower steps started laughing. It was the same one who wanted to know her name the other night. When he finally stopped laughing, he saw the girl staring at him, and with those eyes, the boy could not help but think that he might have made a mistake in thinking the question was funny. The girl only looked at the boy long enough to let him know that he should remain quiet when she was around, then turned back to face Selby.

Even though he did not laugh, he had a look on his face telling the girl that he wanted to ask her more than one question, but he did not. He turned and looked out over the front yard of the building. "Keyota!" he yelled and one of the girls that were running in the yard stopped and came running up the steps to where he was sitting. He waved his hand to let the girl know to bend down so he could whisper something in her ear. When finished, the girl named Keyota stood back up and nodded to Selby. He then turned to look at the girl who had asked him the question. "We don't mention that around here." The girl who had asked the question was about ready to ask another, but Selby continued, "Keyota will take you there though."

The girl looked at the one called Keyota, turned back to Selby, and nodded to let him know that what he had done would suffice. She then turned and walked down the steps. Before she reached the street, the little girl named Keyota was walking beside her.

When they reached the street in front of the building, Keyota pulled on the girl's cloak, and when she saw she had her attention, she pointed straight ahead. The girl took it as that was the way they would be traveling, and Keyota started running in that direction. The girl had to take off running to catch up to Keyota, but since she had spent most of her life chasing rabbits, she had no problem catching up to her guide.

The girl followed Keyota for a while, long enough for Moon to rise to the midpoint of the night. They had gone back into the more populated area of the city, and when more of the citizens appeared, the two stopped running and began to walk.

When Moon was past the midpoint, Keyota had finally come to a halt. The girl saw that there were buildings all around but did not know if they had come to where she wanted to be. "Is it here?" she asked Keyota, who nodded and pointed to her left. The girl turned her head to the right to look at the building Keyota had pointed towards. The building looked nothing like the ones around it.

It was four levels high, and black. It was not because someone dyed it that way, it was the color of the stones used to build the place. Even the windows had black shutters covering them.

At the second level of the building, a balcony ran the entire length of the side facing the street. On that level, instead of windows, there were doors. Seven of them.

There was an iron fence going around the building, but from what the child was looking at, the appearance of the building alone would keep anyone away from the place. That is unless someone had a reason to approach it.

The girl turned to look at Keyota who was standing to her left. She saw that her escort was watching her, and it appeared that she would not even look at the building. The girl turned and looked at the building. She needed Keyota to lead her there, but she would go the rest of the way alone. "Leave," the girl said to her escort, and having done as instructed, started heading back in the direction she had come. More than happy to be away from the one place every child knew that whoever went in through the black front doors, never came out again.

Now that she was alone, she walked towards the building and came to the first set of steps. As she placed her foot on them, she could feel the coldness coming from them, even though she had on her boots. She only hesitated for a moment, when she felt the feeling come over her, but after she realized she did not appear to be in any danger, she continued to climb.

When she reached the first landing and had placed both her feet on the surface, she felt something else. It was not cold like before, this time she felt something inside her. She did not even know the word to describe it, if she had, she would have called it fear. The only thing that came to mind was the image of the girl with the man that night in the room, when she had watched from the other side of the door. It was not the memory she was feeling something about, it was the fact that she did not want the same thing to happen to her. She remembered the young woman she had watched, start crying after the man left. Now the girl had to force herself to realize that it was not her, that night, in the bed with the man, and it never would be.

When the child regained control of what she was feeling, she began walking toward the front door. She had to go up another set of steps, but unlike the first ones, when she stepped on these, there did not seem to be anything unusual about them.

When she reached the top, she stopped and looked down. She saw a wooden beam on the ground and noticed that it ran quite a few paces off to the left and the right. The girl did not know why it was there, but the same type of wood used to make the beam was the same as the shutters across the windows, and like the shutters, the beam was black. Since she did not see what the reason for it was, she stepped over it and continued towards the front door.

When she reached it, for the first time that night, since she had left the building where she was staying, she removed her left hand from the inside of her cloak. The right one she kept within it, so she could keep her knife out of sight. She lifted her hand

and knocked on the door. When she did, the sound that came from it, was hollow and sounded as if she had just banged her fist against a large iron bell. She remembered hearing something like it when she lived in the first city with the woman. A bell would sound throughout the city to let everyone know that one shift in the mines had ended and another one was about to begin. The girl had not struck a bell, but the door made a sound just like it.

She waited for a few breaths then struck the door again with three knocks. She was sure that with the noise she had made, anyone inside would have heard it as well, unless no one was inside, or they would not open the doors at night.

No one came after the second time she knocked, so she was about ready to strike the door again, but before she could, someone spoke behind her. "It is not time yet."

The girl was so surprised to hear the voice, she spun around, and by the time she had turned to face the direction the voice had come from, she already had her knife out in front of her. If the man, who had come up behind her, had not been fast enough, or smart enough, to take a step back, then he would have met the sharp end of the knife the child was holding.

Even though the man saw the knife before the girl had completely turned to face him, he did not give it a second thought. At any time, he would have been able to take the blade from the child but had no need to. In fact, if he wanted to, he would have been able to move all the way to the girl and put his own blade in her before she had made the second knock on the door, and she never would have even known he was there until it was too late.

The man came out to see who was knocking on the door, for very few were brave enough to even come to the first set of steps of the Assassin's Guild, and if they did, the cold spell placed on them would normally let the person know that they should not go any further. If they did, then the spell on the first landing would surely send them running away, when their worst fear came to the surface of their mind. Tonight, someone had passed both of the two wards, and since anyone who did, must have a strong will, the Masters of the guild would want to see who was brave enough to venture to their door.

When the man noticed the knife in the girl's hand, he took two steps backwards. One was so that the girl would not stab him; the other was so that the girl he was looking at would feel a little more at ease, or as much as she could with an assassin sneaking up on her. "I mean you no harm child, and only came to see who has ventured to the doorsteps of our fine establishment."

The girl, knife in hand, looked at the man who had snuck up behind her. Since he had moved away, she did not advance toward him. She heard what the man said, but before she answered him, she looked him over. He was a good size taller than she was, but a lot of adults are. He had on a brown shirt with the end not tucked into his trousers, which were also brown. When she looked down at his feet, she saw that he did not have on any shoes, and if she had to guess, she would say that the man just woke up and came out to her, straight from his bed. Even his hair looked as if he had not taken a comb to it.

"I haven't got all night child, so if you have something to say I suggest you say it so that I can get back to my night's sleep."

The man confirmed what she had thought by the way he looked. Since he had not made any move toward her, the girl decided she was not in any immediate danger. "Is this the Assassin's Guild?" she asked.

The man looked at the child and the left corner of his mouth raised slightly to suppress the rest of his smile. "There is no such thing girl. I suggest you go on home to your mother and leave me to my peace."

The girl was quick to reply, "I have no mother."

"Then go back to your father or whoever it is that wipes your tears and your bottom." The man turned around and started walking away. The girl noticed that if he had wanted to return to his bed then he was heading in the wrong direction because he was walking away from the building.

The girl turned around herself and once again raised her hand and banged on the door, which made the same noise as before.

"Child if you continue to do that, you will bring the city guards to our doorsteps which is not something neither you nor I want. Especially me." The man said, but even though he said it, he knew the city guards would not even think of stepping within the boundaries of the guild. They enjoyed breathing too much.

The girl heard what the man behind her said but raised her hand again and banged on the door. When she stopped, she sensed the man was coming towards her, so she quickly turned around and had her knife out in front of her. It surprised the man at how fast the child had adjusted her position and a small part of him was glad he had not approached any faster, or he might have felt the tip of the small blade, or maybe even more of it.

He saw that the girl was ready to defend herself, but what he acknowledged, even more, was that she would not be going away until she found out about the place she had come to. She had passed all the tests set forth by the Masters for anyone who made it to the door of the Assassin's Guild.

The first two were the steps and the landing. The third was the questions the man had asked her about her parents. The last was any person wanting entrance into the guild, had to show determination in seeking admittance. At least to a certain extent.

The man held his arms up in front of him with his palms facing the child, to show that he was no threat to her. At least for the moment. "What is your name little girl?"

The child remained in her stance with her knife raised up before her, ready to use it if necessary. "I have none."

That answer alone brought a smile to the man's face. A child with no name was a child with no past or a limited one, something the guild looked for. Which was the reason for the question about any parents the child might have. Links to a person's life could hinder them from becoming what the guild trained them to do, and family was always a hindrance. No one who had contact with a mother, father, brother, sister, or even an aunt or uncle could join the guild. Of course, the guild had its ways of finding out if any of those family members were still a part of the person's life.

"Well, I suggest you get one," the man said, referring to her not having a name. He saw the girl was about to say something so he quickly spoke first, "That is if you wish to join my Assassin's Guild." The man noticed that the girl was good at keeping a smile off her face. Good but not great. A trained assassin can notice the slightest body movement of a person to know what the person was thinking, and when he saw the corner of her mouth rise ever so slightly, he knew the child was holding back a smile. "There are some rules which must be followed for you to be admitted though."

"What are they?" the child asked, and not even the man could pick up the smile the child was suppressing. She had control of her feelings after she heard she was at the Assassin's Guild.

"First we will not accept anyone under fifteen seasons or over seventeen." The man knew the girl was about to say something but extended his already raised hand up to stop her before she could. "Yes, it is easy to tell that you are not of the right age yet, and even if you think you are ready, the rule is there for a purpose. Fifteen is the age the Guild feels a child is no longer a child; we are not here to be nursemaids to children. And before you ask, they have ways to ensure no one enters through the door who is not of age or is too old."

The girl did not speak, so the man continued to the next rule. "You will need to acquire something besides that knife you have in your hand." The girl looked from the man to her knife and then back to him. She wanted to tell him that she had killed many animals with the knife and she knew how to use it, but she remained silent. "All you need is a sword or even a bow and a quiver of arrows, any weapon that you can be trained on." The man looked to his right then his left as if he was making sure no one overheard what he was about to say, then faced the child. "Trust me, it doesn't matter even if it is an old sword, when you get inside, they will set you up with nicer weapons better than you could ever imagine." He ended his statement with a big smile. He did not know why but he wanted the girl who had come to the door this night to be part of his guild. He had a feeling she would fit in with his associates and himself, very well.

The assassin continued, "The guild will only take in seven new recruits every five seasons. That is how long it takes to train the last ones who entered through the door behind you. That is unless they just happened to die while inside." He thought his statement would get a reaction from the child, but she did not respond in any way, so he continued, "The next time that seven individuals will be chosen is a little over three full seasons away. A moon-mark before the Masters choose the new recruits, they will fly a red flag from the balcony above our heads." The man noticed her lack of response to his statement. Usually, when someone suggests something that is above them, a person would glance in that direction. The child never took her eyes off him. "Then the day before they choose, they will fly a green flag. On the day of selection, they will fly a black flag, and at precisely midday, they will choose the new recruits. As I said, only seven will enter the door behind you, and usually, more than twenty arrive seeking admittance. That means there are going to be more people walking away from the door, than walking through it." Once again, the child did not turn to look in the direction the man had mentioned. "And finally, the last rule and probably the most important," the man said then stopped talking waiting for the girl to speak.

When she realized, the man was not going to continue, she spoke, "And what is that?"

The man turned around and walked away. When

he was three paces away from the girl, he turned to face her, "Why, not to die between now and the day of selection." He then turned around and walked away from the building. When he reached the street, he turned to his left and out of the girl's sight. All the while, he was sure he would be seeing the girl again.

The child waited until the man was out of her sight, and then for ten breaths more, before she walked away from the door, and down the steps. This time when she crossed them, she did not feel the same feeling she had before.

When she made it to the street, she turned and looked back at the building. She was not old enough; in fact, she was not sure how old she was. Age to her was not important so she never thought much about it or concerned about the fact that she did not know her age. However, she knew someone who would, *"Moon?"*

"Yes child," Moon thought to her.

"When will I be the age of fifteen seasons?"

Moon answered her, *"In just under three full seasons."*

The girl would be old enough by the time the next group of recruits entered the guild. The girl did not doubt that she would be one of them, and neither did Moon.

SIXTEEN

When the girl walked away from the building, the night she knocked on its door, she remembered the last and most important rule, the man had given her, "not to die between now and the day of selection." She had to come up with a way to survive. For that, she would either have to find a place to hunt for her food or find a way to earn coin to purchase what she needed. She still had quite a bit of what she had saved, but it would not last for three seasons.

As she made her way back to the building where she was staying, having remembered every turn the other child had taken to bring her to the Guild, she looked at some of the buildings she passed. When she reached the part of Sarzanac, where the drinking houses and brothels were, she thought about trying to see if she could work in one of them, cleaning like she did when she was young, but the thought of working in one of those places made her feel uncomfortable. Especially since every time she looked at one of the many brothels, she could not stop the memory returning of the girl and the man she had watched and remembered how the thought made her feel when she walked up the steps of the building to the Assassin's Guild. She decided then, that she would not even think about going to work in one of those places ever.

The sun had already started rising in the sky, and the girl had to place the hood of her cloak over her head to keep out the light. When she reached the building where she was staying, she did not see Selby or the other three boys who waited with him, but there were three different boys sitting on the steps. The girl figured they were the ones who guarded the entrance when the sun was up, and since the child had never come out during that time in the few nights she had been in the city, she never saw the ones there now.

Since she did not see Selby, she decided she would wait until she did to ask the question she had. One of the boys currently present might be able to tell her what she wanted to know, but she had talked to Selby previously, and he appeared to be the one who not only ran the place but also would be the one that would give her an answer she could trust.

When she walked up the steps and passed the boys, they did not say anything to her. Even though she had never seen them before, she took it that as long as she was not an adult, then they would not try to stop her.

When she walked inside the building, she noticed more children than what she normally saw in the place. She had arrived at night the first time in the city and came out of her little loft only after the sun went down. Now that she was about in the daytime, she saw just how many children lived in the building.

As she walked up the stairs, she heard talking and laughing on every level she reached. She decided that the majority, if not all of the children living in the building, had one thing in common with her, they all prefer to be up and about when the sun had gone out of the sky and only came inside the house when the sun came up. She did suspect that none of the other children had the same problem with the sun irritating them as it did her.

When she reached the ladder to take her to the upper room, she bent down to retrieve the stone. This time she had to reach behind the ladder to pick it up because it had fallen off the step. She replaced the stone back in one of the pockets inside of her cloak then climbed the ladder, opened the hatch, and went inside the loft. She closed the hatch behind her and settled down to get some sleep. When the sun went down, she would find Selby. Before she closed her eyes, she thought about the second thing she needed to talk to him about.

She was awake before the sun had left the sky. Even with the window to the loft closed, with the shutters covering it, she could tell the sun was still out and decided to wait a little while longer before she would leave. She finished off some of the rat she had but made sure she ate only enough to get her through the night. She did not know when she would be able to replenish her supplies. Water was not a problem, so she filled up on it to make sure that her stomach would not think it was empty.

Once the sun was out of the sky, she put on her cloak and stepped out of the loft. When she reached the bottom of the ladder, she placed the stone on the last step and then went to find Selby.

She found him in his usual spot with his lieutenants, sitting on the front steps of the building. When she reached the one Selby was sitting on, she stopped and looked at him and he turned his head and looked at her. "May I speak with you alone?" she asked him.

He turned his head, looked to his lieutenants, and nodded to them. With the silent command, all three of the boys stood up and walked away. Two of the boys walked down the steps and positioned themselves ten paces from them. The last boy went up the steps and inside, to make sure no one exited the building to interrupt the meeting the two were about to have.

When his lieutenants were in place, Selby made a motion with his right hand to offer the girl a seat beside him. She did not know why but she took him up on it and sat down next to him. Then began to ask her questions. "Are there any woods around this city?"

Selby noticed that the child was not looking at

him, which was something most people would do when trying to have a conversation with the person they were talking with. He followed the direction the girl was looking and saw that she was staring at the back of one of his lieutenants. It was Barret, the one who asked the girl about her name, and the one who laughed at her when she asked about the Assassin's Guild. He turned back to look at the girl and answered her question, "The nearest woods are four sun-cycles away."

Hearing that answer, the girl realized that she was going to have to decide on what she would do. She knew she would not be able to live in the city with no food or coin, and even though Selby had told her the first night she arrived, that she could share in whatever food they collected, the girl wanted to provide for her own needs. She did not have a problem with giving others some of her food, but she did not take what she did not earn.

She thought that maybe she could leave the city and live in the woods until the time came when the Assassin's Guild would select the new recruits, but that was over three seasons away. She did not mind the wilderness and knew she would be able to survive, but something inside her made her feel she needed to stay in the city.

If she traveled to the woods and hunted rabbits, or other animals to bring back to sell, it would take four sun-cycles to get there and another four to return, and a few to do the hunting she would need to do. She would have to hunt enough to supply her the food she would need for the time in the woods, as well as enough to bring some back to sell for coin. It was a plan, but it would take time and the girl did not see it bringing her the funds and food she needed.

She decided she would spend another night walking through the city searching for a way to earn coin or at least food. If she did not find anything, then she could start planning to make the trip to the woods.

"Is that all you wanted to know?" Selby asked since the child was not saying anything.

The girl did not turn to look at him, and he saw that she still had not taken her eyes off Barret. "Someone entered my place while I was away last night." The girl now turned her head to look at Selby, "I cleared it of the rats, and claim it as mine."

Selby did not have a problem with what the girl had done. He and the others had been living in the building for over two seasons, and no one had even attempted to get rid of the rats that had made the top room their home. After the first night the girl sitting next to him arrived, no one had seen a single rat on any of the floors, so he figured the girl had dealt with all of them. He thought that since she took care of the rat infestation for the entire building, she was more than welcome to have the top part of the building for herself.

Now that she had come to him and suggested

that someone had entered her place while she was away, Selby would have to deal with it. He had set the rules for those that wanted to stay, and he was going to make sure that anyone staying in the building followed them. "I will make sure that everyone knows not to enter the place while you are away." The girl gave him a look and he knew what it meant, "Or while you are there."

The girl did not give any indication that she appreciated what he was going to do. She just turned her head away from him and put her focus back on the lieutenant standing a few paces from the steps. The one she believed had entered her place.

"You don't think it was me, do you?" Selby asked.

"No," the child answered without hesitation. She did not know why, but she could tell that Selby would not go against any of the rules he had put in place. She may not have known what the word was that described what she felt about him, but to someone else it was trust.

Selby followed her gaze and saw that she was once again staring at Barret. He had a feeling that she had an idea of who had trespassed on her domain, and now Selby decided he would have a word with the lieutenant. "Is there anything else you wanted to talk about?" he asked without taking his eyes off Barret. For her answer, she stood up and started walking down the steps. As she stepped off the last one Selby called to her, "Hey!" When the child turned to look over her shoulder, he asked his next question, hoping for an answer, "Did you really kill all those rats, or did you just find them dead up there?" For her answer, she turned and walked away, going back out into the city.

Even after she was out of his sight, Selby continued to stare in the direction he saw the girl go. The girl with the deep eyes. The girl with the deep, but pretty eyes.

"That child is creepy."

Selby finally stopped looking out into the city and turned his head to look at Barret who had returned to sit on the step below him. Yes, he was going to have to have a talk with him.

When the girl came back to the building, with no success in finding a place to earn coinage, she saw Selby sitting on his step in his normal place, along with two of his lieutenants.

When she passed by the step where Selby was, he turned his head to look at her and her at him. The glances they exchanged told her that she would not have to worry about anyone entering her place again and that he now had an opening for a new lieutenant. The girl smiled at him, even though she was not aware that she did, and walked up the last of the steps and into the building.

Selby could not help himself and turned around to watch the girl leave his sight. He then went back to looking out into the front of the building. Thinking about what he could do, with the girl with the deep, beautiful eyes.

The next night the child did the same as before. She went into the city to look for a way to earn coin but once again, she was not successful. She might have had better luck if she actually asked someone to hire her but in every place she saw, there were always too many adults about, and she did not want to be around them for a long period of time. She wanted to find something that would allow her to provide what she needed but allow her to be by herself. That was why she enjoyed hunting. At least that was one of the reasons. The other was because she enjoyed the kill.

This night when she returned to the building, she only saw the two lieutenants. Selby was not in his usual spot. When she came up to the steps, she thought about asking the boys where he was but decided that it did not concern her, so she went into the house, and up to the room where she had been staying.

The next night, when she stepped out of the opening and climbed down the ladder, she saw Selby standing at the top of the stairs that led to the level below. When she made it to the bottom of the ladder, she did not replace the stone she used before. She had not used it since she had her talk with Selby, and he gave her confirmation that no one would bother her. The only reason she used the stone at all was to find out if someone would try to get into where she was staying. She did not do it to make sure no one took her belongings because whenever she left the room, she always took everything with her except for the blanket she used. The bags for her water, food, and coin, and of course, her knife always went with her. When Barret went into her room, he actually suffered whatever punishment Selby had given him, for nothing.

He waited for the girl to come to him at the top of the stairs. He was the one in charge of the building, but he was going to show this girl as much respect as he could. She stopped when she reached him and waited for him to tell her what he wanted. "I have a job for you."

The girl was not completely sure what he meant, but she knew that from the last place she had shared with other children, they would go out and steal the food and coins they needed to survive, so the girl gave her response, "I do not steal," she said then started to walk around Selby. She had not lied. The girl knew what stealing was, and decided long ago, never to resort to it. She would earn what she needed, by either hunting or trading for coin, or use coin to purchase what she required. The only things she had ever taken without permission were the two bags and the knife she left with, the night she set out on her own. To her, those were for survival.

"You won't have to steal anything," Selby said behind her, and she turned to look at him. He came down the couple of steps that brought him to stand on the one above, where the girl had stopped. "It is a job that pays coin, but before I tell you what it is, you have to agree to my terms."

The girl did not know what to think. She was curious about what Selby was suggesting, but when he said the word "terms" she had a feeling he would be getting something out of whatever he had planned. "What are they?" the girl asked.

Selby smiled at her and told the girl what he had come up with, "It's simple. For every five copper pieces you receive, you give me two."

"Two?" the girl said, questioning the boy's cut, with her giving away almost half of her coin.

"That is the deal. And just so you know, one of the two copper pieces you give me, goes to supplies and food, which all of us will need on days when we can't get what we need in our usual way."

"And the second one?" the girl asked, thinking that the first purpose sounded reasonable.

Selby smiled and simply said, "It's for the future."

The girl did not understand, but the smile Selby had, made her smile as well, and she gave her answer, "We have a deal."

"Excellent, follow me," Selby said and stepped around the girl to head down the stairs.

The girl did exactly that and followed Selby down the stairs and out of the house. "I will be going out for a while," Selby said to his three lieutenants that were sitting on the steps, the newest one being a girl. When they reached the street, Selby stopped and looked back at his three lieutenants then looked at the girl standing next to him. "You know I could always use another lieutenant, and as you can see,

I have no problem with having a girl as one." The girl that was with him just stared at him. Selby knew that if he asked the girl to be one of his lieutenants, she would decline. He knew this girl was a loner. He turned and started walking into the city knowing that he would never ask her to take the position again because she would not.

Selby led the girl to a part of the city she had never been to since she had arrived. Before they even reached where they were going, she could smell something she had never smelled before. The scent was always in the air, but she was not able to separate it from all the other smells in the city until she came closer to where it was coming from.

Being a child of few words, she kept quiet the entire time she had been following the boy, and he was the one who spoke when they had arrived at their destination. "This is the city's harbor. The ships make dock here to sell their wares or to take on more, or both. They travel all over the world. Some of them leave and won't return for a season or two, and some won't ever come back."

The girl looked out at what she was seeing for the first time in her life, and what she saw, amazed her. Yes, the boats were impressive. They were huge with wooden beams rising from them and reaching into the sky. They were wide but not as wide as they were long. And as much as they impressed her, it was what they were on, and what stretched out behind them that caused her to finally speak, "What is that?"

"What?" Selby asked, not knowing what the girl was referring to.

"The lake," the girl said not knowing what else to call the water she was looking at. She had seen rivers, brooks, and even lakes, but the water now looked as if it went on forever. Like land did, but what she was seeing now, moved.

"That is the ocean," Selby said and looked at the girl. For the first time since he had met her, she showed some sign of emotion. Selby knew the great ocean had that effect on many people. The ones it called to and decided to make a living from it. Either by sailing on one of the merchant vessels, or one of the ships which made its living from attacking those vessels. Even though Selby saw the lure in either of those professions, he had other plans for his life, and it required him to remain on land.

He saw the girl sniff the air. "That is the salt in the water that you smell. When we are in the city, the other scents cover it up, but since we are so close, you can smell it easily. The only thing is that you don't drink the water because it isn't good for you." The girl did not take her eyes off the great water; she heard what Selby had said, even though she could not see how anything so amazing could do her any harm.

Moon was in the sky, and it pleased Moon, to see how the girl marveled at the sight she was seeing. Even though Ocean was one of Ourgós' creations, Moon was still above Ocean, and responsible for watching over Ocean and all the creatures that live in the great water.

"Come on, I will take you to where you need to go and explain what you will be doing." Selby walked away but stopped when he heard the girl ask her question.

"And what is that?"

He turned around and with a smile, answered the girl's question, "Why killing rats of course." He then turned and started heading for the big ships and the docks where they were waiting. If he had waited a moment before turning away, he would have seen the smile on the girl's face.

Selby led the girl to the ship, where he had talked with the captain earlier in the day while explaining to her what his plan consisted of. "When ships come into port, they will unload their cargo and set out again as soon as they are ready. In between the time they arrive and leave, the crew will spend time cleaning the ship and making any repairs it might need. Another task they must do is to get rid of any rats that made it aboard in any one of their previous stops. As hard as the crew tries to keep the rats out of the cargo hold, while they are at a port, some always manage to get on board, and if one of them happens to be a female then soon there could be more than what had found their way on board."

When they reached the beginning of the port, the girl continued to look at the big ships, and the great water, which never seemed to end or remain still, while Selby continued with his explanation as to why they were there. "The crew members that capture the rats sometimes use cats but once a cat has killed a few it loses interest and the crew either have to get another cat or wait until the one they have is ready to start working again. Of course, cats only work when they want to."

"You have arranged it so that I replace the cats?" the girl asked.

"Sort of. I talked to one of the captains and told him that I knew a person who can kill rats better than any cat, and I could guarantee that by the time he left port, his ship would be free of any vermin. I also told him that we would not be responsible for any rats that came on board after they left Sarzanac." The girl heard the word "we" but did not say anything. "The captain of the vessel will pay a copper piece for every two rats you catch. Oh, just so you know, you have to make sure that he or his first mate see the rats. He isn't going to take your word for the number you say you kill, and I can't fault him for that."

Selby stopped talking. "Is there anything else?" the girl asked.

"Nope, that is pretty much it. You get a copper piece for every two rats you kill, and for every five copper pieces you receive you give me two." Selby stopped walking and waited until the girl was looking at him. "I came up with this plan, and yes you could keep all the coinage for yourself and go from ship to ship and offer the captains your service, but I hope we can work together on this, and we both can get something out of it."

The girl never even thought about crossing the boy. He was the one who had come up with the plan, and the girl had no problem with it or with the terms of the arrangement. "You find the ships, I kill the rats," the girl said, and Selby nodded to let her know that was the arrangement. The girl nodded back to let him know that she accepted the terms and that she would not cross him.

"Well then, here we are," Selby said, and extended his arm to his left to point at the dock where he had stopped their journey. They both turned to face the ship, "It is called *The Consort*. The captain said they would be sailing in three sun-cycles." He turned his head to look at the girl, "I hope that will be enough time for you to clear out his rat problem, and you will need to make sure that before they sail no more rats get on board before they leave port. Remember, I promised the captain his ship would be free of rats when he left, and I would hate for it to get around that I wasn't true to my word. Because if it gets out that we can't do what we say we can, then our little business will end before we have a chance to get it started."

She noticed Selby used the word "we" a lot, but she was the one that was going to be doing the majority of the work. She did not have a problem with it though, he had found a way for her, and apparently himself, to earn some coin. "Anything else?" she asked and turned her head to look at him. He shook his head to let her know that he had told her everything. The girl then turned to face the ship and walked up the plank.

"The hold is in the bottom of the ship just in case you didn't know," Selby yelled to her.

She did not, but she would have asked someone where she was supposed to go to kill the rats when she got on board. The sooner she started killing rats, the sooner she would earn some coin.

When led to the ship's hold, she could not believe what she saw. The hold took up a good portion of the bottom of the ship. There was no cargo, so it was completely empty, except for the rats that were scurrying about, either looking for food, or a way out of the place. All the girl could think of was that this was going to be easy. Even with the number she was looking at; she did not think there would be a problem with cleaning out the rats in the time Selby had given her.

Three sun-cycles later, she arrived back at the building where she had been staying. She had remained on the ship for the time it took her to clean out the rats, until the ship left port, to make sure no more of the vermin made it aboard.

She saw Selby in his usual place with his three lieutenants sitting on the steps. She went past them, walked to the step where Selby was, pulled out a bag, and tossed it to him. He could hear the jingling of the coins inside as it traveled through the air and felt the weight of it as it landed in his hand. "That is all of it," the girl said, and Selby took his eyes off the bag he was holding and put them on her, "I figured you would want us to divide it together." All Selby could think of, was that he had come up with a profitable plan. As well as how much he would love to have this girl as one of his lieutenants.

She had killed sixty-five rats over the last three sun-cycles. That brought her a total of thirty-two copper pieces. With that amount, she did not even argue with the captain when he refused to pay for the sixty-fifth one, because the agreement he had made was for one copper piece for every two rats killed. Since he did not give her any coin for it, she tossed it to him and told him it was his. That was after she had taken the coin for the ones she had killed in pairs.

When they divided up the coin, Selby took twelve out of the thirty-two for his share, but when the girl saw that there were two coins left that did not fill the amount of five where she would have to give him two, she gave Selby one of the two. The captain of the ship might have wanted to get the better of the deal, but the girl knew that if it were not for Selby and his plan, she would not have the coins in the first place. She ended up with nineteen copper pieces and Selby kept thirteen for his cut. They were both happy.

Selby told her that he had already arranged her next job with another captain who had just entered port that morning. The captain said it would take him two sun-cycles to empty his cargo, but afterward, he would be happy to pay for the removal of the rats, since the crew members who usually did it, ended up killing only the ones that were almost dead and could barely move. That gave the girl a couple of days to rest before she went back to the harbor.

When the day came that *The Nettie's* hold was empty, Selby walked with her to where the ship was waiting at the dock. As she walked up the plank, he stayed only long enough to see her step on board. He never had the urge to go on a ship. It did not matter if it was at port or sailing the sea, his place was on land, as was his future.

The girl went into the hold and could not help but smile when she saw the rats covering the bottom of the ship. She was sure there was more this time than on the last ship. Selby had said *The Nettie* was one of the ships that stayed away for almost a full season, and that was why he chose it as their next customer because the longer it was on the sea going from port to port, the more rats there would be. With what the girl was seeing now, she knew Selby was correct.

Like the last ship, when she began killing the rats, she had no problems with ending their life, because there were so many of them, and everywhere she stepped, all she had to do was bend over and stab her knife down. With each try, there was not a time when her knife did not go into one of the creatures. Soon the rats learned that the creature after them was more dangerous than others like it and that they had to keep their distance. Unfortunately for the rats, just like she did on the first ship, the child resorted to a different tactic.

The rats learned to stay away from the big creature, and the girl knew they would run away when she tried to get close. She decided that instead of moving toward the rats, she would send the knife, flying through the air, spinning end over end, stopping when it pierced the rat she wanted to kill. Impaling it on the blade, as well as pinning the rat to the floor or side of the ship, so that it could not run away.

The rats knew it was dangerous to get near the deadly sharp object or the creature that wields it and decided to wait until the creature left before they came out. After the second day, they thought the creature was not leaving, that was until she went around and put out all the flames that were in the holders in the area where they lived. When it was dark, they thought it was safe to venture out again. Since rats can sense her in the dark, they knew that the creature was still with them, but they also knew creatures like this one could not see in the amount of darkness that was around them. Feeling safe, they went out and some of the rats even went over to the creature, to try and bite the thing for killing so many of their brothers and sisters. A couple of them got a nip or two in, just before they felt the sharp bite from the thing the creature used to kill the others.

Even in the complete darkness, the creature could end their life.

The rats finally decided that since it was dark, if they just stayed away from the creature then they would be able to survive. Surely, the creature could not kill them if they did not go close to it, especially with it being so dark. The rats came out of their hiding places but made sure they stayed away from the creature.

Rats have exceptionally good hearing, and every so often, they heard first the sound of something flying through the air, then they heard the cry of one of their brothers or sisters, followed by the sound of the sharp object embedding itself in the wood of the ship. Sometimes the cries of their fellow rats continued afterward.

It did not matter, the rats knew that as long as they stayed in the same place with the creature, they were not safe, and since they thought the creature had taken up permanent residence in their home, they decided that to survive, they needed to be someplace else. What few rats remained after the fourth day the child was on the ship, abandoned it and left it to the creature.

She had collected one hundred and twenty rat bodies within the four days she had cleaned out the hold. It was just in time because, on the fifth day, *The Nettie* began to take on cargo. The child stayed for another two cycles of the sun as the crew members stored the cargo in the ship's hold, to make sure no rats got on board.

When she and Selby divided the sixty coins, he kept twenty-four for himself and the girl kept thirty-six. She added them to the nineteen she had, and still had not spent, which gave her a total of fifty-five copper pieces just from killing rats. She was pleased with what she had made. Fifty copper pieces were equal to one silver piece and when she was hunting in the woods it took her a while to make that amount, and she had made it now in just over a moon-mark of being on the ships.

She even enjoyed the work more than hunting because not only did she earn the coin in the same spot without having to trek through the wilderness, but with what she was doing, she knew she was toning her skills with the knife she had. She was able to not only hear a rat in the dark by the sound it made, but she could see it as well and impale it on her knife while she was over eight paces away. It pleased both Selby and the girl with the way the plan had succeeded.

The only one not happy with what the child was doing was Rat. Too many of Rat's subjects suffered and died, because of the child of Moon. It was not that Rat had any deep feelings for the rats that had died, but Rat did not like Moon's plaything interfering in Rat's domain.

Rat was going to tell the rats, that when the child came onto one of the ships, they were to leave and let the child have it. Rat knew the child received payment for what she was doing, and if there were no rats then she would not gain anything. It pleased Rat, with what Rat had devised.

That is until Moon found out from Wind, what Rat had planned. Moon told Rat not to interfere in what the child was doing, or else Moon would make sure Rat suffered for it.

Rat was under the authority of Sun. Rat could go to Sun and let Sun know what Moon was doing, but Rat knew Sun would care less about Rat or the rats, and what was happening to them. Sun might take an interest if Sun found out it was the child of Moon killing the ones belonging to Rat, but Rat knew it would be a waste of time seeking help from Sun. Sun cared about Sun and no one else. Even though Sun is responsible for watching over all life on land.

Moon told Rat not to command any of the rats to leave the ship the child boarded, but Rat could tell all other rats not to enter the ship or any of the cargo the ship took on board. To Moon that was a fair deal. The child could kill rats and survive, and even though Rat would lose a few, Rat would be able to save the ones that did not enter the ship. Of course, it pleased Moon that the child was becoming more of what Moon needed her to be.

She made her living over the next few seasons as an exterminator, and she became very good at it. After about one moon-cycle since she began, word got around about how well the child could clear out a ship's hold and captains would seek out the child the day they docked. Although they were never able to find her, the boy who made all the arrangements, was always at the docks, ready to meet with any captains with a rat problem, to broker a deal.

If the captain had to be back out to sea within two sun-cycles, then the price of clearing the ship went up to one copper piece for each rat killed. Of course, the captains agreed to the deal, because they would make the coin back with the amount of product they would be able to sell since the rats would not get to it before they reached their next destination.

When word got around about what the girl was doing, others tried to get in on the action and start their own little business in clearing out ship's holds. Not surprisingly, they failed. In fact, when someone other than the girl attempted to remove the rats, at a reduced price, there appeared to be more rats in the end than there were when the ship made port. This was due to Moon telling Rat to have more rats enter the ships where someone was trying to interfere with what the girl was doing. Of course, Rat had no choice but to agree.

Moon watched the child kill rats. She became so good at it that most of the time even before she started killing them, she would douse all the lights so that she could make it more interesting for herself. She would clear out the holds within two nights, and only stay on the ship, to make sure no others got on board. Which they did not because of Moon and Rat.

While she was doing all of this, she never forgot the reason she had come to Sarzanac in the first place. Every now and then when she was not working, she would go by the Assassin's Guild. It was not just to see if they had placed the red flag out, she knew it was not time yet, but she made the trip just so she could keep in her mind, and in her heart, of where she wanted to be.

Once every moon-cycle, the girl would ask Moon, "Am I old enough yet?"

Moon would always tell her, "No, you are not."

Then one night while she was in a ship's hold killing rats, Moon thought to her, *"Child."*

"Yes Moon," she replied as she pulled her last kill off her blade.

"You are old enough."

The child smiled and then thrust her arm out behind her. She heard the blade, that she had released, enter into the wood of the ship's haul, a breath after it entered into a rat, then heard the last cry of her latest kill. She had not even turned her head to look in the direction before she let the blade fly.

SEVENTEEN

Every night, after the one Moon told the child she was old enough, she went by the Assassin's Guild to look for the sign she had been waiting for. The red flag that would let her know the Guild was about to select the new recruits.

The child remembered one of the other rules the man had told her. That she needed to find some type of weapon. Something other than the knife she had. She did not see why she needed to, she had become very efficient with the blade, and since the man also told her she would receive other weapons when she entered the Guild, she thought the knife would be sufficient. However, she would purchase a weapon to meet the requirement. Not doing so, may stop her from entering the Guild, and that was not something that she would allow.

She did not have to worry about having the funds for what she needed. She had collected a good deal of coinage in the amount of time she had been killing rats. Selby had even hired her talents out to some of the shops in the city on the days when she did not have work on one of the ships. Of course, since the number of rats was greatly less than what was on a ship, the price went up to cover the difference. Any rat the child killed in a shop was worth two copper pieces per rat. The owners were more than happy to pay because they knew the girl was good at what she did and they would get what they paid for.

Funds were not a problem for the child, even after she paid for food, and some new clothes every now and then, when she wore out the ones she had or outgrew them because she got older. The problem was that in every shop she went into that sold weapons, she never found anything she liked.

Swords were plentiful, and even though she was not the height of an adult, she had no problem finding a blade weighted properly for her to wield. But when she picked one out and worked with it, she could tell right away it was not the weapon for her.

She tried a couple of bows, but to her, it seemed too awkward to carry. Not only would she have to either carry the bow in her hands, or string it over her shoulder, she would have to carry a quiver of arrows, and since one only held about twenty arrows, when she ran out, she would be defenseless, which she never wanted to be.

She tried a couple of hand axes and some small maces, but they felt too clumsy, and she would have to put more strength into a single swing, just to make an effective hit. When it came down to what was available, she decided to keep to her knife, for now. When the day came that the Assassin's Guild would be making their selections, and if she had not found a weapon to her liking, she would purchase the cheapest sword available, and trust that when she entered the Guild, they would have a weapon to suit her.

One night when she was coming from one of the upper-class districts, having finished the job of removing the rats from the lower levels of a very fancy home, she was making her way to the building of the Assassin's Guild to do her daily check. When she arrived, she saw what she had been waiting for. On the second-floor balcony, directly in the center, there was the red flag. The sign which let everyone know that the Guild would soon be choosing the new recruits.

She remembered what the man had told her that night. About how after the red flag flew on the balcony, a green flag would replace it, to let everyone wanting to try for admittance to the Assassin's Guild, know that selection would take place on the following day. On that morning, a black flag would hang in its place. The girl knew that it would not be long before she would be walking through the door. She never had a doubt, because if for some reason, they did not except her this time, then by the time the Guild made its next selection, five seasons would have passed, and she would be too old to be part of the selection. When the day came this time, she would enter the place, there was no other option for her.

She walked away from the building, more excited than she had ever been in her life. She had waited for over three seasons to see the red flag, and now that she had, there was nothing else to do, but wait, and still purchase a weapon, but that was nothing. She would wait until the day of the green flag and then just buy any sword she could find cheap. That way she would meet the requirement.

She remembered the three requirements told to her. One was she had to be between fifteen and seventeen seasons of age. Two she had to have a weapon, and three, she had to stay alive, while waiting for the day. The last one was just as easy as getting the weapon.

Since she had come to Sarzanac, there was only one time she had to defend herself against someone else alone. One night when she had been making her way home after going by the Assassin's Guild, just to see it, she sensed someone following her. She did not see them, but she was sure there was a person behind her, and that they were not just traveling in the same direction she was.

She confirmed this when she turned down an alley and could still feel the presence behind her. She never turned around to look at the person, until she was midway into the alley. When she did, she saw that it was someone she had almost forgotten about, Barret, the ex-lieutenant of Selby. She had not seen him for over two seasons, which did not bother her at the least. Now that he had followed her into the alley, she had no doubt that this meeting was not a coincidence, nor was it going to be a pleasant one, at least not for Barret.

"Did you want something?" the girl asked.

Both of the children in the alley had aged since the last time they had seen each other, but only the girl had grown in height. She did not know how old Barret was, but since he looked to be the same height as he was when she had last seen him, the girl figured that either he was waiting for his next growth spurt, or the boy would not be any bigger than he was now. He was about a head taller than she was, and even though she had grown taller, she still was not at her full height, being only over fourteen seasons.

"I've been hoping to see you again, so I could get even for what you did to me."

The girl had no idea of what the boy was talking about, but she wanted to drag this out a little longer, to see what he would say, and maybe, for some fun. "And what is it you think I did to you?"

The boy took a step closer to the girl. They were now about fifteen paces apart. "You ratted me out to Selby. You were the one who told him I went into that room of yours."

The girl did not hesitate to give her reply, "I did not." Which she knew she had not. She never said a word to Selby about who she thought the person was who entered the loft she claimed as her own. "But it was you, wasn't it?" she asked to see if he would confirm what she had guessed.

"Yes, but no one saw me, and you must have had some way to know it was me. I don't know how, but after you had that meeting with Selby, he…" the boy paused for a breath, "…he confronted me."

The girl did not know what that meant, but she had a feeling that Selby did not just have a pleasant talk with the boy, and then sent him on his way. She even thought about maybe asking Selby exactly how he "confronted" the boy. Not that she cared, but it might be an interesting story. "I didn't tell Selby what you had done. But since you have confirmed that you were the one who trespassed into my area, then whatever he did to you, you earned it yourself."

"I didn't deserve to be kicked out, just because I went into that place. Especially since you had only been there a couple of nights."

"And in that couple of nights, I had claimed the area as my own. You should stay away from places you should not be." The boy thought the girl was talking about the loft, and she was to a certain extent, but what she was referring to more, was the place the boy was now. He had gone into her area at the house when she was not there; now he had come into this alley. He had come in with her. "I suggest you turn around and forget about what you thought you were going to do this night."

"Not just this night, every night."

"What?" the girl asked.

"Every night since Selby kicked me out, I thought about how if I ever saw you again, I was going to

342

make you pay for what happened to me. You were all I could think about."

"I'm flattered but I am not interested in you, in that way," the girl could not help snickering at her remark. Barret did not think her comment, or her smile, was amusing.

The boy started walking towards her slowly. "Because of what you did, I ended up living on the streets again by myself. I had to go hungry, and I had to sleep in the cold. I finally found a group of people that I could team up with but the life I have with them is nothing compared to the life I had as one of Selby's lieutenants. Because of you, he kicked me out."

The girl had no sympathy for the boy, and if he was looking for some, he was not going to get it from the girl, who herself had spent a good portion of her life alone. She never had a problem with sleeping in the cold, and between her and Moon, she never had to worry about going hungry. To her, if Barret's hardships bothered him so much then he should have done something about them himself and stopped blaming her. It was not her fault for what happened to him. He was the one who broke the rule. He brought his punishment on himself.

"Because of you, I had to do things I never wanted to do. I didn't like killing but the ones I work for now expect results. They don't care if it is a man, woman, or child, if they tell me to kill, then that is what I have to do. And now, I am going to do the one thing

I have dreamt of since you had me tossed out on the street. The one good thing that has come from me having to leave Selby is that I have no problem with killing you. I guess in a way, because of what you did, you made me into the person I am now, and now you are going to see, just what you made me into."

The girl knew the boy was thinking he was the victim; and in a way, he may be, but she did not cause the suffering he had brought on himself. Although, she was going to cause him some if he thought she was going to let him do anything to her.

The boy took off running towards the girl. She did not move when she saw him coming closer, not even when she saw that he pulled a knife from behind his back with his right hand, one with a longer blade than the one she had.

He came running towards her, and when he was almost two paces from her, she raised her left hand to the clasp at her neck that held her cloak together. At the same time, she moved her right hand inside of the cloak, grabbed it, then pulled her cloak off and flung it out in front of her. She did it in a way that when it was in the air, it spread out, and for a brief moment, it was between her and the boy coming towards her, causing them to be out of each other's sight. She knew it would not stop him, but that was not her goal. The cloak was only in the air for a breath, but as the boy reached it, he continued forward, knocking the cloak to the side. He did not decrease his momentum, thinking he would simply brush the obstacle out of his way, and continue with his plan. Only his plan did not consider the part that as he moved the cloak out of his view, he continued to run towards the girl, impaling himself on the knife she had in her right hand, just high enough to enter his mid-section.

Even though he felt the knife cut into his stomach, he still had the determination to kill the child, who he believed was the reason he had suffered. While still having the knife's blade in him, he thrust his right hand, and his own knife out, trying to pierce the girl's upper body. He was fast but the girl, who had spent her time killing rats, in the dark, was faster.

She easily avoided the boy's knife, by leaning the top part of her body to her left. This allowed the boy's arm to pass on her right and as it did so, she executed three moves. She brought up her left hand and grabbed the boy's arm at the wrist as it passed her. She also used her right hand, to pull the knife out of the boy's body, and then brought it up and over her left arm to stab him in his chest. To the boy, it appeared that all three of those things happened at the same time.

The boy knew when he felt the pain in his chest that the girl was more than what he had expected. For so many nights, before he fell asleep, he would imagine what he would do when he saw this girl again. He would use his knife to slit the girl's throat and as he did, he would look into her eyes and smile, letting her know that she would pay for all the suffering that she put him through.

In a way, maybe not by his thinking, he would never suffer again.

The boy could only look into those deep eyes staring back at him. He did not move until the girl pulled her knife out of his chest, and with one fluid motion, she brought the blade across the back of his right hand, causing him to drop his knife to the ground.

The girl, while still holding onto the boy's right arm, brought it between the two of them, bending it towards him and to his right. With the pressure, she was putting on the limb, and the fact that he now had two additional holes in his body compared to the ones he had before he came into the alley, the boy fell to his knees.

The girl still held onto the boy's wrist. Now that he was on his knees, his head was at the height of her midsection, so she had to bend over to move closer to his face. When she did, she looked directly into his eyes, and he into hers, "You were forced to leave because you were not smart enough. It is for that same reason you will not walk out of this alley." The boy swallowed hard, and tears rolled down his cheeks. That did not stop the girl from thrusting her knife into his throat.

She pulled the knife out and let go of the boy's arm at the same time. He tried to take a couple more breaths, but either the hole in his chest or the one in his throat stopped any air from entering his lungs. He was able to stay alive long enough to see the child walk over, pick her cloak up off the ground, and place it back on. He then saw her walk away, down the alley.

He remembered what she had said to him, that he would not walk out of this alley, and she was right.

Someone else saw the entire incident that night. He had traveled across the rooftops following the girl since she walked away from the Assassin's Guild. He recognized her as the one he had talked to over two seasons ago, and since she impressed him that night, and since he had nothing else planned for this night, he decided to follow her and see what she had been up to. He was glad he had made that choice.

He was not sure what impressed him more. That she had sensed someone had been following her, without turning around, or the fact she led the boy into an alley so that she could deal with him. Or maybe it was the way she remained in control of herself the entire time. Or it could have been when she did the maneuver with her cloak to distract the boy, causing him to run directly into the child's trap and onto the blade. Then again, it could have been the second maneuver she had done, grabbing the boy's arm, and stabbing him in his chest.

As the assassin played the scene over in his mind, he decided that the entire event was something he was glad to have witnessed and was sure that any of the Masters of his Guild would have loved to have seen this child's performance.

He thought about continuing to follow the girl but decided he would let her alone, at least for the rest of the night. He would check in on her now and again, to see if he could see just how this girl grew as she waited for the day the Guild would once again take in new recruits. He thought about the last rule he relayed to the girl but had no worries about her having a problem staying alive. No, he was sure she would be present when the Guild made their selections. In fact, he was sure she would be one of the chosen, and to increase her chances, which were already high, he would have a talk with the seven Masters who would be making the selection. Once he told the girl's story, each of them would have an interest in her, he was sure of that.

EIGHTEEN

The girl knew that when she saw the red flag on the balcony, her new life would soon be upon her. It also meant she had to end the old one.

She reached the building she had made her home for over three seasons. She still claimed the loft as her own, and she never had a problem with rats after the first night she arrived.

The guards that stood on the front steps of the building were no longer lieutenants. There were always four present, as well as another six positioned at various locations over the front of the building. They had replaced the lieutenants about a season after the girl began her rat duties.

In the beginning, when they took up their post, they armed themselves with sticks and small knives. Since then, they have advanced their weapons to swords. Every guard carried one and knew how to use it to defend the building where the girl lived, as well as the buildings to each of its sides. Yes, Selby, in the three seasons the girl has known him, had expanded his territory.

She walked across the yard and up the front steps, and more than one of the guards gave the girl a nod to show her the respect she has earned. Even though she was not a lieutenant or even a guard, to everyone living in one of the three buildings, the girl was only second to Selby, and even that was not by much.

As she walked into the building, she heard the noise that had been going on for over two seasons. There was always some part of the building under repair, or renovation, to the way Selby wanted it. Not just in this building but in the other two as well. Since almost everyone that had taken up residence in the place, was sleeping while the sun was up, most of the remodeling took place at night, which was good for the girl as well since she would sleep when the sun was out. What little bit of construction that did go on during that time did not bother her.

She walked up the stairs but instead of taking the last flight leading to the fifth floor and her loft, she walked further onto the fourth floor. On this level as well, there were two guards posted at the beginning of the hallway and in the middle. There would be another two standing at the door she was heading for.

When she reached it, the two guards looked at her and she nodded to them. The guard on her right, a girl no more than thirteen, turned, opened the door, and stuck her head inside, "She is here to see you sir." The guard then pulled her head out of the doorway but did not close the door. Like everyone else who stood at this door, Selby would never deny the girl entrance into the room he took as his command post.

The guard nodded and the girl walked through the opened door. When she entered and was far enough into the room, the guard in the hallway closed the door behind her. She walked ten more steps inside and stopped, waiting for Selby to finish with the twelve lieutenants he was meeting with. Even this number was only a third of all the ones he had placed in command to oversee the operations of the three buildings he was now in control of.

While he was talking, he made sure his eyes met the girl's and when he smiled at her, the lieutenants knew the meeting was about to be over. They have all been in this room at some time with Selby to discuss some topic of concern, but once the girl came in, Selby would end the meeting abruptly so that he could see why she had come to his office.

He ended the meeting after three more statements and then dismissed his lieutenants. They did not mind though, because whenever they met with their leader, Selby made sure he told them everything he wanted them to know, but even more importantly, at least to Selby, he made sure they told him, everything they or the ones under their command, had done, seen, or heard throughout the city. Selby was thorough in his questioning because the most important thing to Selby was the need to know every bit of information. Once told, he would be the one to decide just how important it was and whether or not he should retain it. Of course, he retained everything reported to him.

The lieutenants left the room and the last to leave closed the door behind him. When those two met, no one else attended.

The girl looked at the boy, no, looked at the young man making his way towards her. As he stepped around his desk, she saw how the boy had grown into who he is now. Selby stood over twenty-four handbreadths. He was fourteen when she had met him, but after a season, he shot up in height so fast that everyone said that he would not stop growing until his head was in the clouds, which most people thought it was there already.

Selby never told anyone what his great secret plan was. Not even the girl he would talk to with no one else around. After a season of the girl killing rats and handing over part of her coins to Selby, he began to purchase things. The first were the swords for all the guards to carry. After he felt they had enough training and practice, he then started buying supplies to rebuild the building they lived in. Even though he never said why, the girl knew the reason he purchased the swords and trained the guards and lieutenants first. Selby was preparing himself, and the ones under his command, for when someone took notice of what he was doing, and they decided that he and the children who had taken up residence in the building, would be better off somewhere else. A couple groups of adults tried but failed. Even the girl defended the place she had made her home, and when she did, more than one adult died.

After the two attempts by adults, another group of children attacked the building but before there was a single fist or sword raised from either group, Selby asked to speak privately to the leader who invaded his territory. They went inside the building and when they both returned, the leader of the other group told the ones who had come with him, that they all would now follow Selby. No one knew what Selby had said to the other child, but even though he was older than Selby, he was now one of his lieutenants, and there was no doubt in the loyalty he had for his leader.

It was the next day, with all the children combined, they evicted the humans out of the buildings to the left and the right, to add to their holdings. One building belonged to a group of adults who would supply hapweed to anyone that wanted it. Since it deadens the mind and the body, Selby had always wanted to do away with the people running it, but never had the power, until now. The second building had adults which dealt with the selling of women, against their will. Selby hated it even more than the first building and since the ones who ran the city did nothing about either of the buildings, Selby decided that he would.

He crossed the room over to the girl, and when

he was within an arm's reach of her, she could see the stubble on his face he had for a beard. He might be seventeen and taller than most men, but he still could not grow a full beard no matter how long he went without shaving. The girl never said it to him, but she liked the way it made him look as if he was too much of a street person to care if he shaved or not, but also that he was old enough not to care at all what someone might think about him.

When he stopped in front of her, she was about ready to tell him why she had come to see him, but he did not give her the opportunity, "I know," he said and looked into her eyes. All her life, Selby was the only person that would look directly into her eyes, and not turn away after a few breaths. Of course, Selby was the only person who had ever thought she had the most beautiful eyes.

When he said, "I know," the girl knew what Selby had meant, and even more importantly, he knew why she came to see him. He turned around and walked back behind his desk then turned to face her. "I have already canceled the job I had arranged for you and have put the word out that we are no longer in the rat killing business." The girl could hear a bit of sadness in what he just said, a part of her felt the same way. The rat killing business had brought these two together. She needed it to make a living for herself while she waited for the Assassin's Guild to announce that they would be accepting recruits. Selby needed it so that he could fund whatever he needed the funding for. He never told her, so she never asked.

They each had a reason for what they had done, but together they built something which made each of them realize they may not need to rely on anyone else to survive, but it was nice to have someone around just in case they did.

Neither one of them talked about their past, to each other or anyone else. That was probably because both of them had their focus on the future. For the girl, it was the Assassin's Guild, for Selby it was whatever Selby looked towards, but kept to himself.

Even though they never talked about it, he knew that someday the girl would be leaving. The night she asked about the Assassin's Guild, and he had sent Keyota, now one of his lieutenants, to lead the girl to the building where the Guild resides, Selby knew what the girl had planned. Silently he wished her the best of luck in what she wanted to do, but also, silently, he wished she would stay with him. Maybe even becoming one of his lieutenants, or maybe something even more. Selby always thought that a king should have a queen.

"I was informed that the red flag had been placed out on the balcony at that place." Selby still would not say the words "Assassin's Guild." To him, to do so, might just bring their eyes to focus on him, and he was not ready for that, at least not yet. "I was told today, and even though you would probably have found out yourself, I was going to tell you when you returned tonight."

The girl did not know that she would finish the job she had started yesterday until she had left the place earlier tonight. Somehow, Selby knew she had, and that she would be returning this night. That was the thing about him, he always knew.

He put his hands in his trousers pockets, looked down at the top of his desk, and took a deep breath, to prepare himself to begin the speech he had been working on for half a season. When he looked up and was about to speak, he saw the girl shaking her head. Without saying a word, he knew what she was telling him. That she could not accept his offer to remain with him. That she could not be one of his lieutenants, or even what he wanted more than that. She had a great deal of respect for him, but it did not matter how she felt, she had a bigger calling than just living in a building in Sarzanac and killing rats.

To give a silent answer to her silent reply, Selby nodded his head, to let her know that he understood and that he would not say anything else about her staying. "While you are away, I will make sure no one takes up residence in your room. I mean with the exception of some rats, but I am sure that when you return, you will be able to deal with them."

"I'm sure I will." She said it, but both knew that if she did return, she would not be staying long, in the place she had called home for over three seasons.

Selby walked back around the desk and came to stand in front of the girl. He stood there looking at her, while she looked at him. Neither one of them said anything for a few moments. The girl did not because she had always been one of few words. Selby stood there holding that position because he wanted one last time to look into those deep, beautiful eyes. Eyes that he feared he would never see again.

When the girl thought the moment had lasted long enough, she turned around and walked to the door. When she opened it, she stepped through and closed it behind her. The guards, which should have been at their posts, were not in the hallway. Someone must have told them that the meeting the two were about to have, was going to be more private than any of the others which had taken place before.

The girl walked down the hall and took the last flight of stairs to the fifth floor, then climbed the ladder to her loft. She would get some sleep, and when the sun went down, she would go to the Assassin's Guild to see if they had put out the green flag. It was the only thing that mattered now. Her life of killing rats was over, and even though she never thought she was beneath that type of work, she knew her life was about to change, for better and grander things.

Selby stayed in the same spot where he had been when the girl walked out of the room. He had lived on the streets for as long as he could remember. Not a day went by that he did not think about his mother and sister who had died before he had even seen his fourth season of life.

His family had never been rich, and barely had enough coinage to feed themselves. But they had each other. One night while they were eating dinner, three men burst into their home and beat him until he was almost dead. In fact, the men thought they had completed the task. Even though he had been slipping in and out of conciseness, he heard the men taking advantage of his mother and sister. As much as he tried, he was not able to force himself to stand up and fight their attackers, and either make them go away or die while trying.

When he finally came to, he saw his mother, and his sister of fourteen seasons lying on the floor. They were not moving and never did again. He left his home and never returned. He started living on the streets. Stealing what he could to live, and when he could not find food to steal, like the girl with the deep beautiful eyes, he had to rely on the rats he could catch and kill to survive. It was when the girl had said the word "rat" that night that he felt a bond with her. As if there was nothing wrong with rat. It was meat and if that was all a person had available, they should be thankful for it.

A few seasons after the death of his mother and sister, he found out that a wealthy man wanted to claim his home, and others around it, to build warehouses. He paid the men who had come to his home. Selby always thought that if he had known the man was sending those men to his home, then he could have warned his mother and sister, and they would still be alive. He blamed himself for lacking that information, and from that day on, information was something he would never lack again.

Selby had plans, and to begin those plans he needed others to join him. He started out with just one child. It was the first lieutenant, he ever had. Then he found another child to join him. Then another and then another. By the time Selby was thirteen, he had already gathered over forty other children looking to him for leadership. He set rules in place to make sure everyone who joined his band was safe, because never again would he allow someone to hurt those he was responsible for.

He had acquired his first building, abandoned for as long as Selby could remember, but he knew that for him to continue with his plan, he would need funds. Which was hard to come by, especially since he made his living on the streets. Picking pockets was only enough to get by, not enough to build an empire.

Then the girl with the deep beautiful eyes came to where he was, and a few nights later, they had started their own business. She would kill the rats, and he would find her the work. Everything was finally going according to his plan, and he thought he would be able to reach his goal. When the girl with the deep beautiful eyes appeared, he had to make a slight change to his plans for her. The only problem was she did not want to be a part of them.

Selby knew he would never be able to change her mind, so he had to accept the fact that just because he might plan something, it does not necessarily mean it will happen. Maybe not about the girl, but the plan he had come up with all those seasons ago, would. He was progressing faster than he could ever imagine and within a few more seasons, he would see his hard work pay off. He just was not sure if he would see the girl with the deep beautiful eyes again.

He stood there looking at the door she had exited. He would make sure he had someone go to the Assassin's Guild every day to see if the green flag was flying. Better yet, to be sure he knew the minute it was, Selby decided he would have a couple of his lieutenants assign one or two lookouts near the Guild so they could relay the message to him as soon as they saw the new flag. Yes, that was what he would do. That way he would have that bit of information even sooner.

Until then he would stay in this room. He would cancel all the meetings he normally would have unless it was someone telling him about the flag. The green flag was the signal that the next day the Guild would choose the new recruits. Then the girl either would enter the Guild or not. If not then maybe, just maybe she would come back to him and become one of his lieutenants or maybe even something more.

He only held onto that thought for a breath, because he knew that if anyone had a chance to enter the Guild it would be the girl. He never knew her name because she had said she did not have one. When he wanted to get her attention, he would just say "Hey," that is what he called to her. What she did not hear him call her was the name he had chosen for her not long after they began their rat killing business, and that was "My Queen."

NINETEEN

Hanna replaced the container underneath the opening in the relief shack. She had burned the contents this morning, the same as she has ever since she took over the task. She has been doing it for so long, and so use to the stench, she does not even use her hand anymore to cover her mouth and nose to reduce the smell. This task, just like everything Hanna does, is just one more routine, which makes up her life.

Even though she is fifteen, Hanna has accepted the fact that this is what she will be doing for the remainder of her life. She wakes up in the morning, before the sun rises, and starts with the list of chores for the day; the same chores, which she did the day before and will be doing tomorrow.

When Hanna finished outside, she went back in the house where she washed up and helped Mama serve breakfast; first to the guest staying in the boarding house, then to Papa, Mama, and herself. Hanna ate because if she did not then she would not live, but if it were up to her, she would not even bother doing that, because, to Hanna, there is no purpose in life.

Everything Hanna loved she ended up losing. First, the village where she and her family lived; even though she does not remember much of the place or even the names of the people she knew. Then those men took her father from her, and then her mother. After her mother passed away, she made sure she remained detached from Mama and Papa. The two who helped raise her when her parents were alive, and after they both passed away. They tried to fill a part of Hanna's life with some of what she had lost. They tried, but Hanna, even though she appreciated everything they did for her, would not bring herself to come to love them. Why, when she knew they would leave her one day as well. To Hanna, everyone leaves her.

While Mama continued to work in the kitchen, Hanna served the guests their breakfast. She performed her duties with no complaints and was polite to anyone who spoke to her. But more than one guest over the seasons Hanna had lived and worked at the boarding house, had asked her and even Mama and Papa if she ever smiled. Mama and Papa never had an answer, or at least they never gave one. Hanna, the child they had come to love as their own, had not smiled in a long time. When someone asked Hanna the question directly, she did respond. She simply said, "Why," then would walk away.

It was not that she just did not smile. When others saw her or even talked to her, everyone could see the young woman appeared to have, or show, no feelings at all. As if every bit of emotions inside had been frozen, and there was nothing that could thaw the coldness which had wrapped her heart.

One reason Hanna was like this, was because of the things she had gone through in her short life. But the main reason was because Hanna wanted it that way. If she did not let anyone enter her heart, then she would not have to suffer what comes when someone breaks it. Mostly by leaving in some manner. To Hanna, everyone leaves her.

Now that the serving of the morning meal was over, Hanna would spend the rest of the day taking care of the other chores she was responsible for. A couple of the guests who had been staying in the boarding house had left, so she had to change the linens on the beds and wash the ones she removed. The task took a good portion of her time to complete, since she had to heat the water over the fire pit, and then fill up the tub to wash the linen; and after she had wrung them out as much as she could, she would take them to the roof, to hang them in the sun. During the entire time the chore took, she would not have to worry about someone trying to talk to her, and it helped pass the day away. Not that Hanna was waiting for something, other than the chores she performed.

She finished washing the linens and went to the roof to hang them. It was not midday yet, so the sun was not at its highest point. Hanna had not talked to

Sun for seasons, and since she would not reply when Sun tried to talk to her, Sun had stopped trying many seasons ago. They had not spoken to one another for so long that Hanna had convinced herself that everything she had thought had happened when she was a child was just a dream.

The problem Hanna had in believing what she told herself, was the fact that she clearly remembers the day when the Mountain Raiders came to her village, and Sun made the fire rise and stretch across the field, burning every one of the Raiders to ash, or maybe it had all been a dream as well, a very vivid dream.

She had even convinced herself that the red mark on the back of her right hand had either been there since she was born, or she had burnt herself somehow when she was younger and had forgotten. There have been many times, while heating water over the fire pit, that she moved too close and received a slight burn from the fire. Maybe when she was younger, even before she came to the city, she had somehow stuck her hand in a fire, which is how she received the mark.

It was always a light shade of red. The color of someone's complexion who had worked in the sun too long and the rays from the sun had burnt their skin. The color also matched that of the sun itself. She has seen it on many of the people who made their living working outside and did not wear a covering on their heads. Although that never happened to her. No matter how long she was out in the sun, it never bothered her skin. To her, the only reason for having the mark must be because she must have received a burn at one point in her life. It could not have come from the sun rising high in the sky, higher than what it should have, and then a ray of the sun had shined down on her hand she had placed on a big rock. It must have been a dream as well. Just like the Mountain Raiders. Just like the wall of fire.

As Hanna was working with the linen, she heard the door leading from the inside to the roof open. Since she was standing with one of the bed linens in front of her, securing it to the line, she was not able to see who it was. She figured that it was probably either Mama or Papa, coming to get her to help them with something. Since they did not say anything, when Hanna finished hanging the linen she was working with, she stepped to the other side of it to see what they wanted.

She saw that it was not Mama or Papa, but Colton. Even though he had used the door a few times before, it surprised her for him to use it now. Usually, the only time he did, was when he had stopped by the boarding house and was already inside talking to Hanna, then decided to follow her up to the roof when she had some linen to hang up to dry. Of course, when they made it to the roof, Hanna would hang up the wash, while Colton would sit against the ledge and talk to her. Colton always seemed to be talking.

While Hanna was hanging the linen, Colton would talk to her but most of the time she did not even pay attention to what he was saying. If he asked her a question, usually, he would have to call her name to get her attention and then repeat what he had just asked her. Hanna would then reply in a manner to let him know that she could care less what he asked her or even what he was talking about, but that did not bother him. When he first met the girl with the golden hair, he had made it his assignment in life to get her to smile and to show her that she did not have to be unhappy all the time.

He even told her that once, but all she said was "I'm not unhappy, I'm just who I am." Colton did not understand her response and took it that she was too unhappy to know what she was saying, so he continued to try to make Hanna see that life was good, and that she could enjoy it.

If Hanna had gotten to know Colton, not just as someone who came around to talk to her while she did her chores but had taken the time to become friends with him, then maybe she would have noticed something was different about him this day. Not only had he used the door to come to the roof, but Colton, who was always the first to speak, and the last, had not said a word since he had stepped onto the rooftop.

When Hanna saw that it was only Colton, she walked back to the other side of the linen she had just hung, reached down into the basket, grabbed the next one, and began hanging it up. By the time she had finished with it, Colton still had not said a word. Usually, by now, he would have already begun talking about all the things he had done since the last time he saw her, and since he usually stopped by almost every other sun-cycle, it surprised Hanna at how much a person of his age could accomplish so much in so little amount of time, over the entire city.

By the time Hanna had finished with the second piece of linen since his arrival, she had not heard a word out of Colton and even thought that maybe he had gone back inside but realized she had not heard the door make its normal squeaking noise. She also knew that using the door to leave the roof was not something Colton normally did. He had told her one time that there was no reason to go through the house to get back outside since he was already outside, to begin with, and it was easier to go over the side of the building. She thought that was just the way he was and did not even try to tell him that it was dangerous. Danger was not something Colton ever considered.

Since she did not hear a word from him, Hanna stepped around the last piece of linen she hung and saw that he was still there, looking at her. She turned and grabbed the next linen in the basket and started hanging it up from the side she was now standing on. She had her back to Colton, but at least he could see her, so he would be able to start telling her all the things he had accomplished recently.

He still did not say anything, and before she had finished hanging the linen up, for the first time since they had known each other, Hanna spoke first. She turned her head so that she was looking over her right shoulder at him, "Someone finally cut out your tongue," she said then turned back to continue with what she was working on, "I knew that one day someone would get tired of hearing you talk." He still did not reply, even though it was the first time Hanna tried a bit of light banter.

Hanna finished with the piece of linen and turned to face Colton. She finally noticed that he was acting differently and was now looking down at the rooftop. "What's the matter with you?" Hanna asked.

Colton took a moment then gave his answer, "I'm leaving."

"You just got here," Hanna said because when he showed up, he usually spent quite some time talking Hanna to death before he decided he had some other place to be.

Colton lifted his head, and looked at Hanna, "I mean I am leaving for a while."

Hanna may not have shown it on her face, but inside, was the first time she had ever reacted to anything Colton had ever said to her in a way, where she thought he might be untruthful with her. Even with some of the things he would tell her that he had gotten into, or even more spectacular, the way he had to get out of something, Hanna always believed he was telling her the truth. Even though he would tell her that there were times when he had to stretch the truth, which was his way of saying that he had lied, she knew he never lied to her. Now he must be. Because even though she would not allow herself to become close to him, she knew that if there was someone who would always be around, it would be Colton. He was the only person Hanna knew that had less in life than she did. He just took to it differently.

Now, Hanna thought he was lying to her, and she did not like it.

She turned around and went to the other side of the linen she had just hung. She reached down into the basket and pulled out the next one, then began to work with it. Colton came to the side she was on and stood behind her. When he realized that she was not going to turn to look at him, he began to tell her what he had meant. "I am joining the priesthood."

Hanna could not help but turn her head to look behind her. As many times as Colton had tried to get her to smile, by saying something funny, at least to him, or by doing something that would get almost everyone else to smile, and with the exception of the first day they met, he had never succeeded with her. Now, not only was she smiling but she also appeared that she was going to start laughing.

Maybe she did not want him to see her smile, or maybe she had to turn away before she did burst out laughing, but she went back to working with the linen, trying hard to suppress the smile trying to appear on her face.

"It's true. I am heading to the temple after I leave here," Colton said, and he could not help but say it with the sadness he had in his heart. Not for what he was about to do, but because he knew that he would not see Hanna, his friend, for a long time, and may never again. Colton knew that with him not coming to see her, there was no other person that would try to show Hanna that there is more than just chores and that joy and happiness can be a part of a person's life if they choose to have those things.

Hanna could not fight what she was feeling inside nor the smile forcing its way to her lips. Ever since she had known Colton, he had always been trying to get her to smile. He succeeded on the first day they met when he had jumped over the side of the house. Since that day, especially after her mother had passed away, she had no reason to smile, even though he had tried many different ways. From telling some funny story involving him and usually some other person that ended up losing something of theirs, or he would do something to get her to laugh, like the time he stuffed his mouth full of nuts and was acting like a squirrel. A couple of times, she had to force herself not to. Her mouth might have wanted to smile, but her heart always made sure it was the one in control. Until this time.

She turned around and could not hide the smile

she had. She could not see it herself, but she was sure that once Colton had, he would finally say something like, "Got you to smile!" When she finally focused on his face, she realized that she was the only one smiling.

"It's true," Colton said, taking Hanna's expression that she did not believe him. As much as he wanted to see her smile for all these seasons, he knew that when she realized he was being honest with her, she would not be smiling, or maybe she never would.

"So, what is your plan? You go to the temple and pretend you want to be a priest and after a mooncycle or two, you walk out of there with every bit of coin they have." Hanna was impressed with herself because she thought she had uncovered his scheme. She turned around to go back to her work, but still had the smile on her face, and waited for him to let her know that was his plan.

"I will be away for at least six seasons. That is how long they said it will take me to make the first rank as a priest of Ourgós."

Hanna did not turn around, because she did not want to let him think she was believing what he had said. She was even kind of angry with him because he had made her smile, and with that, she remembered she had not done so in a long time. "Well, you let me know how that goes," she said without turning to face him, because she still did not want him to see her smiling, "But don't come running back here to get me to hide you when they catch you with your hands in their coin purses." She waited for him to say something, but he remained silent. It appeared that this time she was the one who was doing most of the talking, and Colton was quiet. Since he was not saying anything, she turned around to look at him. He was not smiling like her, and Colton always had a smile on his face, even though he had lived his entire life on the streets of Maridian.

"It's true," he said, and when he did, two things happened. First, Hanna knew he was telling her the truth, and second, she stopped smiling. The last one bothered Colton more than she would ever know.

"Why?" Hanna was finally able to ask.

Colton knew that she would want to know why he had made this decision, and even knew what he was going to say to her. He just did not think she would understand, because a part of him did not either even though he was the one about to enter the priesthood. "I feel as if I am being called to do this. Ever since I turned fourteen, I have been thinking about becoming a priest."

"But you have lived on the streets your entire life," Hanna said as if to try to convince him, and even herself, that he could not be a priest. "You have stolen from people or tricked them out of whatever they had that you wanted, so how are you going to become a priest?"

Colton gave her the only answer he had, "I don't know?" His confusion was just as great as Hanna's, about what he was going to do. He never kept anything from her. He told her the good and the not so good things he had done living on the street, and the items in the not so good column were greater. However, he never told her about the pull he felt in his heart. He knew that becoming a priest and serving Ourgós the Creator is what he wanted to do. It was what he needed to do.

For the majority of his life, Colton thought he would spend the rest of his life living on the streets. Maybe when he became older, maybe around twenty, he might set off on his own and see other parts of the world. There were many nights when he was lying in whatever place he ended up at when he wanted to sleep that he would think about traveling the world, traveling it with Hanna. He always thought that if he could get her out of the city where she has lived for most of her life, and where she suffered so much sadness, then maybe, just maybe he could get her to smile. He did not think that telling her he was joining the priesthood, would be the one thing to bring a smile to her face. At least until she realized he was being serious, then the smile, he so longed to see, disappeared.

When the desire came over Colton to become a priest, he was the first to laugh at the idea. Being who he was and the things he had done since he was a young boy, becoming a priest was the funniest idea he had ever thought of. Until he realized it was not funny at all, and it was something he wanted to do, more than anything he had ever planned in his life.

Colton even went to the man he had called Father to see what he thought about what he had decided. A part of Colton wanted the man to tell him it was a foolish idea, but there was another part, the part bigger than the first, that wanted the man to tell him that he was doing the right thing. The man told Colton that he would make a very good priest, and if anyone could get the stuffy rich people to give up their coinage to the temple, then Colton would be the one. Colton took it as a compliment, and it was.

The man also told him that usually the second or third son of a wealthier family, or a family with some means would join the priesthood. For a person to do so, they had to make a stipend to join. This rule was in place for a few reasons. One was that if the family or individual had to give a substantial monetary gift to the temple, then the priests knew the person was serious about what they had decided to do. The second reason was because it cost to give shelter, food, and teaching to an individual for the number of seasons the person would be in training, so the church needed the funds to meet those needs. The third reason was because if there was no financial requirement, anyone could join, and that would lead to individuals who had no coinage, joining only so they could have a place to stay and food to eat.

When the man he called Father mentioned this to Colton, he told him that he would help with as much of the funding as he could. Colton told him that it would not be necessary.

Colton had been making his living on the streets of Maridian ever since he was seven. He was now fourteen. For seven seasons, he had been acquiring coin from the different schemes he had conceived. Acquiring, but spending very little. The most he ever used at one time was for the flowers he had bought for Hanna when her mother passed away. When he went to the nearest temple to discuss with the priests about him joining, they told him, that as an orphan, he would not be able to donate the standard tribute for them to take him in. There was not a set amount, it just had to be big enough to make the priests see that the person was taking their decision to join seriously.

The next day, Colton returned to the temple with three bags, full of coins and other items. Not only were there copper pieces, but there were a few silver, six pieces of gold, and even one platinum. This was the first time any of the priests had even seen one. Copper was most common and even silver. They would receive gold, but only when someone was giving their offering to join their ranks, but they had never even seen a platinum coin. They were just that rare. In one of the bags, mixed in with the coins, there were also quite a few rings, which would bring the church at least a few more copper, and maybe some silver.

When Colton emptied out the contents of the bags in front of the priests, he saw them stare at the small treasure he had brought. He was the one who had to speak to get them to look at him, "Will that cover it?" he asked, and the only thing the priests could do was nod. They did not even ask him how he was able to come by the items they were looking upon. They knew about Colton, almost everyone in the city of Maridian did. They knew he would do odd jobs for some of the citizens and that he had been at it for quite some time, but never did they think that a child living on the street and making a living from being generous, kind, and helpful, could obtain so much wealth. Even though they were priests in the Order of Ourgós, they forgot, at least at the moment, being generous, kind, and helpful, was what Ourgós the Creator wanted everyone to be, and if they were, then he would reward them greater than they could imagine.

Colton had spent the two sun-cycles before he came to see Hanna, going to all the people he had helped over the seasons, to say his goodbyes. If he had known what some of them were going to do, then he would have taken more than just two.

In almost every house he stopped by, they insisted he stay for a meal, because they knew that with being a priest, he would have to get used to going without large amounts of food, and they would not hear of him leaving their presence without being fed. By the fifth meal at the fifth house, he had to pretend to be eating the food placed in front of him because he just could not eat another bite. He did think that if the people he had come to know, would have fed him so well for joining the priesthood, he would have done so a long time ago. At least he would have said he would.

A couple of people offered him coins to take with him. To stay true to his manner, Colton only took half of what they presented, and gave his patented reply, "As not to offend your generosity." Since he was truly joining the priesthood, he had no reason to keep the coinage, so when he did go back to the temple, he would give it to the priests and tell them it was to go with his initial offering. Colton knew that when the priests saw the two gold coins, they would once again wonder how a person like this young man could always have funds.

The day before Colton went to say goodbye to Hanna, he stopped by the shop of the man he called Father. That night, for the first time, Colton accepted the man's offer to have dinner with him, his wife, and their son. It was one of the best meals, Colton ever had. Before dinner was over, both he and the man started relating stories of some of the things Colton had done over the seasons since they had met. There was a great deal of laughter in the house that night, but before it was over there were also a few tears.

Colton had even accepted the offer to stay there that night, since he was going to the temple the next day to begin his training. He made sure he was the first to rise, before the sun had even come up, so that he could leave without anyone seeing him. He did not make it.

As he was about to step out the front door, he heard behind him, "I'm proud of you son," from the man he called Father. Colton turned around and saw the man looking at him. The man did not move and neither did Colton. All he did, was give the man a nod of his head, to let him know that what his father had just said, meant a lot, because he might have started out calling the man Father, but after all these seasons, Colton realized the man, was his father and he was his son. Not by blood, or by adoption, but because that was what they were to each other.

The day had come when he was to start his new life. There was one last part of the old one he had to say goodbye to. He stopped by the boarding house at a time when he knew Hanna would be alone on the roof. He always knew when she would be up there because he always made sure he knew when one of the patrons who had been staying was leaving. He knew it was one of Hanna's chores, to replace the linen, and wash the ones she removed.

When he arrived, he said his goodbyes to Mama and Papa, and he could tell by the look on their faces that when he told Hanna, she was going to take it hard. If anyone asked Hanna if she had any friends, she would say no. Mama and Papa knew there was one person who was her friend, even if she did not think so.

Now Colton was standing there looking at Hanna and had taken the smile from her face. He had finally succeeded and still, he failed.

"I won't be able to come and see you. Until I take my vows I will have to remain in the temple, and I know for a while, I will have limited contact with anyone. That is unless you come to any of the services." Colton paused to see if Hanna heard the invitation he was making to her. He might not be able to talk to her, but at least they may be able to see one another, and smile. Either she did not understand what he was saying, or she had no intention of attending any of the services. Colton knew that when it came to anything spiritual, Hanna had no need for it. To her, Ourgós was just someone who gave a person a family, then took them away. She did not need or want anything from someone she could not even see.

When Colton decided that he had kept quiet long enough he continued. "Do you know that for the first season I am there, I am not allowed to say a single word?" He let out a small chuckle at what he had just said, but Hanna gave no response. "I figure if I can get through that, then the rest of what I have to do, will be easy. You know better than anyone I like to talk." Once again, Hanna did not respond. At least not in the way, he was hoping.

Hanna, not knowing what to say, did the one thing she knew. She turned around and went back to hanging up the wet linen. For Hanna, no matter what happens in life, there will always be chores. They never leave.

Colton did not want to leave with Hanna not talking

to him. He was about to go over to her and spin her around to look at him so that he would not have to talk to her back. He stopped after he took the first step because he knew that no matter what he said, she still would not understand why he was doing this. It was not about Hanna, it was not even about himself, to Colton, it was about serving Ourgós, and from the first time he had decided to, nothing else mattered.

He stayed where he was but continued to talk to her, "When I am done and have taken my vows, I will come back and see you. If you are still here, I hope we can be friends." He waited to see if that would bring a response from her, but it did not. He turned and headed for the door to take him back inside. Even though the linen was blocking his view of her, and hers of him, when he turned around, he said one last thing. "I know it is hard for you, but I do hope that someday you will smile, and never stop." He did not wait to see if she would say anything. He went inside, leaving Hanna to do her chores.

She was so surprised by what had just happened, Hanna, not realizing what she was doing, started taking down the linen she had just hung up to dry; even though it was just as wet as when she started. She tried not to think about how she would never see Colton again. That she would never hear any more of his stories or see the stupid bow he would give her, or the stupid salute he would do with his hand. She decided that it did not matter, because to Hanna, everyone leaves her.

Before she took the last of the wet linen down, she realized what she was doing and even thought, how it was Colton's fault that she would have to rehang all the linen. It was just another one of her many chores, working at the boarding house. She knew it was what she would be doing for quite some time, more than likely for the rest of her life.

Colton left Hanna's and went straight to the Temple of Ourgós. He had taken care of the last item he needed to, and it was time to start down the path he had chosen for himself, but to him, it was not so much as what he had chosen, it was more as if it was his calling.

He arrived at the temple and stood outside looking at the front doors, which were twice the size of a tall man. Here he would be staying; learning to become a priest and serving Ourgós the Creator of all things. He knew it was what he would be doing for quite some time, more than likely for the rest of his life.

TWENTY

The third night after the girl saw the red flag at the guild, as she was leaving her loft, and reached the midpoint on the ladder, she saw Keyota standing at the top of the stairway. By the way the lieutenant was smiling, the girl knew why the younger girl had come up to meet her.

The girl never told anyone what she was planning to do when it came to the Assassin's Guild, but like Selby, everyone under his command made sure they knew what was going on, not only in the three buildings they resided in, but the entire city. So that meant every person in the three buildings knew the girl who barely spoke to anyone, the one with the deep eyes was about to enter the Assassin's Guild. Keyota was especially thrilled about this since she had begun looking up to the girl who had made a profession at killing rats.

The other reason Keyota idolized the girl was because on one of those incidences when a group of adults attacked their home, one man was about to bring his sword down on her. As he raised his arms up over his head, the girl with the deep eyes jumped on his back and brought her knife across his throat ending his life and saving Keyota's. Since that day, Keyota looked up to the girl as if she were her big sister, so much, that when she turned fifteen, she would also try to enter the Assassin's Guild, just like the one who had saved her life.

The girl knew the reason Keyota was waiting for her, so she rushed past her, ran down the stairs, and out the front door. Keyota followed her all the way down the front steps, but once there, she stopped. She knew the girl was going to the Assassin's Guild to verify what she had gone to tell the girl in the first place. Keyota did not mind that the girl had to check for herself, she understood the girl was just that way.

When Keyota turned around to go back into the building, she just happened to look up to the fourth floor and saw Selby staring out the window. He too had seen the girl run off into the night.

The girl ran down the street. She had made the trip so many times, she did not have to think about which turn she needed to make. Her body moved without instructions from her thoughts, the same way she went about killing rats.

When she finally made it to the building, she saw what she had been waiting for since she saw the red flag. Now, on the balcony from the second floor of the Guild, the green flag was flying.

Tomorrow would be the day the Guild took in the new recruits. She remembered what the man had told her, about how only seven out of the number who tried to obtain entrance would be walking through the door of the Guild. She would be one of those seven.

She had one more thing to do which was to acquire a weapon. Since the sun had already gone down then most of the shops would have closed for the night. She would still have time in the morning to make it to one of the shops before midday. Usually, she never went out until the sun had gone down, but since tomorrow was the day of the selection, she would be up and about and would bear the annoyance of the sun. She still had her cloak, and even though it did not reach the ground any longer, because she had grown in height, it would cover her head and face to keep her out of the sun's light. She never worried about the rest of her body, since she always wore shirts with long sleeves to cover her arms, and her trousers and boots covered her legs and feet.

Since there was nothing else she could do for now, she took one more look at the green flag, then turned to her right to head back to her building where she would wait. As soon as she faced the direction she needed to travel, she saw someone she had not seen in quite a while, even though he made sure he had kept an eye on her.

Dressed differently from the first time they had met, he stood before the girl. The previous time they saw one another he had no shoes on, but now wore a black leather shirt, with black leather pants.

His boots, which rose up to his knees, were also the same color and material. The girl did not see or hear him move close to her, and that bothered the child a bit since she saw a sword sheathed at his left hip. With the way he had it positioned, the girl could tell he used his right hand to wield it, so that was the one she would keep an eye on.

The man had waited for the girl to arrive and only came up to her after she had seen the green flag. He had never spoken to the child since the first time they met, but he had followed her on a number of nights when he was in the city and not on assignment.

He had taken a liking to the girl the first time he saw her, and since then his approval of her had grown. He had even seen her fight alongside the children that lived in the building with her and when she had killed three of the attackers, he reported back to the Masters of the Guild of how she handled herself and the situation. Of course, she had killed in defense of her home, so the Masters did not show much interest, because to them, being an assassin, as all the Masters were, knew that many people can kill when faced with very few options. The assassin who had reported on the girl understood, but he also knew, the girl he had taken an interest in, was exactly what the Guild was looking for.

The man had approached the girl and even though she was good, the man, trained as an assassin, had no problem coming up to her without her noticing him. Although he was able to, when she turned and saw him, he noticed that she had her knife out in front of her before her body was completely facing him.

"Tomorrow is the day you have been waiting for," he said to her, but she did not reply, nor did she take her eyes off him. If he wanted to, the man could have told the girl that he had no intention of harming her, but he did not. As an assassin, he knew that at any moment in their life, any person you might trust could turn on you, for no reason, or for a reason, which does not even make sense. The Guild had taught him that, and the girl might as well learn it as well. Which from the way she kept her knife out, pointing at him; she would not have a problem with it. "I see you still have that knife. I hope you have something better when you arrive tomorrow."

The girl did not say anything, so the man decided he would end the meeting. He lifted his arms up with his hands positioned at the height of his shoulders, his palms facing toward the girl to show her he had no intention of drawing his sword. He then stepped into the street and circled around the girl, all the while making sure he faced her. What he thought was more intriguing, was that as he walked around the girl, she turned with him, never taking her eyes off him.

When he was on the other side of her, he took five steps backwards, to put more distance between the two of them, then nodded to the girl. What she did next even surprised him. She turned around and walked away. A part of him felt insulted, because he was certain, the girl knew what he was, and to turn her back on him, told him that she was not afraid of him, at the least. He could not help but smile. "Hey," he said to the girl and she turned around to face him, this time without her knife drawn. "My name is Dodge." He waited for the girl to return his offer of exchanging names but when she did not, he continued, "So what is yours?"

The girl waited for one breath then answered, "I don't have one." She then turned around and started walking away.

"You might want to get one before tomorrow," Dodge yelled to her.

She could not help herself, and looked over her shoulder, but saw that the assassin Dodge was no longer standing where he had been. She turned her head and started back to her building. Tomorrow morning, she would purchase a sword. That would be easy to obtain. As for getting a name, she had no idea on what to go by. She never had one, and since she had survived this long without a name, she did not see a reason in having one now. The man had told her she should. She decided she would listen to the assassin. He said his name was Dodge, and she could not help but wonder if that was the name given to him when he came into the world, or for some other reason.

As she walked through the city, she passed by

some of the shops that sold weapons, and even though they would not be open until morning, she looked at the ones in the windows. She was not going to spend a lot of coin on whichever one she would purchase, but she stood there looking, and wondered just what they would teach her when she entered the Assassin's Guild.

As she stepped away from the shop she had stopped in front of, she thought that maybe she would just ask Selby to sell her one of the swords he had in his stock. Even though he made sure each of his lieutenants and his guards had a sword, the other people living in the building and working with him, were not allowed to carry one. A good portion of those people were ten seasons or younger, and he did not want any of them hurting someone or themselves, because they did not know how to use a weapon. Because of that, Selby always had a stash of swords kept locked up and would only arm every member of his band if it was a matter of life or death. Selby would say that if your life is on the line, then you are never too young to wield a sword or take another's life. Something else the girl agreed with him on.

They had not talked since the night she had gone to see him, and he realized she would be leaving soon. He had not come to see her, and she stayed away from him. Partly because that was just the way she was, but there was a small part of her that if she had spent more time with him, then she might just decide that living in the building and killing rats for the rest of her life might not be that bad after all. Which was the deciding reason she would purchase a sword from one of the many shops in the city. There was no need to see Selby before she entered the Guild. At least none greater than entering the Guild itself.

Before she made it back to her building, she heard Moon in her thoughts. *"Child, come to the great water."*

Over the last few seasons, Moon rarely spoke to her. Since she did not need to find food or water, there was not much Moon helped her with, and Moon preferred it that way. Every now and then, she would ask Moon if she were old enough, referring to the age she needed to be to enter the Guild, and Moon would tell her, *"Not yet,"* until the night when Moon told her she was. Other than that bit of exchange, they seldom spoke to each other. So, when the girl heard Moon, it was unexpected, but since it was Moon, she would do what Moon wanted her to.

She walked through the city and made her way to the docks where she had spent a great deal of time. She thought this was where Moon wanted her to be. *"Walk to where the sand meets the water then turn to your left and continue."*

She walked to the edge of the water where she had come many times, to feel the coldness of it, and to hear the rushing of the waves. It was a peaceful sound and was one of the few things that made the child feel as if there was no reason to be anywhere else. Tonight though, Moon wanted her to travel somewhere else, so when she reached the water, she turned to her left and went in the direction which Moon instructed her to.

She continued to walk, thinking that Moon would tell her when to stop. When the girl reached the end of the shoreline Moon still had not spoken letting her know where she was to go next. She believed she had not reached where Moon wanted her to be, so she continued.

She had to climb over many of the big rocks that were in her path. Some were so big that instead of going over them, she climbed into the water and made her way around them, until she could climb back onto shore. When she did this, the water was shallow and she was still able to touch the bottom of the ocean, so she did not have to swim. Which was a good thing because she did not know how. Still, she never had a fear of drowning because she knew the great water would never do her any harm. It was under the control of Moon, so Moon would make sure Ocean would not take her under, and if she happened to go below the surface, Moon would make sure Ocean brought her back.

She continued to travel down the shore and only stopped when Moon spoke, *"That is far enough."*

The girl looked around and saw that wherever Moon had brought her, she was by herself. She looked up into the sky and saw Moon was at the midpoint, which meant she had been traveling for almost half the night. The first thing she thought of was that if she did not start heading back before the sun rose, she would miss the only thing she had been waiting for, and not even Moon would stop her from entering the Guild. "Where am I?" the child asked aloud to Moon since there was no one else around to hear her.

She could speak words to Moon, but Moon still had to think thoughts to her. *"Where is not important. I have brought you here to give you a gift."*

"A gift?" the child said when she heard Moon's last word to her.

"Yes, child. I have watched you since you came into this world and have seen how much you have grown into who you are."

"With your help Moon," the girl said, and the words came from her heart.

Moon did not reply to the comment, because to Moon, what the child had said was the truth. Moon believed the girl would not have made it in the first city where she lived if it had not been for Moon. *"I have brought you here to give you more of my help. Turn and face the water."* The girl did as Moon commanded. She suddenly saw the water that came to the land begin to move. Not in the way it normally would. Usually, it would move onto the shore and then back. Now it moved backwards only, clearing an area of the land normally covered by water. Moon's control over the tide pulled the water back farther than what it normally would.

When Moon finished, the shoreline stretched another twenty paces towards the water. Since Ocean covered the part of land, and Ocean is under the authority of Moon, the land belonged to Moon. *"Remove your clothes child,"* Moon thought to the girl, and she did not hesitate to do as instructed. Moon was going to give her a gift and she did not want Moon to take back the offer because she hesitated.

She stood there unclothed, waiting for what Moon wanted her to do next. Suddenly a light from the sky fell onto the land that a moment ago was covered by water. With the light positioned ten paces from the original shoreline, the girl followed it with her eyes, from the land towards the sky; she saw the light was coming from Moon.

It was a moonbeam; something very few people have ever witnessed. Yes, Moon usually shown in the sky and some of the light from Moon would reflect off surfaces, especially water. But what the girl was seeing now, was something Moon very seldom would do, and that was to send a beam of light to the world below. A beam of light that if someone were to touch it, they would feel Moon on their skin.

"Step into the light, child." The girl did not hesitate to do as instructed. She left the shore and stepped into the area clear of water and entered the circle of light coming from Moon.

As soon as she stepped into it, she could feel the cold of Moon. She had never felt so safe in all her life. To someone else, they might compare what the girl was feeling to standing in the warm comforting light of the sun, or maybe in the arms of a loving parent. Since the girl had never known either of those experiences, she could not explain what she was feeling. She felt so safe that all she could do was close her eyes and tilt her head so that it was facing Moon. There she stood, completely free of clothing with her entire body basking in the light of Moon.

She did not realize it but even the soles of her feet, which touched the light from Moon when she entered the area, were feeling the same way as the rest of her body.

Moon knew this, and it was what Moon had planned for this evening. It was just one of Moon's gifts to the child. *"Open your eyes child and look upon yourself."*

The girl did, but before she took her eyes and placed them on herself, she looked directly at Moon. She saw the brightness of Moon's glow, and never had she seen anything so beautiful. She then lowered her eyes and looked down at her body. Even though Moon's light was still shining on her, she could tell what Moon had done. Somehow, the light of Moon had changed the color of her skin to the same shade of white as Moon.

She raised her hands and arms to get a better look at them, and they were the same color as the rest of her body. She did not look, but if she had, the soles of her feet would have shown the color as well.

She was the color of the full moon, from head to toe. All except for her eyes, and hair, which she had never cut, and flowed over halfway down her back. It had always been black, and Moon would not change it. For part of Moon was always in darkness, and the child would represent all of what Moon is, the child's hair and eyes would remain the color of darkness. Which only accentuated the pale white of the child's skin.

"Do you like the gift, my child?" Moon thought to the girl.

Never before had the child shed a tear because someone gave her something. She did not this time but came close. "You have made me to look like you," the child said, taking another glance at her arms and body, then looked back to the sky at Moon, "It is beautiful, as you are Moon," she said, and of course, Moon agreed with her.

"I have another gift for you," Moon said, and before the girl could speak, two more beams of light from Moon landed just outside of the area of light where the child was standing. *"Kneel down and take them."*

The child did as Moon instructed. She bent down so that only her right knee touched the ground, but she was still able to see what was in the two small circles of light. One at each of her sides, and a single step forward. She grabbed hold of each of the handles and brought the items up so she could look at them.

What she was holding was something she thought was even more beautiful than what she looked like. In her hands, she held two daggers. When she picked them up, she positioned them so that the blades were pointing upwards. Even though this was the first time she had seen them, let alone hold them, she knew the length of the blades, from the tips to the hilts. The blades were six handbreadths in length. It began with a tip sharper than anything the child had ever seen. As she looked down the blades, she knew the width of them were no more than two finger widths at its widest section and went into the cross-guards, which was a third of the length of the full blade. Which also happened to be the same length as the hilts. The ends of the hilts ended in circular orbs. The girl noticed they looked exactly like Moon when Moon is full in the sky.

The two daggers were almost exactly alike. Their measurements were the same but what made them different were their colors. The weapon she held in her left hand was completely black. From the tip of the blade to the end of the hilt was as dark as the child's hair, and as dark as the part of Moon no one saw. The weapon in her right hand was pale white. The color of the child's skin, and the face of Moon shining in the night sky.

"The name of the blade you hold in your left hand is Umbra. It comes from the part of me, which

is always in shadow, and it will cast you in a shadow so dark, no one will see you." The child looked at the weapon in her left hand, then put her focus on the one in her right, waiting to hear about it. *"Full is the name of the weapon in your right. As Umbra comes from shadow, Full comes from the part of me, that when all creatures drawing breath, raise their eyes to the night sky, and see the light I shine on them, they become mesmerized. To the sentient creatures of the land, it is what is known as moonstruck. When you call to Full, it will send out a light that will mesmerize the ones who look upon it."*

The child gazed on Full for a moment longer, then put her focus on Umbra. She could not tell which one she loved more, because she loved them both the same.

"I have one more gift for you child," Moon said, and even though the girl wanted to say something about what Moon had already given her, she was too overwhelmed to speak.

The next thing she felt, was Moon doing something in her mind. The pain was almost unbearable. There was even a point when she had to grind her teeth together so she would not scream. She did not want to offend Moon, for what Moon had done and what Moon was doing. When Moon had finished, the child could not stop herself from moving forward a bit and only stayed upright because she placed her hands on the ground before she fell to it.

Moon then explained. *"I have existed for as long as the first creatures have walked the world. In that time, I have witnessed countless battles. A single being against a single being, as well as armies against armies. Human, elf, dwarf, troll, and gnome. Each of them has fought against the other, and some against their own kind. What I have seen I have passed on to you. I have seen how one being would defend against their attacker, as well as the attacker ending the life of their chosen victim. Now, what I know about combat, you do as well."*

Moon had spoken the truth as Moon always did. She knew what to do in every situation Moon had ever observed. She knew how to take on one combatant as well as numbers that would overwhelm her. She knew how to use her new blades to block multiple attacks, while at the same time, she knew how to strike with her own weapons to end the life of another. The child knew how to fight.

She had always felt there was something about her, which allowed her to take a life. She had developed it when she hunted and when she killed rats. Now with what Moon had given her, she knew exactly what to do in every situation. Whether it was to stand and fight, or to turn and flee because the situation called for it. This was the third gift from Moon and the child was more than grateful for what Moon had done.

"Do you like what I have given you child?" Moon asked.

"Yes, Father," the child said, because for some reason it seemed right to refer to Moon in that manner.

Moon knew what the word father meant but never thought anyone would use it to refer to Moon. Moon was a Guardian. Moon was neither male nor female. Moon was neither he nor she. Moon was Moon. The child called Moon, Father. A title the sentient creatures in the world would call the male who procreated with a woman to bring a child into the world. Moon thought that when it came to the child, the word father suited Moon perfectly. For was it not Moon who had raised the child and made her into what she is now? Was not that the role of the one called Father? Moon used another word for the first time referring to the child. *"Rise my daughter."* The girl did not do as Moon had instructed her. *"What is wrong my child?"*

She waited for a few breaths before she spoke, "Father I am grateful for all that you have done for me, and especially for the gifts you have given me this night. Because of that, I fear to anger you by asking for anything more."

A part of Moon did anger. Moon had given the child three precious gifts, and the child wanted more. As quick as Moon angered, Moon, overcame it. For was it not the responsibility of a father to give a daughter what she desires. *"Do not fear me daughter. Ask."*

The child had to take another few breaths before she could speak. Not because she was afraid to ask, but because even after all Moon had done, Moon had instructed her to ask for something else. The child thought to herself, is that not the sign of a loving father? "Father, I thank you for the wonderful gifts you have presented to me this night, and if you will, I ask for only one more, and that is a name." The child raised her head so that she could see Moon in the sky, shining down on her. "Please, give me a name Father."

How could Moon deny the child's request? Moon knew that many fathers would give a child the name they would go by, long after they had entered and left the world. Why should Moon be any different? *"As you wish my child. For I am Moon your father, and since I will always be with you, so you shall be known by what is always with me. Rise my child, my daughter, my Nyght."*

The girl could not hold back the tears any longer. Moon had granted her so much; she felt she would never earn what Moon had given so freely.

Moon removed the moonbeam from the world, and the child walked back to the shore to retrieve her clothes. As she dressed, she never let go of the wonderful blades her father had given her. When she placed her cloak on, she closed the front of it, keeping her new blades in her hands inside the cloak. She kept her hood off her head, so Moon could see her features; the pale white skin of her face; surrounded by the blackness of her hair. When the sun came up, she knew it would bother her even more than it had before; for now, she would keep her hood pulled back since it was night, and she is Nyght.

TWENTY-ONE

She made it back to the part of the city where the Assassin's Guild was located but did not approach the building. She stayed in the alley across the street and waited. The sun had just started to rise, and Nyght made sure she had her hood over her head before the sun's rays even came into the sky. To ensure she stayed out of the sun's light and out of sight from anyone else, she kept to the middle of the alleyway. There were still six sun-marks before it was midday. She could have headed back to her building but decided there was nothing she needed from there.

When she had left the place last night, she had left behind the water and food bag, since she did not need them at that moment. As usual, she took her knife and some of her coins with her but left the majority of them in her room. She did not worry if someone would take what she had earned over the past seasons, no one had ever tried to enter her place, and Selby would make sure no one would. When she finally did walk out of the Guild when her training was complete, she was not sure if she would return for the coinage or not. She had needed it to survive, but there was no telling where the path, she was about to start down, would take her.

As the sun rose in the sky, Nyght noticed a lot of movement in the street. She made her way closer to the entrance of the alley, to get a better look. What she saw, made her believe that even though the Assassin's Guild was something that was not mentioned in the city, it did not stop a vast majority of people from coming to the area to see who the new recruits would be.

As the morning passed, more people took up positions that would allow them to get the best view possible of what was to come. Nyght even saw street vendors set up their portable carts to make a bit of coin for themselves. There was even some walking through the crowds, carrying items they had for sale. The Assassin's Guild might not have been something people talked about, out in the open, but on this day, it was the only topic people were discussing.

As midday grew closer, and the crowd grew thicker, it hindered her view of the building. If she had been able to see what was happening at the front of it, she would have seen the hopeful start making their way closer to the door of the Guild. Some of them did not make it past the first step. That was because the spell that caused a person to feel the coldness, which Nyght had felt over three seasons ago, forced them to turn around, deciding that they had made a mistake in trying to gain entrance. Fifty-five children had passed the first set of steps. Less than half that number made it past the first landing, and more than a few of those that did not, ran back the way they came when forced to face their fear.

Throughout the morning and before midday, only twenty-four children between the ages of fifteen and seventeen passed the two tests that led to the front door of the Guild. Twenty-four made it but three of them fell to the ground the moment they came within an arm's reach of the black wood beam in front of the building. Two of the children were under the age of fifteen, and the third was over the age of seventeen. All of them thought they would be able to ignore the age limit rule. They were still alive and six people, not known by anyone, came out of the crowd and up to where the three had fallen to take them away.

When the older child woke, they would send him on his way, but the Guild would make sure he would know that if he tried to gain entrance again, he would not wake up. The message given to the small boy and girl under the age would be different. The next time the selection of new recruits took place, and if they were still within the age limit, the Guild would be more than happy to allow them to try again. Especially since they were under the age of requirement but were still able to pass the two tests. It showed they had strong wills.

Nyght did not see any of what had happened,

staying in the alley. She knew she still had time, so she did not need to rush in like the other children, hoping to gain admission into the Guild. As she waited, she did not even turn around when she felt someone coming up behind her. She knew who it was. "Hello Dodge," she said.

Not only did she know who was behind her, but she did not turn around to look at him, nor did she bring out her knife as she had the two previous times they met. Since she did not face him, Dodge moved to stand to her right. "You're waiting until all the other children have made it to the choosing area then you will make your entrance," he said. Not to ask her if that was her plan, but to let her know, he knew why she was waiting in this alley. "You will enter alone so that all eyes will be on you. Not that you care about the ones belonging to the other children, but so the Masters will get to see you without any distractions."

Nyght did not respond, but the man to her right was correct. When she took the task of killing rats in the dark, she always chose first the ones that were the loudest, because they drew her attention to them. She was not going to squeak like the rats, but with what she had planned, she would definitely get the attention of the ones doing the choosing. "How did you get the name Dodge?" the child asked without looking to her right. She kept her head forward and tilted downwards, just enough so that the hood of her cloak obscured Dodge's view of her face.

"I'll make a deal with you. You survive the next five seasons, and I will tell you my story." The girl nodded her head enough so that he knew she would be hearing how he got his name. "I don't see any weapon, but I have a feeling you have something under that cloak of yours." Once again, the girl nodded her head so that Dodge knew she did, and then he asked his last question, "So do you have a name?"

The girl waited two breaths then turned her head and raised it enough so that he could see her face. She waited until he did and saw the color of her skin that was inside the hood of her cloak, surrounded by her black hair. When he saw the way the girl looked now, different from the previous night, Dodge could not stop his eyes from growing wider. "I am Nyght," the girl said, then turned her head and stepped out of the alleyway.

Dodge was an assassin and had seen many things that would cause grown men to stop and think. There were very few times that he felt that way, but when he saw the color of the child's skin, he thought that maybe he should not have taken an interest in the girl. He realized that she was going to use the way she looked, to get the attention of the Masters to increase her chances to enter the Guild. She did not know it, but there was no need for her to make the extra effort.

As Nyght made her way through the crowd, she used her shoulders and body to push people aside and out of her way, since she kept her arms inside her cloak. When she came in contact with a couple of men, they thought the child should learn some respect, but when she looked up at their faces and they saw the pale white color of her skin and the deep black eyes, they took one last quick look to make sure they had actually seen what they thought they saw, then turned their eyes away.

Nyght made it to the front of the building when it was almost midday. She walked up to the first set of steps, but when she touched them, she did not feel the cold she had the first time. It was the same when she reached the first landing. She did not know it, but the spell on them, had tested her the first night she came to the building, and there was no need to do so again. She had passed.

She moved to where the other children were standing, which was directly behind the black wooden beam on the ground. When she reached it, she used her body to push the boy to her right to take the spot directly in the middle.

"Hey!" the boy said and even reached for the sword he had in the scabbard on his right hip. Before he could draw it, Nyght turned toward him and made sure she had raised her head enough so the boy would see her face. When he did, not only did he remove his hand from the hilt of his sword, but he also stepped out of line and walked to the far-right end, not wanting to be next to the newest arrival.

When the sun was directly overhead, the seven doors located on the second level balcony opened and seven adults walked out of them. They were the Masters who would be training the new recruits. Every Master trained at the Guild as well, and when they reached an age where they could do more for their organization than just kill, they took on the roles of teachers.

If any of the children waiting below, had been talking to one of their companions, when the seven Masters made their appearance, they went silent. Here was their chance to become something more than just another adult living their life in the city. Each child had one hope, and that was to become an assassin.

What the children did not know was that the Masters had already decided who would be entering the Guild. This farce of the selection day was something the Guild organized to remind the citizens of Sarzanac that no matter what happens, the Assassin's Guild was always around and would not go away.

It was assassins, like Dodge, who did the recruiting for the Guild. Every so often, word would get out about some child who had killed an individual, or the child showed up at their front door wanting to enter the Guild. When one of these things occurred, the Guild would send one of their assassins to assess the child. If the assassin felt the child had potential, then they would pass on the rules to the child that would allow them to present themselves on the day of recruitment. Even the rule about getting a certain type of weapon was to see if the child would do as instructed. If the child happened to already have a sword or another weapon, then the assassin would simply tell them they needed to find a different one.

Another task the assassin had to do was to make sure the child had no living relatives or at least any the child knew about or associated with. They would follow the child and soon they would be able to tell if the child talked to any adults. Then the assassin would simply find out who the adults were and if related to the child, the Guild would simply not select them on the day of recruitment.

With the twenty-two possible selections, seven, previously chosen, would be stepping into the Guild.

The Masters walked up to the railing of the balcony. It was then that Nyght removed her right hand from inside her cloak, reached up, and pulled back her hood. This caused every Master to notice her, and more than one child did as well. Even though the sun above, not only bothered her but hurt her, she waited until she reached the count of ten before she replaced her hood over her head and returned her right arm to the inside of her cloak. She then made a slight adjustment to return Full, back to her right hand.

With the pause in the ceremony over, the children remained quiet, and some of them even stopped breathing when all the Masters raised their bows, with arrows already set. The Masters all at once pulled the strings of their bows back and released their arrows. More than one child flinched when they saw the arrows let loose, but the Masters decided previously not to select them.

All the children looked down. In front of seven of the children, at their feet, an arrow was sticking into the wood beam. Then the Master in the center of the balcony spoke, "If you have an arrow in front of you, congratulations, you have been selected. For those of you who do not, you may leave. The ones chosen, please retrieve the arrow at your feet and proceed through the door ahead of you." All the Masters then turned to walk back into the building but stopped when they heard one child who was not happy with the decision the Masters had made.

"No! It is not fair! I deserve to be admitted into the Guild!" As the boy spoke up, he stepped over the wood beam and yelled what he had to say to the Masters above. They showed him courtesy, by turning around, and walking back to the railing to hear what the boy thought they should do. "I am seventeen this season, so this is my only chance to be trained as an assassin. But you will let in a freak like that one." As he spoke the last words, he turned his head and pointed directly at Nyght.

Part of her wanted to silence the fool, for calling her a freak, but also because the boy was nothing but an obnoxious spoiled brat. She could tell, by the way he talked. He thought he should be one of the chosen just because he said so. Nyght also suspected that if the child had ever killed anyone, he must have done it while they were asleep or with their backs to him. Not that there was anything wrong with killing a person that way; unless the one doing the killing, did it because they were a coward and afraid to face their target.

"I should be chosen before that piece of cow muck," the boy said to end his argument.

He did not have a chance to say anything else, because seven arrows pierced his body, and he fell to the ground. He landed on his back so those around saw the seven arrows that had struck the boy in his chest. It was obvious to everyone present that the arrows created a circle. They struck the boy all at once, not one missing the mark the Masters aimed for.

The Master who spoke before, spoke again, "As I said, if you have an arrow in front of you, congratulations, you have been selected. For those of you who do not, you may leave. The ones chosen please retrieve the arrow at your feet and proceed through the door ahead of you." The Masters then turned and went back through the doors they used to enter onto the balcony.

The children who did not have an arrow at their feet decided it was best if they ran away from the area; not one of them stayed to remove the body of the boy who had thought he had known better than the Masters.

The chosen seven walked towards the door that had opened for them. Nyght made sure she was the last one to enter. Just before she did, she thought to herself, that this is where she would be spending the next few seasons of her life, becoming an assassin. She knew that it was what she would be doing for quite some time, more than likely for the rest of her life.

And happy that she would be.